"You are such *a jerk, Lieutenant Catalanotto!"* Veronica snapped.

"Why can't you take me seriously for one damned minute? Or are you *trying* to foul this up, so you won't have to place yourself in danger?"

Joe's smile disappeared instantly, and Veronica knew with deadly certainty that she'd gone too far. He took a step toward her, and she took a step back. He was very tall, very broad—and *very* angry.

Then he reached out and, with one finger underneath her chin, lifted her head so that she was forced to look up into his eyes.

The connection was there between them again—instant and hot. The look in his eyes was mesmerizing. It erased everything—all the angry words, all the misunderstandings—and left only this almost primitive attraction, this simplest of equations. Man plus woman.

"You're wrong, Veronica," he murmured. "I take you *very* seriously...."

Dear Reader,

We've got some great reading for you this month, but I'll bet you already knew that. Suzanne Carey is back with *Whose Baby?* The title already tells you that a custody battle is at the heart of this story, but it's Suzanne's name that guarantees all the emotional intensity you want to find between the covers.

Maggie Shayne's *The Littlest Cowboy* launches a new miniseries this month, THE TEXAS BRAND. These rough, tough, ranchin' Texans will win your heart, just as Sheriff Garrett Brand wins the hearts of lovely Chelsea Brennan and her tiny nephew. If you like mysterious and somewhat spooky goings-on, you'll love Marcia Evanick's *His Chosen Bride*, a marriage-of-convenience story with a paranormal twist. Clara Wimberly's hero in *You Must Remember This* is a mysterious stranger—mysterious even to himself, because his memory is gone and he has no idea who he is or what has brought him to Sarah James's door. One thing's for certain, though: it's love that keeps him there. In *Undercover Husband*, Leann Harris creates a heroine who thinks she's a widow, then finds out she might not be when a handsome—and somehow familiar—stranger walks through her door. Finally, I know you'll love *Prince Joe*, the hero of Suzanne Brockmann's new book, part of her TALL, DARK AND DANGEROUS miniseries. This is a royal impostor story, with a rough-around-the-edges hero who suddenly has to wear the crown.

Don't miss a single one of these exciting books, and come back next month for more of the best romance around—only in Silhouette Intimate Moments.

Yours,

Leslie Wainger

Leslie Wainger
Senior Editor and Editorial Coordinator

Please address questions and book requests to:
Silhouette Reader Service
U.S.: 3010 Walden Ave., P.O. Box 1325, Buffalo, NY 14269
Canadian: P.O. Box 609, Fort Erie, Ont. L2A 5X3

PRINCE JOE

SUZANNE BROCKMANN

INTIMATE MOMENTS

Published by Silhouette Books

America's Publisher of Contemporary Romance

SILHOUETTE BOOKS

ISBN 0-373-07720-3

PRINCE JOE

Books by Suzanne Brockmann

Silhouette Intimate Moments

Hero Under Cover #575
Not Without Risk #647
A Man To Die For #681
*Prince Joe #720

*Tall, Dark and Dangerous

SUZANNE BROCKMANN

wrote her first romance novel in 1992, and fell in love with the genre. She writes full-time, along with singing and arranging music for her professional a cappella singing group called Vocomotive, organizing a monthly benefit coffeehouse at her church and managing the acting careers of her two young children, Melanie and Jason. She and her family are living happily ever after in a small town outside of Boston.

For Eric Ruben, my swim buddy.

Prologue

Baghdad, January 1991

Friendly fire.

It was called friendly because it came from U.S. bombers and missile launchers, but it sure as hell didn't feel friendly to Navy SEAL Lieutenant Joe Catalanotto, as it fell from the sky like deadly rain. Friendly or not, an American bomb was still a bomb, and it would indiscriminately destroy anything in its path. Anything, or anyone, between the U.S. Air Force bombers and their military targets was in serious danger.

And SEAL Team Ten's seven-man Alpha Squad was definitely between the bombers and their targets. They were deep behind enemy lines, damn near sitting on top of a factory known to manufacture ammunition.

Joe Catalanotto, commander of the Alpha Squad, glanced up from the explosives he and Blue and Cowboy were rigging against the Ustanzian Embassy wall. The city was lit up all around them, fires and explosions hellishly illuminating the night sky. It seemed unnatural, unreal.

Except it was real. Damn, it was *way* real. It was dangerous with a capital *D*. Even if Alpha Squad wasn't hit by
friendly fire, Joe and his men ran the risk of bumping into
a platoon of enemy soldiers. Hell, if they were captured,
commando teams like the SEALs were often treated like
spies and executed—after being tortured for information.

But this was their job. This was what Navy SEALs were
trained to do. And all of Joe's men in Alpha Squad per-
formed their tasks with clockwork precision and cool confidence. This wasn't the first time they'd had to perform a
rescue mission in a hot war zone. And it sure as hell wasn't
going to be the last.

Joe started to whistle as he handled the plastic explosives, and Cowboy—otherwise known as Ensign Harlan
Jones from Fort Worth, Texas—looked up in disbelief.

"Cat works better when he's whistling," Blue explained
to Cowboy over his headset microphone. "Drove me nuts
all through training—until I got used to it. You *do* get used
to it."

"Terrific," Cowboy muttered, handing Joe part of the
fuse.

His hands were shaking.

Joe glanced up at the younger man. Cowboy was new to
the squad. He was scared, but he was fighting that fear, his
jaw tight and his teeth clenched. His hands might be shaking, but the kid was doing his job—he was sticking it out.

Cowboy glared back at Joe, daring him to comment.

So of course, Joe did. "Air raids make you clausty, huh,
Jones?" he said. He had to shout to be heard. Sirens were
wailing and bells were ringing and antiaircraft fire was
hammering all over Baghdad. And of course there was also
the brain-deafening roar of the American bombs that were
vaporizing entire city blocks all around them. Yeah, they
were in the middle of a damned war.

Cowboy opened his mouth to speak, but Joe didn't let
him. "I know how you're feeling," Joe shouted as he put
the finishing touches on the explosives that would drill one
mother of a hole into the embassy foundation. "Give me a
chopper jump into cold water, give me a parachute drop
from thirty thousand feet, give me a fourteen-mile swim,

hell, give me hand-to-hand with a religious zealot. But this... I gotta tell you, kid, inserting into Baghdad with these hundred-pounders falling through the sky is making me a little clausty myself."

Cowboy snorted. "Clausty?" he said. "You? Shoot, Mr. Cat, if there's anything on earth *you're* afraid of, they haven't invented it yet."

"Working with nukes," Joe said. "That sure as hell gives me the creeps."

"Me, too," Blue chimed in.

The kid wasn't impressed. "You guys know a SEAL who *isn't* freaked out by disarming nuclear weapons, and I'll show you someone too stupid to wear the trident pin."

"All done," Joe said, allowing himself a tight smile of satisfaction. They'd blow this hole open, go in, grab the civilians and be halfway to the extraction point before ten minutes had passed. And it wouldn't be a moment too soon. What he'd told Ensign Jones was true. Jesus, Mary and Joseph, but he hated air raids.

Blue McCoy stood and hand-signaled a message to the rest of the team, in case they'd missed hearing Joe's announcement in the din.

The ground shook as a fifty-pound bomb landed in the neighborhood, and Blue met Joe's eyes and grinned as Cowboy swore a blue streak.

Joe laughed and lit the fuse.

"Thirty seconds," he told Blue, who held up the right number of fingers for the rest of the SEALs to see. The squad scrambled to the other side of the street for cover.

When a bomb is about to go off, Joe thought, there's always a moment, sometimes just a tiny one, when everything seems to slow down and wait. He looked at the familiar faces of his men, and he could see the adrenaline that pumped through them in their eyes, in the set of their mouths and jaws. They were good men, and as always, he was going to do his damnedest to see that they got out of this city alive. Forget alive—he was going to get them out of this hellhole untouched.

Joe didn't need to look at the second hand on his watch. He knew it was coming, despite the fact that time had seemed to slow down and stretch wa-a-a-ay out....

Boom.

It was a big explosion, but Joe barely heard it over the sounds of the other, more powerful explosions happening all over the city.

Before the dust even settled, Blue was on point, leading the way across the war-torn street, alert for snipers and staying low. He went headfirst into the neat little crater they had blown into the side of the Ustanzian Embassy.

Harvard was on radio, and he let air support know they were going in. Joe was willing to bet big money that the air force was too busy to pay Alpha Squad any real attention. But Harvard was doing his job, same as the rest of the SEALs. They were a team. Seven men—seven of the armed forces' best and brightest—trained to work and fight together, to the death if need be.

Joe followed Blue and Bobby into the embassy basement. Cowboy came in after, leaving Harvard and the rest of the team guarding their backsides.

It was darker than hell inside. Joe slipped his night-vision glasses on just in time. He narrowly missed running smack into Bobby's back and damn near breaking his nose on the shotgun the big man wore holstered along his spine.

"Hold up," Bob signaled.

He had his NVs on, too. So did Blue and Cowboy.

They were alone down there, except for the spiders and snakes and whatever else was slithering along the hard dirt floor.

"Damned layout's wrong. There's supposed to be a flight of stairs," Joe heard Blue mutter, and he stepped forward to take a look. Damn, they had a problem here.

Joe pulled the map of the embassy from the front pocket of his vest, even though he'd long since memorized the basement's floor plan. The map in his hands was of an entirely different building than the one they were standing in. It was probably the Ustanzian Embassy in some other city, in some country on the other side of the damned globe. Damn! Someone had really screwed up here.

Blue was watching him, and Joe knew his executive officer was thinking what *he* was thinking. The desk-riding genius responsible for securing the floor plan of this embassy was going to have a very bad day in about a week. Maybe less. Because the commander and XO of SEAL Team Ten's Alpha Squad were going to pay him a little visit.

But right now, they had a problem on their hands.

There were three hallways, leading into darkness. Not a stairway in sight.

"Wesley and Frisco," Blue ordered in his thick Southern drawl. "Get your butts in here, boys. We need split teams. Wes with Bobby. Frisco, stay with Cowboy. I'm with you, Cat."

Swim buddies. Blue had read Joe's mind and done the smartest thing. With the exception of Frisco, who was baby-sitting the new kid, Cowboy, he'd teamed each man up with the guy he knew best—his swim buddy. In fact, Blue and Joe went back all the way to Hell Week. Guys who do Hell Week together—that excruciating weeklong torturous SEAL endurance test—stay tight. No question about it.

Off they went, night-vision glasses still on, looking like some kind of weird aliens from outer space. Wesley and Bobby went left. Frisco and Cowboy took the right corridor. And Joe, with Blue close behind him, went straight ahead.

They were silent now, and Joe could hear each man's quiet breathing over his headset's earphones. He moved slowly, carefully, checking automatically for booby traps or any hint of movement ahead.

"Supply room," Joe heard Cowboy breathe into his headset's microphone.

"Ditto," Bobby whispered. "We got canned goods and a wine cellar. No movement, no life."

Joe caught sight of the motion the same instant Blue did. Simultaneously, they flicked the safeties of their MP5s down to full fire and dropped into a crouch.

They'd found the stairs going up.

And there, underneath the stairs, scared witless and shaking like a leaf in a hurricane, was the crown prince of

Ustanzia, Tedric Cortere, using three of his aides as sand-bags.

"Don't shoot," Cortere said in four or five different languages, his hands held high above his head.

Joe straightened, but he kept his gun raised until he saw all four pairs of hands were empty. Then he pulled his NVs from his face, squinting as his eyes adjusted to the dim red glow of a penlight Blue had pulled from his pocket.

"Good evening, Your Royal Highness," he said. "I am Navy SEAL Lieutenant Joe Catalanotto, and I'm here to get you out."

"Contact," Harvard said into the radio, having heard Joe's royal greeting to the prince via his headset. "We have made contact. Repeat, we have picked up luggage and are heading for home plate."

That was when Joe heard Blue laugh.

"Cat," the XO drawled. "Have you looked at this guy? I mean, Joe, have you really looked?"

A bomb hit about a quarter mile to the east, and Prince Tedric tried to burrow more deeply in among his equally frightened aides.

If the prince had been standing, he would have been about Joe's height, maybe a little shorter.

He was wearing a torn white satin jacket, reminiscent of an Elvis impersonator. The garment was amazingly tacky. It was adorned with gold epaulets, and there was an entire row of medals and ribbons on the chest—for bravery under enemy fire, no doubt. His pants were black, and grimy with soot and dirt.

But it wasn't the prince's taste in clothing that made Joe's mouth drop open. It was the man's face.

Looking at the Crown Prince of Ustanzia was like looking into a mirror. His dark hair was longer than Joe's, but beyond that, the resemblance was uncanny. Dark eyes, big nose, long face, square jaw, heavy cheekbones.

The guy looked exactly like Joe.

Chapter 1

All of the major network news cameras were rolling as Tedric Cortere, crown prince of Ustanzia, entered the airport.

A wall of ambassadors, embassy aides and politicians moved forward to greet him, but the prince paused for just a moment, taking the time to smile and wave a greeting to the cameras.

He was following her instructions to the letter. Veronica St. John, professional image and media consultant, allowed herself a sigh of relief. But only a small one, because she knew Tedric Cortere very well, and he was a perfectionist. There was no guarantee that Prince Tedric, the brother of Veronica's prep-school roommate and very best friend in the world, was going to be satisfied with what he saw tonight on the evening news.

Still, he would have every right to be pleased. It was day one of his United States goodwill tour, and he was looking his best, oozing charm and royal manners, with just enough blue-blooded arrogance thrown in to captivate the royalty-crazed American public. He was remembering to gaze directly into the news cameras. He was keeping his eye movements steady and his chin down. And, heaven be praised, for a man prone to anxiety attacks, he was looking calm and collected for once.

He was giving the news teams exactly what they wanted—a close-up picture of a gracious, charismatic, fairy-tale-handsome European prince.

Bachelor. She'd forgotten to add "bachelor" to the list. And if Veronica knew Americans—and she did; it was her business to know Americans—millions of American women would watch the evening news tonight and dream of becoming a princess.

There was nothing like fairy-tale fever among the public to boost relations between two governments. Fairy-tale fever—and the recently discovered oil that lay beneath the parched, gray Ustanzian soil.

But Tedric wasn't the only one playing to the news cameras this morning.

As Veronica watched, United States Senator Sam McKinley flashed his gleaming white teeth in a smile so falsely genuine and so obviously aimed at the reporters, it made her want to laugh.

But she didn't laugh. If she'd learned one thing during her childhood and adolescence as the daughter of an international businessman who moved to a different and often exotic country every year or so, she'd learned that diplomats and high government officials—particularly royalty—take themselves very, *very* seriously.

So, instead of laughing, she bit the insides of her cheeks as she stopped several respectful paces behind the prince, at the head of the crowd of assistants and aides and advisers who were part of his royal entourage.

"Your Highness, on behalf of the United States Government," McKinley drawled in his thick Texas accent, shaking the prince's hand, and dripping with goodwill, "I'd like to welcome you to our country's capital."

"I greet you with the timeless honor and tradition of the Ustanzian flag," Prince Tedric said formally in his faintly British, faintly French accent, "which is woven, as well, into my heart."

It was his standard greeting; nothing special, but it went over quite well with the crowd.

McKinley started in on a longer greeting, and Veronica let her attention wander.

She could see herself in the airport's reflective glass windows, looking cool in her cream-colored suit, her flame-red hair pulled neatly back into a French braid. Tall and slender and serene, her image wavered slightly as a jet plane took off, thundering down the runway.

It was an illusion. Actually, she was giddy with nervous excitement, a condition brought about by the stress of knowing that if Tedric didn't follow her instructions and ended up looking bad on camera, she'd be the one to blame. Sweat trickled down between her shoulder blades, another side effect of the stress she was under. No, she felt neither cool nor serene, regardless of how she looked.

She had been hired because her friend, Princess Wila, knew that Veronica was struggling to get her fledgling consulting business off the ground. Sure, she'd done smaller, less detailed jobs before, but this was the first one in which the stakes were so very high. If Veronica succeeded with Tedric Cortere, word would get out, and she'd have more business than she could handle. *If* she succeeded with Cortere...

But Veronica had also been hired for another reason. She'd been hired because Wila, concerned about Ustanzia's economy, recognized the importance of this tour. Despite the fact that teaching Wila's brother, the high-strung Prince of Ustanzia, how to appear calm and relaxed while under the watchful eyes of the TV news cameras was Veronica's first major assignment as an image and media consultant, Wila trusted her longtime friend implicitly to get the job done.

"I'm counting on you, Véronique," Wila had said to Veronica over the telephone just last night. She had added with her customary frankness, "This American connection is too important. Don't let Tedric screw this up."

So far Tedric was doing a good job. He looked good. He sounded good. But it was too early for Veronica to let herself feel truly satisfied. It was her job to make sure that the prince *continued* to look and sound good.

Tedric didn't particularly like his younger sister's best friend, and the feeling was mutual. He was an impatient, short-tempered man, and rather used to getting his own way. *Very* used to getting his own way.

Veronica could only hope he would see today's news reports and recognize the day's success. If he didn't, she'd hear about it, that was for sure.

Veronica knew quite well that over the course of the prince's tour of the United States she was going to earn every single penny of her consultant's fee. Because although Tedric Cortere was princely in looks and appearance, he was also arrogant and spoiled. And demanding. And often irrational. And occasionally, not very nice.

Oh, he knew his social etiquette. He was in his element when it came to pomp and ceremony, parties and other social posturing. He knew all there was to know about clothing and fashion. He could tell Japanese silk from American with a single touch. He was a wine connoisseur and a gourmet. He could ride horses and fence, play polo and waterski. He hired countless aides and advisers to dance attendance upon him, and provide him with both his most trivial desires and the important information he needed to get by as a representative of his country.

As Veronica watched, Tedric shook the hands of the U.S. officials. He smiled charmingly and she could practically hear the sound of the news cameras zooming in for a close-up.

The prince glanced directly into the camera lenses and let his smile broaden. Spoiled or not, with his trim, athletic body and handsome face, the man was good-looking.

Good-looking? No, Veronica thought. To call him good-looking wasn't accurate. Quite honestly, the prince was gorgeous. He was a piece of art. He had long, thick, dark hair that curled down past his shoulders. His face was long and lean with exotic cheekbones that hinted of his mother's Mediterranean heritage. His eyes were the deepest brown, surrounded by sinfully long lashes. His jaw was square, his nose strong and masculine.

But Veronica had known Tedric since she was fifteen and he was nineteen. Naturally, she'd developed a full-fledged crush on him quite early on, but it hadn't taken her long to realize that the prince was nothing like his cheerful, breezy, lighthearted yet business-minded sister. Tedric was, in fact, quite decidedly dull—and enormously preoccupied with his appearance. He had spent endless amounts of time in front of a mirror, sending Wila and Veronica into spasms of giggles as he combed his hair, flexed his muscles and examined his perfect, white teeth.

Still, Veronica's crush on Prince Tedric hadn't truly crashed and burned until she'd had a conversation with him—and seen that beneath his facade of princely charm and social skills, behind his handsome face and trim body, deep within his dark brown eyes, there was nothing there.

Nothing *she* was interested in, anyway.

Although she had to admit that to this day, her romantic vision of a perfect man was someone tall, dark and handsome. Someone with wide, exotic cheekbones and liquid brown eyes. Someone who looked an awful lot like Crown Prince Tedric, but with a working brain in his head and a heart that loved more than his own reflection in the mirror.

She wasn't looking for a prince. In fact, she wasn't looking, period. She had no time for romance—at least, not until her business started to turn a profit.

As the military band began to play a rousing rendition of the Ustanzian national anthem, Veronica glanced again at their blurry images in the window. A flash of light from the upper-level balcony caught her eye. *That was odd.* She'd been told that airport personnel would be restricting access to the second floor as a security measure.

She turned her head to look up at the balcony and realized with a surge of disbelief that the flash she'd seen was a reflection of light bouncing off the long barrel of a rifle—a rifle aimed directly at Tedric.

"Get down!" Veronica shouted, but her voice was drowned out by the trumpets. The prince couldn't hear her. No one could hear her.

She ran toward Prince Tedric and all of the U.S. dignitaries, well aware that she was running toward, not away from, the danger. A thought flashed crazily through her head—*This was not a man worth dying for.* But she couldn't stand by and let her best friend's brother be killed. Not while she had the power to prevent it.

As a shot rang out, Veronica hit Tedric bone-jarringly hard at waist level and knocked him to the ground. It was a rugby tackle that would have made her brother Jules quite proud.

She bruised her shoulder, tore her nylons and scraped both of her knees when she fell.

But she saved the crown prince of Ustanzia's life.

When Veronica walked into the hotel conference room, it was clear the meeting had been going on for quite some time.

Senator McKinley was sitting at one end of the big oval conference table with his jacket off, his tie loosened, and his shirtsleeves rolled up. Henri Freder, the U.S. ambassador to Ustanzia, sat on one side of him. Another diplomat and several other men whom Veronica didn't recognize sat on the other. Men in dark suits stood at the doors and by the windows, watchful and alert. They were FInCOM agents, Veronica realized, high-tech bodyguards from the Federal Intelligence Commission, sent to protect the prince. But why were they involved? Was Prince Tedric's life still in danger?

Tedric was at the head of the table, surrounded by a dozen aides and advisers. He had a cold drink in front of him, and was lazily drawing designs in the condensation on the glass.

As Veronica entered the room, Tedric stood, and the entire tableful of men followed suit.

"Someone get a seat for Ms. St. John," the prince ordered sharply in his odd accent. "Immediately."

One of the lesser aides quickly stepped away from his own chair and offered it to Veronica.

"Thank you," she said, smiling at the young man.

"Sit down," the prince commanded her, stony-faced, as he returned to his seat. "I have an idea, but it cannot be done without your cooperation."

Veronica gazed steadily at the prince. After she'd tackled him earlier today, he'd been dragged away to safety. She hadn't seen or heard from him since. At the time, he hadn't bothered to thank her for saving his life—and apparently he had no intention of doing so now. She was working for him, therefore she was a servant. He would have expected her to save him. In his mind, there was no need for gratitude.

But she wasn't a servant. In fact, she'd been the maid of honor last year when his sister married Veronica's brother, Jules. Veronica and the prince were practically family, yet Tedric still insisted she address him as "Your Highness," or "Your Majesty."

She sat down, pulling her chair in closer to the table, and the rest of the men sat, too.

"I have a double," the prince announced. "An American. It is my idea for him to take my place throughout the remaining course of the tour, thus ensuring my safety."

Veronica sat forward. "Excuse me, Your Highness," she said. "Please forgive my confusion. Is your safety still an issue?" She looked down the table at Senator McKinley. "Wasn't the gunman captured?"

McKinley ran his tongue over his front teeth before he answered. "I'm afraid not," he finally replied. "And the Federal Intelligence Commission has reason to believe the terrorists will make another attempt on the prince's life during the course of the next few weeks."

"Terrorists?" Veronica repeated, looking from McKinley to the ambassador and finally at Prince Tedric.

"FInCOM has ID'd the shooter," McKinley answered. "He's a well-known triggerman for a South American terrorist organization."

Veronica shook her head. "Why would South American terrorists want to kill the Ustanzian crown prince?"

The ambassador took off his glasses and tiredly rubbed his eyes. "Quite possibly in retaliation for Ustanzia's new alliance with the U.S.," he said.

"FInCOM tells us these particular shooters don't give up easily," McKinley said. "Even with souped-up security, FInCOM expects they'll try again. What we're looking to do is find a solution to this problem."

Veronica laughed. It slipped out—she couldn't help herself. The solution was so obvious. "Cancel the tour."

"Can't do that," McKinley drawled.

Veronica looked down the other side of the table at Prince Tedric. He, for once, was silent. But he didn't look happy.

"There's too much riding on the publicity from this event," Senator McKinley explained. "You know as well as I do that Ustanzia needs U.S. funding to get their oil wells up and running." The heavyset man leaned back in his chair, tapping the eraser end of a pencil on the mahogany table. "But the prospect of competitively priced oil isn't enough to secure the size funds they need," he continued, dropping the pencil and running his hand through his thinning gray hair. "And quite frankly, current polls show the public's concern for a little-nothing country like Ustanzia—beg pardon, Prince—to be zilch. Hardly anyone knows who the Ustanzians are, and the folks who *do* know about 'em don't want to give 'em any of their tax dollars, that's for sure as shootin'. Not while there's so much here at home to spend the money on."

Veronica nodded her head. She was well aware of everything he was saying. It was one of Princess Wila's major worries.

"Besides," the senator added, "we can use this opportunity to nab this group of terrorists. And sister, if they're who we think they are, we want 'em. Bad."

"But if you know for a fact that there'll be another assassination attempt...?" Veronica looked down the table at Tedric. "Your Majesty, how can you risk placing yourself in such danger?"

Tedric crossed his legs. "I have no intention of placing myself in any danger whatsoever," he said. "In fact, I will remain here, in Washington, in a safe house, until all danger has passed. The tour, however, will continue as planned, with this lookalike fellow taking my place."

Suddenly the prince's earlier words made sense. He'd said he had a double, someone who looked just like him. He'd said this person was an American.

"This man," McKinley asked. "What was his name, sir?"

The prince shrugged—a slow, eloquent gesture. "How should I remember? Joe. Joe Something. He was a soldier. An American soldier."

"'Joe Something,'" McKinley repeated, exchanging a quick, exasperated look with the diplomat on his left. "A soldier named Joe. Should only be about fifteen thousand men in the U.S. armed forces named Joe."

The ambassador on McKinley's right leaned forward. "Your Highness," he said patiently, "when did you meet this man?"

"He was one of the soldiers who assisted in my escape from the embassy in Baghdad," Tedric replied.

"A Navy SEAL," the ambassador murmured to McKinley. "We should have no problem locating him. If I remember correctly, only one seven-man team participated in that rescue mission."

"SEAL?" Veronica asked, sitting up and leaning forward. "What's a SEAL?"

"Part of the Special Forces Division," Senator McKinley told her. "They're *the* most elite special-operations force in the world. They can operate anywhere—on the sea, in the air and on the land, hence the name, SEALs. If this man who looks so much like the prince really is a SEAL, standing in as the prince's double will be a cakewalk for him."

"He was, however, quite unbearably lower-class," the prince said prudishly, sweeping some imaginary crumbs from the surface of the table. He looked at Veronica. "That is where you would come in. You will teach this Joe to look and act like a prince. We can delay the tour by—" he frowned down the table at McKinley "—a week, is that what you'd said?"

"Two or three days at the very most, sir." The senator grimaced. "We can announce that you've come down with the flu, try to keep up public interest with reports of your health. But the fact is, after a few days, you'll no longer be news and the story will be dropped. You know what they say: Out of sight, out of mind. We can't let that happen."

Two or three days. Two or three days to turn a rough American sailor—a Navy SEAL, whatever that really meant—into royalty. Who were they kidding?

Senator McKinley picked up the phone to begin tracking down the mysterious Joe.

Prince Tedric was watching Veronica expectantly. "Can you do it?" he asked. "Can you make this Joe into a prince?"

"In two or three *days?*"

Tedric nodded.

"I'd have to work around the clock," Veronica said, thinking aloud. If she agreed to this crazy plan, she would have to be right beside this sailor, this SEAL, every single step of the way. She'd have to coach him continuously, and be ready to catch and correct his every mistake. "And even then, there'd be no guarantee...."

Tedric shrugged, turning back to Ambassador Freder. "She can't do it," he said flatly. "We *will* have to cancel. Arrange a flight back to—"

"I didn't say I couldn't do it," Veronica interrupted, quickly adding, "Your Majesty."

The prince turned back to her, one elegant eyebrow raised.

Veronica could hear an echo of Wila's voice. "I'm counting on you, Véronique. This American connection is too important." If this tour were canceled, all of Wila's hopes for the future would evaporate. And Wila's weren't the only hopes that would be dashed. Veronica couldn't let herself forget that little girl waiting at Saint Mary's....

"Well?" Tedric said impatiently.

"All right," Veronica said. "I'll give it a try."

Senator McKinley hung up the phone with a triumphant crash. "I think we've found our man," he announced with a wide smile. "His name's Navy Lieutenant Joseph P.—" he glanced down at a scrap of paper he'd taken some notes on "—Catalanotto. They're faxing me an ID photo right now."

Veronica felt an odd flash of both hot and cold. Good God, what had she just done? What had she just agreed to? What if she couldn't pull it off? What if it couldn't be done?

The fax alarm began to beep. Both the prince and Senator McKinley stood and crossed the spacious suite to where the fax machine was plugged in beneath a set of elegant bay windows.

Veronica stayed in her seat at the table. If this job couldn't be done, she would be letting her best friend down.

"My God," McKinley breathed as the picture was slowly printed out. "It doesn't seem possible."

He tore the fax from the roll of paper and handed it to the prince.

Silently, Tedric stared at the picture. Silently, he walked back across the room and handed the sheet of paper to Veronica.

Except for the fact that the man in the picture was wearing a relaxed pair of military fatigues, with top buttons of the shirt undone and sleeves rolled up to his elbows, except for the fact that the man in the picture had dark, shaggy hair cut just a little below his ears, and the strap of a submachine gun slung over one shoulder, except for the fact that the camera had caught him mid-grin, with good humor and sharp intelligence sparkling in his dark eyes, the man in this picture could very well have been the crown prince of Ustanzia. Or at the very least, he could have been the crown prince's brother.

The crown prince's *better-looking* brother.

He had the same nose, same cheekbones, same well-defined jawline and chin. But his front tooth was chipped. Of course, that was no problem. They could cap a tooth in a matter of hours, couldn't they?

He was bigger than Prince Tedric, this American naval lieutenant. Bigger and taller. Stronger. Rougher edged. Much, *much* more rough-edged, in every way imaginable. Good God, if this picture was any indication, Veronica was going to have to start with the basics with this man. She was going to have to teach him how to sit and stand and walk....

Veronica looked up to find Prince Tedric watching her.

"Something tells me," he said in his elegant accent, "your work is cut out for you."

Across the room, McKinley picked up the phone and dialed. "Yeah," he said into the receiver. "This is Sam McKinley. *Senator* Sam McKinley. I need a Navy SEAL by the name of Lieutenant Joseph—" he consulted his notes "—Catalanotto. Damn, what a mouthful. I need that lieutenant here in Washington, and I need him here yesterday."

Chapter 2

Joe lay on the deck of the rented boat, hands behind his head, watching the clouds. Puffs of blinding white in a crystal blue California sky, they were in a state of constant motion, always changing, never remaining the same.

He liked that.

It reminded him of his life, fluid and full of surprises. He never knew when a cream puff might turn unexpectedly into a ferocious dragon.

But Joe liked it that way. He liked never knowing what was behind the door—the lady or the tiger. And certainly, since he'd been a SEAL, he'd had his share of both.

But today there were neither ladies nor tigers to face. Today he was on leave—shore leave, it was called in the navy. Funny he should spend the one day of shore leave he had this month far from the shore, out on a fishing boat.

Not that he'd spent very much time lately at sea. In fact, in the past few months, he'd been on a naval vessel exactly ninety-six hours. And that had been for training. Some of those training hours he'd spent as an instructor. But some of the time he'd been a student. That was all part of being a Navy SEAL. No matter your rank or experience, you always had to keep learning, keep training, keep on top of the new technology and methodology.

Joe had achieved expert status in nine different fields, but those fields were always changing. Just like those clouds that were floating above him. Just the way he liked it.

Across the deck of the boat, dressed in weekend grunge clothes similar to his own torn fatigues and ragged T-shirt, Harvard and Blue were arguing good-naturedly over who had gotten the most depressing letter from the weekly mail call.

Joe himself hadn't gotten any mail—nothing besides bills, that is. Talk about depressing.

Joe closed his eyes, letting the conversation float over him. He'd known Blue for eight years, Harvard for about six. Their voices—Blue's thick, south-of-the-Mason-Dixon-Line drawl and Harvard's nasal, upper-class-Boston accent—were as familiar to him as breathing.

It still sometimes tickled him that out of their entire seven-man SEAL team, the man that Blue was closest to, after Joe himself, was Daryl Becker, nicknamed Harvard.

Carter "Blue" McCoy and Daryl "Harvard" Becker. The "redneck" rebel and the Ivy League-educated Yankee black man. Both SEALs, both better than the best of the rest. And both aware that there was no such thing as prejudices and pre-judgments in the Navy SEALs.

Out across the bay, the blue-green water sparkled and danced in the bright sunshine. Joe took a deep breath, filling his lungs with the sharp salty air.

"Oh, Lord," Blue said, turning to the second page of his letter.

Joe turned toward his friend. "What?"

"Gerry's getting married," Blue said, running his fingers through his sun-bleached blond hair. "To Jenny Lee Beaumont."

Jenny Lee had been Blue's high school girlfriend. She was the only woman Blue had ever talked about—the only one special enough to mention.

Joe exchanged a long look with Harvard.

"Jenny Lee Beaumont, huh?" Joe said.

"That's right." Blue nodded, his face carefully expressionless. "Gerry's gonna marry her. Next July. He wants me to be his best man."

Joe swore softly.

"You win," Harvard conceded. "Your mail was much more depressing than mine."

Joe shook his head, grateful for his own lack of entanglement with a woman. Sure, he'd had girlfriends down through the years, but he'd never met anyone he couldn't walk away from.

Not that he didn't like women, because he did. He certainly did. And the women he usually dated were smart and funny and as quick to shy away from permanent attachments as he was. He would see his current lady friend on occasional weekend leaves, and sometimes in the evenings when he was in town and free.

But never, ever had he kissed a woman good-night—or good-morning, as was usually the case—then gone back to the base and sat around daydreaming about her the way Bob and Wesley had drooled over those college girls they'd met down in San Diego. Or the way Harvard had sighed over that Hawaiian marine biologist they'd met on Guam. What was her name? Rachel. Harvard *still* got that kicked-puppy look in his brown eyes whenever her name came up.

The truth was, Joe had been lucky—he'd never fallen in love. And he was hoping his luck would hold. It would be just fine with him if he went through life without *that* particular experience, thank you very much.

Joe pushed the top off the cooler with one bare toe. He reached into the icy water to pull out a beer, then froze.

He straightened, ears straining, eyes scanning the horizon to the east.

Then he heard it again.

The sound of a distant chopper. He shaded his eyes, looking out toward the California coastline, to where the sound was coming from.

Silently, Harvard and Blue got to their feet, moving to stand next to him. Silently, Harvard handed Joe the binoculars that had been stowed in one of the equipment lockers.

One swift turn of the dial brought the powerful lenses into focus.

The chopper was only a small black dot, but it was growing larger with each passing second. It was undeniably heading directly toward them.

"You guys wearing your pagers?" Joe asked, breaking the silence. He'd taken his own beeper off after it—and he—had gotten doused by a pailful of bait and briny seawater.

Harvard nodded. "Yes, sir." He glanced down at the beeper he wore attached to his belt. "But I'm clear."

"Mine didn't go off, either, Cat," Blue said.

In the binoculars, the black dot took on a distinct outline. It was an army bird, a Black Hawk, UH-60A. Its cruising speed was about one hundred and seventy miles per hour. It was closing in on them, and fast.

"Either of you in any trouble I should know about?" Joe asked.

"No, sir," Harvard said.

"Negative." Blue glanced at Joe. "How 'bout you, Lieutenant?"

Joe shook his head, still watching the helicopter through the binoculars.

"This is weird," Harvard said. "What kind of hurry are they in, they can't page us and have us motor back to the harbor?"

"One damn big hurry," Joe said. God, that Black Hawk could really move. He pulled the binoculars away from his face as the chopper continued to grow larger.

"It's not World War Three," Blue commented, his troubles with Jenny Lee temporarily forgotten. He had to raise his voice to be heard above the approaching helicopter. "If it was World War Three, they wouldn't waste a Hawk on three lousy SEALs."

The chopper circled and then hovered directly above them. The sound of the blades was deafening, and the force of the wind made the little boat pitch and toss. All three men grabbed the railing to keep their footing.

Then a scaling rope was thrown out the open door of the helicopter's cabin. It, too, swayed in the wind from the chopper blades, smacking Joe directly in the chest.

"Lieutenant Joseph P. Catalanotto," a distorted voice announced over a loudspeaker. "Your shore leave is over."

Veronica St. John went into her hotel suite, then leaned wearily back against the closed door.

It was only nine o'clock—early by diplomatic standards. In fact, if things had gone according to schedule today, she would still have been at a reception for Prince Tedric over at the Ustanzian Embassy. But things had gone very much *not* according to schedule, starting with the assassination attempt at the airport.

She'd gotten a call from the president of the United States, officially thanking her, on behalf of the American people, for saving Prince Tedric's life. She hadn't expected that. Too bad. If she'd been expecting the man in the White House to call, she might have been prepared to ask for his assistance in locating the personnel records of this mysterious navy lieutenant who looked so much like the crown prince of Ustanzia.

Nobody, repeat *nobody* she had spoken to had been able to help her find the files she wanted. The Department of Defense sent her to the Navy. The Navy representatives told her that all SEAL records were in the Special Forces Division. The clerk from Special Forces was as clandestine and unhelpful as James Bond's personal assistant might have been. The woman wouldn't even verify that Joseph Catalanotto existed, let alone if the man's personnel files were in the U.S. Special Forces Office.

Frustrated, Veronica had gone back to Senator McKinley, hoping that he could use his clout to get a fax of Catalanotto's files. But even the powerful senator was told that, for security reasons, personnel records for Navy SEALs were never, repeat *never,* sent via facsimile. It had been a major feat just getting them to fax a picture of the lieutenant. If McKinley wanted to see Joseph P. Catalanotto's personnel file, he would need to make a formal request, in writing. After the request was received, it would take a mandatory three days for the files to be censored for his—and Ms. St. John's—level of clearance.

Three *days.*

Veronica wasn't looking to find Lieutenant Catalanotto's deepest, darkest military secrets. All she wanted to know was

where the man came from—in which part of the country he'd
grown up. She wanted to know his family background, his level
of education, his IQ scores and the results of personality and
psychological tests done by the armed forces.

She wanted to know, quite frankly, how big an obstacle this
Navy SEAL himself was going to be in getting the job done.

So far, she only knew his name, that he looked like a rougher,
wilder version of Tedric Cortere, that his shoulders were very
broad, that he carried an M60 machine gun as if it were a large
loaf of bread, and that he had a nice smile.

She didn't have a clue as to whether she'd be able to fool the
American public into thinking he was a European prince. Until she met this man, she couldn't even guess how much work
transforming him was going to take. It would be better to try
not to think about it.

But if she didn't think about this job looming over her, she
would end up thinking about the girl at Saint Mary's Hospital, a little girl named Cindy who had sent the prince a letter
nearly four months ago—a letter Veronica had fished out of
Tedric's royal wastebasket. In the letter, Cindy—barely even ten
years old—had told Prince Tedric that she'd heard he was
planning a trip to the United States. She had asked him, if he
was going to be in the Washington, D.C., area, to please come
and visit her since she was not able to come to see him.

Veronica had ended up going above the prince—directly to
King Derrick—and had gotten the visit to Saint Mary's on the
official tour calendar.

But now what?

The entire tour would have to be rescheduled and re-
planned, and Saint Mary's and little Cindy were likely to fall,
ignored, between the cracks.

Veronica smiled tightly. Not if *she* had anything to say about
it.

With a sigh, she kicked off her shoes.

Lord, but she ached.

Tackling royalty could really wear a person out, she thought,
allowing herself a rueful smile. After the assassination attempt, she had run on sheer adrenaline for about six hours
straight. After that had worn off, she'd kept herself fueled with
coffee—hot, black and strong.

Right now what she needed was a shower and a two-hour nap.

She pulled her nightgown and robe out of the suitcase that she hadn't yet found time to unpack, and tossed them onto the bed as she all but staggered into the bathroom. She closed the door and turned on the shower as she peeled off her suit and the cream-colored blouse she wore underneath. She put a hole in her hose as she took them off, and threw them directly into the wastebasket. It had been a bona fide two-pairs-of-panty-hose day. Her first pair, the ones she'd been wearing at the airport, had been totally destroyed.

Veronica washed herself quickly, knowing that every minute she spent in the shower was a minute less that she'd be able to sleep. And with Lieutenant Joseph P. Catalanotto due to arrive anytime after midnight, she was going to need every second of that nap.

Still, it didn't keep her from singing as she tried to rinse the aches and soreness from her back and shoulders. Singing in the shower was a childhood habit. Then, as now, the moments she spent alone in the shower were among the few bits of time she had to really kick back and let loose. She tested the acoustics of this particular bathroom with a rousing rendition of Mary Chapin Carpenter's latest hit.

She shut off the water, still singing, and toweled herself dry.

Her robe was hanging on the back of the bathroom door, and she reached for it.

And stopped singing, mid-note.

She'd left her robe in the bedroom, on the bed. She hadn't hung it on the door.

"No...you're right. You're *not* alone in here," said a husky male voice from the other side of the bathroom door.

Chapter 3

Veronica's heart nearly stopped beating, and she lunged for the door and turned the lock.

"I figured you didn't know I was in your room," the voice continued as Veronica quickly slipped into her white terry-cloth bathrobe. "I also figured you probably wouldn't appreciate coming out of the bathroom with just a towel on—or less. Not with an audience, anyway. So I put your robe on the back of the door."

Veronica tightened the belt and clutched the lapels of the robe more closely together. She took in a deep breath, then let it slowly out. It steadied her and kept her voice from shaking. "Who are you?" she asked.

"Who are *you?*" the voice countered. It was rich, husky, and laced with more than a trace of blue-collar New York. "I was brought here and told to wait, so I waited. I've been hustled from one coast to the other like some Federal Express overnight package, only nobody has any explanations as to why or even *who* I'm waiting to see. I didn't even know my insertion point was the District of Columbia until the jet landed at Andrews. And as long as I'm complaining I might as well tell you that I'm tired, I'm hungry and my shorts have not managed to dry in the past ten hours, a situation that makes me very, very cranky. I would damn near sell my soul to get into that shower that you just stepped out of. Other than that, I'm sure I'm very pleased to meet you.''

''Lieutenant Catalanotto?'' Veronica asked.

''Bingo,'' the voice said. ''Babe, you just answered your own question.''

But had she? ''What's your first name?'' she asked warily.

''Joe. Joseph.''

''Middle name?''

''Paulo,'' he said.

Veronica swung open the bathroom door.

The first thing she noticed about the man was his size. He was big—taller than Prince Tedric by about two inches and outweighing him in sheer muscle by a good, solid fifty pounds. His dark hair was cut much shorter than Tedric's, and he had at least a two-day growth of beard darkening his face.

He didn't look as exactly like the prince as she'd thought when she saw his photograph, Veronica realized, studying the man's face. On closer inspection, his nose was slightly different—it had been broken, probably more than once. And, if it was possible, this navy lieutenant's cheekbones were even more exotic-looking than Tedric's. His chin was slightly more square, more stubborn than the prince's. And his eyes... As he returned her inquisitive stare, his lids dropped halfway over his remarkable liquid brown eyes, as if he was trying to hide his innermost secrets from her.

But those differences—even the size differences between the two men—were very subtle. They wouldn't be noticed by someone who didn't know Prince Tedric very well. Those differences certainly wouldn't be noticed by the array of ambassadors and diplomats Tedric was scheduled to meet.

''According to the name tag on your suitcase, you've gotta be Veronica St. John, right?'' he said, pronouncing her name the American way, as if it were two words, *Saint* and John.

''Sinjin,'' she said distractedly. ''You don't say Saint John, you say 'Sinjin.''''

He was looking at her, examining her in much the same way that she'd looked at him. The intensity of his gaze made her feel naked. Which of course, underneath her robe, she was.

But he didn't win any prizes himself for the clothing he was wearing. From the looks of it, his T-shirt had had its sleeves forcibly removed without the aid of scissors, his army fatigues had been cut off into ragged shorts, and on his feet he wore a pair of dirty canvas deck shoes with no socks. He looked as if he hadn't showered in several days, and, Lord help her, he smelled that way, too.

"Dear God," Veronica said aloud, taking in all of the little details she'd missed at first. He wasn't wearing a belt. Instead, a length of fairly thick rope was run through the belt loops in his pants, and tied in some kind of knot at the front. He had a tattoo—a navy anchor—on his left biceps. His fingers were blackened with stains of grease, his fingernails were short and rough—a far cry from Prince Tedric's carefully manicured hands. Lord, if she had to start by teaching this man the basics of personal hygiene, there was no way she'd have him impersonating a prince within her three-day deadline.

"What?" he said with a scowl. Defensiveness tinged his voice and darkened his eyes. "I'm not what you expected?"

She couldn't deny it. She'd expected the lieutenant to arrive wearing a dress uniform, stiff and starched and perfectly military—and smelling a little more human and a little less like a real-life marine mammal-type seal. Wordlessly, she shook her head no.

Joe gazed silently at the girl. She watched him, too, her eyes so wide and blue against the porcelain paleness of her skin. It was hard for him to tell the color of her hair—it was wet. It clung, damp and dark, to the sides of her head and neck.

Red, he guessed. It was probably some shade of red, maybe even strawberry blond, probably curly. Yet, if there really was a God and He was truly righteous, she would have nondescript straight hair, maybe the color of mud. It didn't seem fair that this girl should have wealth, a powerful job, refined manners, a pair of beautiful blue eyes *and* curly red hair.

Without makeup, her face looked alarmingly young. Her features were delicate, almost fragile. She wasn't particularly pretty, at least not in the conventional sense. But her cheekbones were high, showcasing enormous crystal blue eyes. And her lips were exquisitely shaped, her nose small and elegant.

No, she wasn't pretty. But she was incredibly attractive in a way he couldn't even begin to explain.

The robe she wore was too big for her. It drew attention to her slight frame, accentuating her slender wrists and ankles.

She looked like a kid playing dress up in her mommy's clothes.

Funny, from the cut and style of the business suits that had been neatly packed in her suitcase, Joe had expected this Veronica St. John—or "Sinjin," as she'd pronounced it with her slightly British, extremely monied upper-class accent—to be, well . . . less young. He'd expected someone in their mid-forties at least, maybe even older. But this girl couldn't be a day over twenty-five. Hell, standing here like this, just out of the shower, still dripping wet, she barely looked sixteen.

"You aren't what I expected, either," Joe said, sitting down on the edge of the bed. "So I guess that makes us even."

He knew he was making her nervous, sitting there like that. He knew she was nervous about him getting the bedspread dirty, nervous about him leaving behind the lingering odor of dead fish—bait from the smelly bucket Blue had knocked over earlier that morning. Hell, he was nervous about it himself.

And damn, but that made him angry. This girl was somehow responsible for dragging him away from his shore leave. She was somehow responsible for the way he'd been rushed across the country without a shower or a change of clothes. Hell, it was probably her fault that he was in this five-star hotel wearing his barnacle-scraping clothes, feeling way out of his league.

He didn't like feeling this way. He didn't like the barely concealed distaste he could see in this rich girl's eyes. He didn't like being reminded that he didn't fit into this opulent world of hers—a world filled with money, power and class.

Not that he *wanted* to fit in. Hell, he wouldn't last more than a few months in a place like this. He preferred his own world—the world of the Navy SEALs, where a man wasn't judged by the size of his wallet, or the price of his education, or the cut of his clothes. In *his* world, a man was judged by his actions, by his perseverance, by his loyalty and stamina. In his world, a man who'd made it into the SEALs was treated with honor and respect—regardless of the way he looked. Or smelled.

He leaned back on the big, fancy, five-star bed, propping himself up on his elbows. "Maybe you could give me some kind of clue as to what I'm doing here, honey," he said, watching her wince at his term of endearment. "I'm pretty damn curious."

The rich girl's eyes widened, and she actually forgot to look disdainful for a few minutes. "Are you trying to tell me that no one's told you *any*thing?"

Joe sat up. "That's *exactly* what I'm telling you."

She shook her head. Her hair was starting to dry, and it was definitely curly. "But that's impossible."

"Impossible it ain't, sweetheart," he said. A double wince this time. One for the bad grammar, the other for the "sweetheart." "I'm here in D.C. without the rest of my team, and I don't know why."

Veronica turned abruptly and went into the hotel suite's living room. Joe followed more slowly, leaning against the frame of the door and watching as she sifted through her briefcase.

"You were supposed to be met by—" she pulled a yellow legal pad from her notebook and flipped to a page in the back "—an Admiral Forrest?" She looked up at him almost hopefully.

The navy lieutenant just shrugged, still watching her. Lord, but he was handsome. Despite the layers of dirt and his dark, scowling expression, he was, like Prince Tedric, almost impossibly good-looking. And this man was nearly dripping with an unconscious virility that Tedric didn't even *begin* to possess. He was extremely attractive underneath all that grime—if she were the type who went for that untamed, rough-hewn kind of man.

Which, of course, Veronica wasn't. Dangerous, bad-boy types had never made her heart beat faster. And if her heart seemed to be pounding now, why, that was surely from the scare he'd given her earlier.

No, she was not the type to be attracted by steel-hard biceps and broad shoulders, a rough-looking five o'clock shadow, a tropical tan, a molten-lava smile, and incredible brown bedroom eyes. No. Definitely, positively not.

And if she gave him a second glance, it was only to verify the fact that Lieutenant Joseph P. Catalanotto was *not* going to be mistaken for visiting European royalty.

Not today, anyway.

And not tomorrow. But, for Wila's sake, for her own career, and for little Cindy at Saint Mary's, Veronica was going to see to it that two days from now, Joe would be a prince.

But first things first. And first things definitely included putting her clothes back on, particularly since Lieutenant Catalanotto wasn't attempting to hide the very, *very* male appreciation in his eyes as he looked at her.

"Why don't you help yourself to something to drink," Veronica said, and Joe's gaze flickered across the suite, toward the elaborate bar that was set up on the other side of the room. "Give me a minute to get dressed," she added. "Then I'll try to explain why you're here."

He nodded.

She walked past him, aware that he was still watching right up to the moment she closed the bedroom door behind her.

The man's accent was atrocious. It screamed New York City—blue-collar New York City. But okay. With a little ingenuity, with the right scheduling and planning, Joe wouldn't have to utter a single word.

His posture, though, was an entirely different story. Tedric stood ramrod straight. Lieutenant Catalanotto, on the other hand, slouched continuously. And he walked with a kind of relaxed swagger that was utterly un-princely. How on *earth* was she going to teach him to stand and sit up straight, let alone *walk* in that peculiar, stiff, princely gait that Tedric had perfected?

Veronica pulled fresh underwear and another pair of panty hose—number three for the day—from her suitcase. Her dark blue suit was near the top of the case, so she pulled it on, then slipped her tired feet into a matching pair of pumps. A little bit of makeup, a quick brush through her almost-dry hair . . .

Gloves would cover his hands, she thought, her mind going a mile a minute. Even if that engine grease didn't wash off, it could be hidden by a pair of gloves. Tedric himself often wore a pair of white gloves. No one would think that was odd.

Joe's hair was an entirely different matter. He wore his hair short, while Tedric's flowed down past his shoulders.

They could get a wig for Joe. Or hair extensions. Yes, hair extensions would be even better, and easier to keep on. Provided Joe would sit still long enough to have them attached . . .

This was going to work. This was *going* to work.

Taking a deep breath and smoothing down her suit jacket, Veronica opened the door and went back into the living room.

And stopped short.

The living room of her hotel suite was positively crowded.

Senator McKinley, three different Ustanzian ambassadors, an older man wearing a military dress uniform covered with medals, a half-dozen FInCOM security agents, Prince Tedric *and* his entire entourage all stood frozen and staring at Joe Catalanotto, who had risen to his feet in front of the sofa. The tension in the room could have been cut by a knife.

The man in uniform was the only one who spoke. "Nice to see that you dressed for the occasion, Joe," he said with a chuckle.

Joe crossed his arms. "The guys who shanghaied me forgot to bring my wardrobe trunk," he said dryly. Then he smiled. It was a genuine, sincere smile that warmed his face and touched his eyes. "Good to see you, Admiral."

Joe looked around the room, his gaze landing on Prince Tedric's face. Tedric was staring at him as if he were a rat that had made its way into the hotel room from the street below.

Joe's smile faded, and was replaced by another scowl. "Well," he said. "I'll be damned. If it isn't my evil twin."

Veronica laughed. She couldn't help it. It just came bubbling out. She bit down on the inside of her cheek, and all but clamped her hand across her mouth. But no one seemed to notice—no one but Joe, who glanced over at her in surprise.

"Don't you know who you're talking to, young man? This is the crown prince of Ustanzia," Senator McKinley said sternly to Joe.

"Damn straight I know who I'm talking to, Pop," Joe said tightly. "I'm the kind of guy who never forgets a face—particularly when I see it every morning in the mirror. My team of SEALs pulled this bastard's sorry butt out of Baghdad." He turned back to Tedric. "Keeping free and clear of war zones these days, Ted, you lousy bastard?"

Everyone in the room, with the exception of Joe and the still-grinning admiral, drew in a shocked breath. Veronica was amazed that her ears didn't pop from the sudden drop in air pressure.

The crown prince's face turned an interesting shade of royal purple. "How dare you?" he gasped.

Joe seemed to grow at least three feet taller and two feet broader. He took a step or two toward Tedric, and everyone in the room—with the exception of the admiral—drew back.

"How dare *you* put yourself into a situation where my men had to risk their lives to pull you back out?" Joe all but snarled. "One of my men spent *months* in intensive care because of you, dirtwad. I'll tell you right now, you're damned lucky—*damned lucky*—he didn't die."

The deadly look in Joe's eyes was enough to make even the bravest man quiver with fear. They were *all* lucky that Joe's friend hadn't died, Veronica thought with a shiver, or else they'd be witnessing a murder. And unlike the morning's assassination attempt, she had no doubt that Joe would succeed.

"Mon Dieu," Tedric said, hiding the fact that his hands were shaking by slipping into his native French and turning haughtily to his aides. "This...this...*creature* is far more insolent than I remembered. Obviously we cannot risk sending him into public, masquerading as *me*. He would embarrass my heritage, my entire *country*. Send him back to whatever rock he crawled out from under. There is no other option. Cancel the tour."

On the other side of the room, one of the senator's assistants quickly translated Tedric's French into English, whispering into McKinley's ear.

With a humph, the prince stalked toward the door, taking with him Senator McKinley's hopes for lower-priced oil and Wila's dreams of economic security for her country.

But McKinley moved quickly, and cut Prince Tedric off before he reached the door.

"Your Highness," McKinley said soothingly. "If you're serious about obtaining the funding for the oil wells—"

"He's a monster," Tedric proclaimed loudly in French. McKinley's assistant translated quietly for the senator. "Even Ms. St. John cannot turn such a monster into a prince."

Across the room, Joe watched as Veronica hurried over to the prince and Senator McKinley and began talking in a lowered voice. Turn a monster into a prince, huh? he thought.

"You always did know how to liven up a party, son."

Joe turned to see Admiral Michael "Mac" Forrest smiling at him. He gave the older man a crisp salute.

The admiral's familiar leathery face crinkled into a smile. "Cut the bulldinky, Catalanotto," he said. "Since when did you start saluting? For criminy's sake, son, shake my hand instead."

The admiral's salt-and-pepper hair had gone another shade whiter, but other than that, the older man looked healthy and fit. Joe knew that Mac Forrest, a former SEAL himself, still spent a solid hour each day in PT—physical training—despite the fact that he needed a cane to walk. Ever since Joe first met him, the Admiral's left leg had been shorter than his right, courtesy of the enemy during the Vietnam War.

Mac's handclasp was strong and solid. With his other hand, he clapped Joe on the shoulder.

"It's been nearly a year and you haven't changed the least bit," Admiral Forrest announced after giving Joe a once-over. The older man wrinkled his nose. "Including your clothes. Jumping Jesse, what hole *did* we drag you out of?"

"I was on leave," Joe said with a shrug. "I was helping Blue pull in a major tuna and the bait bucket spilled on me. The boys in the Black Hawk didn't give me a chance to stop at my apartment to take a shower and pick up a change of clothes."

"Yeah." The admiral's blue eyes twinkled. "We were in kind of a hurry to get you out here, in case you didn't notice."

"I noticed," Joe said, crossing his arms. "I take it I'm here to do some kind of favor for him." With his chin, Joe gestured across the room toward Prince Tedric, who was still deep in discussion with Senator McKinley and Veronica.

"Something tells me you're not happy about the idea of doing Tedric Cortere any favors," Mac commented.

"Damn straight," Joe said, adding, "sir. That bastard nearly got Frisco killed. We were extracting from Baghdad with a squad of Iraqi soldiers on our tail. Frisco took a direct hit. The kid nearly bled to death. What's maybe even worse, at least in his eyes, is that his knee was damn near destroyed. Kid's in a wheelchair now, and fighting hard to get out."

Mac Forrest stood quietly, just letting Joe tell the story.

"We'd reached the Baghdad extraction point when Prince Charming over there refused to board the chopper. We finally had to throw him inside. It only gave us about a thirty-second delay, but it was enough to put us into the Iraqi soldiers' firing range, and that's when Frisco was hit. Turns out His Royal Pain-in-the-Butt refused to get into the bird because it wasn't luxurious enough. He nearly got us all killed because the interior of an attack helicopter wasn't painted in the colors of the Ustanzian flag."

Joe looked steadily at the admiral. "So go ahead and reprimand me, Mac," he added. "But be warned—there's nothing you can say that'll make me do any favors for *that* creep."

"I'm not so sure about that, son," Mac said thoughtfully, running his hand across the lower part of his face.

Joe frowned. "What's going on?"

"Have you seen the news lately?" Mac asked.

Joe looked at him for several long moments. "You're kidding, right?"

"Just asking."

"Mac, I've been in a chopper, a transport jet and a jeep tonight. None of them had in-flight entertainment in the form of the evening news," Joe said. "Hell, I haven't even seen a newspaper in the past eighteen hours."

"This morning there was an assassination attempt on Tedric."

Aha. Now it suddenly all made sense. Joe nodded. "Gee, sir," he said. "And I already smell like bait. How appropriate."

Mac chuckled. "You always *were* a smart mouth, Catalanotto."

"So what's the deal?" Joe asked. "Where am I inserting? Ustanzia? Or, oh joy, are we going back to Baghdad?"

Inserting. It was a special-forces term for entering—either stealthily or by force—an area of operation.

The admiral perched on the arm of the sofa. "You've already inserted, son," he said. "Here in D.C. is where we want you—for right now. That is, if I can convince you to volunteer for this mission." Briefly, he outlined the plan to have Joe stand in for the crown prince for the remainder of the American tour—at least until the terrorists made another assassination attempt and were apprehended.

"Let me get this straight," Joe said, sitting down on the couch. "I play dress-up in Cortere's clothes—which is the equivalent of painting a giant target on my back, right? And I'm doing this so that the United States will have more *oil?* You've got to do better than that, Mac. And don't start talking about protecting Prince Ted, because I don't give a flying fig whether or not that bastard stays alive long enough to have his royal coffee and doughnut tomorrow morning."

Mac looked across the room, and Joe followed the older man's gaze. Veronica was nodding at Prince Tedric, her face serious. Red. Her hair was dry, and it was definitely red. Of course. It *had* to be red.

"I don't suppose working with Veronica St. John would be an incentive?" Mac said. "I had the opportunity to meet her several weeks ago. She's a real peach of a girl. Rock-solid sense of humor, though you wouldn't necessarily know it to look at her. Pretty, too."

Joe shook his head. "Not my type," he said flatly.

"Mrs. Forrest wasn't my type when I first met her," Mac stated.

Joe stood. "Sorry, Mac. If that's the best you can do, I'm outta here."

"Please," Mac said quietly, putting one hand on Joe's arm. "I'm asking for a personal favor here, Lieutenant. Do this one for me." The admiral looked down at the floor, and when he looked back at Joe, his blue eyes were steely. "Remember that car bomb that took out a busload of American sailors in London three years ago?"

Silently, Joe nodded. Oh, yeah. He remembered. Mac Forrest's nineteen-year-old son had been one of the kids killed in that deadly blast, set off by a terrorist organization called the Cloud of Death.

"My sources over at Intelligence have hinted that the assassins who are gunning for Prince Tedric are the same terrorists who set off that bomb," the admiral said. His voice trembled slightly. "It's Diosdado and his damned Cloud of Death again. I want them, Lieutenant. With your help, I can get them. Without your help . . ." He shook his head in despair.

Joe nodded. "Sir, you've got your volunteer."

Chapter 4

It was nearly two-thirty in the morning before Veronica left the planning meeting.

All of the power players had been there—Senator McKinley, whose million-dollar smile had long since faded; Henri Freder, the Ustanzian Ambassador; Admiral Forrest, the salty-looking military man Veronica had met several weeks ago at an embassy function in Paris; stern-faced Kevin Laughton, the Federal Intelligence Commission agent in charge of security; and Prince Tedric's four chief aides.

It had been decided that Prince Tedric should be spirited away from the hotel to a safe house where he'd be guarded by FInCOM agents and Ustanzian secret service men. The American sailor, Joe Catalanotto, would simply move into Tedric's suite of rooms on the tenth floor, thus arousing no suspicion among the hotel staff and guests—or even among the prince's own lesser servants and assistants, who would not be told of the switch.

After convincing the prince to give Veronica St. John a chance to work with the sailor, McKinley had gotten the ball rolling. Prince Tedric was gone, much to everyone's relief.

Veronica and the prince's main staff were working to reschedule the beginning of the tour. The idea was to organize a schedule that would require Joe to have the least amount of contact with diplomats who might recognize that he was not the real prince. And the FInCOM agents put in *their* two cents worth, trying to set up times and places for Joe to appear in public that would provide the assassins with an obvious, clear target without putting Joe in more danger than necessary.

"Where's Catalanotto?" Admiral Forrest kept asking. "He should be here. He should be part of this op's planning team."

"With all due respect, Admiral," Kevin Laughton, the FInCOM chief, finally said, "it's better to leave the strategizing to the experts." Laughton was a tall man, impeccably dressed, with every strand of his light brown hair perfectly in place. His blue eyes were cool, and he kept his emotions carefully hidden behind a poker face.

"In that case, Mr. Laughton," Forrest said tartly, "Catalanotto should definitely be here. And if you paid close attention, sir, you might even learn a thing or two from him."

"From a navy *lieutenant*?"

"Joe Cat is a Navy SEAL, mister," Forrest said.

There was that word again. SEAL.

But Laughton didn't look impressed. He looked put-upon. "I should've known this was going too smoothly," he said tiredly. He turned to Forrest. "I'm sure you're familiar with the expression, Admiral: Too many cooks spoil the broth?"

The admiral fixed the younger man with a decidedly fishlike stare. "This man is going to be your bait," he said. "Can you honestly tell me that if your roles were reversed, you wouldn't want in on the planning stages?"

"Yes," Laughton replied. "I can."

"Bulldinky." Forrest stood. He snapped his fingers and one of his aides appeared. "Get Joe Cat down here," he ordered.

The man fired off a crisp salute. "Yes, sir." He turned sharply and disappeared.

Laughton was fuming. "You can't pull rank on me. I'm FInCOM—"

"Trust me, son," Forrest interrupted, sitting down again and rocking back in his chair. "See these do-hickeys on my uniform? They're not just pretty buttons. They mean when I say 'stop,' you stop. And if you need that order clarified, I'd be more than happy to call Bill and have him explain it to you.''

Veronica bit the insides of her cheeks to keep from smiling. By Bill, the admiral was referring to the President. Of the United States. The look on Kevin Laughton's face was not a happy one.

The admiral's young aide returned and stood patiently at attention just behind Forrest's chair. Forrest tipped his head to look up at him, giving him permission to speak with a nod.

"Lieutenant Catalanotto is unable to attend this meeting, sir," the aide said. "He's getting a tooth capped, and... something done with his hair, sir. I think."

"Thank you, son," Forrest said. He stood, pushing his chair back from the conference table. "In that case, I suggest we adjourn and resume in the morning, when Lieutenant Catalanotto can attend."

"But—"

The admiral fixed Laughton with a single look. "Don't make me make that phone call, mister," he said. "I may have phrased it kind of casually, but my suggestion to adjourn *was* an order." He straightened and picked up his cane. "I'm going to give you a little hint, Laughton, a hint that most folks usually learn the first day of basic training. When an officer gives an order, the correct response is, 'Yes, sir. Right away, sir.'"

He glanced around the table, giving Veronica a quick wink before he headed toward the door.

She gathered up her papers and briefcase and followed, catching up with him in the corridor.

"Excuse me, Admiral," she said. "I haven't had time to do any research—I haven't had time to *think*—and I was hoping you could clue me in. What exactly is a *SEAL?*"

Forrest's leathery face crinkled into a smile. "Joe's a SEAL," he said.

Veronica shook her head. "Sir, that's not what I meant."

His smile became a grin. "I know," he said. "You want me to tell you that a Navy SEAL is the toughest, smartest, deadliest warrior in all of the U.S. military. Okay. There you have it. A SEAL is the best of the best, and he's trained to specialize in unconventional warfare." His smile faded, giving his face a stern, craggy cast. "Let me give you an example. Lieutenant Catalanotto took six men and went one hundred miles behind the lines during the first night of Operation Desert Storm in order to rescue Tedric Cortere—who was too stupid to leave Baghdad when he was warned of the coming U.S. attack. Joe Cat and his Alpha Squad—they're part of SEAL Team Ten— went in undetected, among all the bombs that were falling from U.S. planes, and pulled Cortere and three aides out without a single fatality."

Admiral Forrest smiled again as he watched an expression of disbelief flit across Veronica's face.

"How on earth . . . ?" she asked.

"With a raftload of courage," he answered. "And a whole hell of a lot of training and skill. Joe Cat's an expert in explosives, you know, both on land and underwater. And he knows all there is to know about locks and security systems. He's a top-notch mechanic. He understands engines in a way that's almost spiritual. He's also an expert marksman, a sharpshooter with damn near any ordnance he can get his hands on. And that's just the tip of the iceberg, missy. If you want me to continue, then we'd better find a place to sit and get comfortable, because it's going to take a while."

Veronica tried hard to connect everything she'd just heard with the grimy, unkempt, seemingly uneducated man who had appeared in her hotel room. "I see," she finally said.

"No, you don't," Forrest countered, a smile softening his words. "But you will. Best thing to do is go find Joe. And when he talks to you, really listen. You'll know soon enough what being a SEAL means."

Joe sat in the hairdresser's portable chair, looking at himself in the hotel-room mirror.

He looked . . . different.

A dentist had come in and capped the tooth he'd chipped three years ago while on a training mission and had never had fixed.

Joe had stopped noticing it after a while. He'd had the rough edges filed down the day of the accident, but he'd never had the time or inclination to get the damn thing capped.

The capped tooth wasn't the only thing different about him now. Joe's short dark hair was about six inches longer—and no longer short—thanks to the hair extensions the tired-looking stylist had almost finished attaching.

It was odd, seeing himself with long hair like this.

Joe had grown his hair out before, when he'd had advance warning of covert operations. But he liked wearing his hair short. It wasn't military-regulation short, just a comfortable length that was easy to deal with.

Long hair got in the way. It worked its way into his mouth, hung in his face, and got in his eyes at inopportune moments.

And it made him look like that cowardly idiot, Tedric Cortere.

Which was precisely the point, right now.

God help them, Joe vowed, if they expected him to wear those satin suits with the ruffles and metallic trim, and those garish rings on his fingers. No, God help *him*. This was a job, and if the powers that be wanted him to dress like an idiot, he was going to have to dress like an idiot. Like it or not.

Joe stared into the mirror at the opulence of the hotel room. This place gave him the creeps. He was nervous he might break something or spill something or touch something he wasn't supposed to touch. And his nervousness really annoyed him. Why *should* he be nervous? Why *should* he feel intimidated? It was only a lousy hotel room, for Pete's sake. The only difference between this room and the cheap motel rooms he stayed in when he traveled was that here the TV wasn't chained down. Here there was a phone in the bathroom. And the towels were thick and plentiful. And the carpets were plush and clean. And the wallpaper wasn't stained, and the curtains actually closed all the way, and the furniture wasn't broken and mismatched. Oh yeah, and the price tag for a one-night stay—that was different, too.

Sheesh, this place was as different from the places he usually stayed as night was to day, Joe reminded himself.

But the truth was, he wished he *was* staying at a cheap motel. At least then he could lie on the bed and put his feet up without being afraid he'd ruin the bedspread. At least he wouldn't feel so goddammed out of his league.

But he was stuck here until another assassination attempt was made or until the prince's U.S. tour ended in five weeks.

Five weeks.

Five weeks of feeling out of place. Of being afraid to touch anything.

"Don't touch!" he could still hear his mother say, when as a kid, he went along on her trips to Scarsdale, where she cleaned houses that were ten times the size of their tiny Jersey City apartment. "Don't touch, or you'll hear from your father when we get home."

Except Joe didn't have a father. He had a whole slew of stepfathers and "uncles," but no father. Still, whoever was temporarily playing the part of dear old dad at home would have leaped at any excuse to kick Joe's insolent butt into tomorrow.

Jeez, what was wrong with him? He hadn't thought about *those* "happy" memories in years.

The hotel-room door opened with an almost-inaudible click and Joe tensed. He looked up, turning his head and making the hairdresser sigh melodramatically.

But Joe had been too well-trained to let someone come into the room without giving them the once-over. Not while he was looking more and more like a man who'd been an assassin's target just this morning.

It was only the media consultant. Veronica St. John.

She posed no threat.

Joe turned his head, looking back into the mirror, waiting for the rush of relief, for the relaxation of the tension in his shoulders.

But it never came. Instead of relaxing, he felt as if all of his senses had gone on alert. As if he'd suddenly woken up. It was as if he were about to go into a combat situation. The colors in the wallpaper seemed sharper, clearer. The sounds of the hairdresser behind him seemed louder. And his sense of smell heightened to the point where he caught a whiff of Veronica St. John's subtle perfume from all the way across the room.

"Good God," she said in her crisp, faintly British-accented voice. "You look . . . amazing."

"Well, thank you, sweetheart. You're not so bad yourself."

She'd moved to where he could see her behind him in the mirror, and he glanced up, briefly meeting her gaze.

Blue eyes. Oh, baby, those eyes were blue. Electric blue. Electric-*shock* blue.

Joe looked up at her again and realized that the current of awareness and attraction that had shot through him had gone through her, as well. She looked as surprised as he felt. Surprised, no doubt, that a guy from his side of the tracks could catch her eye.

Except he didn't look like himself anymore. He looked like Prince Tedric.

It figured.

"I see you had the opportunity to take a shower," she said, no longer meeting his eyes. "Did your clothes get taken down to the laundry?"

"I think so," he said. "They were gone when I got out of the bathroom. I found this hotel robe.... I'd appreciate it if you could ask Admiral Forrest to send over a uniform in the morning. And maybe some socks and shorts . . . ?"

Veronica felt her cheeks start to heat. Lord, what was wrong with her? Since when did the mention of men's underwear make her face turn as red as a schoolgirl's?

Or maybe it wasn't the mention of unmentionables that was making her blush. Maybe it was the thought that this very large, very charismatic, very handsome, and very, *very* dangerous man was sitting here, with absolutely nothing on underneath his white terry-cloth robe.

From the glint in his dark brown eyes, it was clear that he was able to read her mind.

She used every ounce of her British schooling to keep her voice sounding cool and detached. "There's no need, Your Majesty," she said. "We go from here to your suite. A tailor will be arriving soon. He'll provide you with all of the clothing you'll need for the course of the next few weeks."

"Whoa," Joe said. "Whoa, whoa! Back up a sec, will ya?"

"A tailor," Veronica repeated. "We'll be meeting with him shortly. I realize it's late, but if we don't get started with—"

"No, no," Joe said. "Before that. Did you just call me 'Your *Majesty*'?"

"I'm done here," the hairdresser said. In a monotone, he quickly ran down a quick list of things Joe could and could not do with the extensions in his hair. "Swim—yes. Shower—yes. Run a comb through your hair—no. You have to be careful to comb only above and below the attachment." He turned to Veronica. "You have my card if you need me again."

"Find Mr. Laughton on your way out," Veronica said as Joe stood and helped the man fold up his portable chair. "He'll see that you get paid."

She watched, waiting until the hairdresser had closed the hotel-room door tightly behind him. Then she turned back to Joe.

"Your Majesty," she said again. "And Your Highness. *And* Your Excellency. You'll have to get used to it. This is the way you're going to be addressed."

"Even by *you?*" Joe stood very still, his arms folded across his chest. It was as if he were afraid to touch anything. But that was ridiculous. From the little information Veronica had gleaned from Admiral Forrest, Joe Catalanotto, or Joe Cat as the admiral had called him, wasn't afraid of *any*thing.

She crossed the room and sat down in one of the easy chairs by the windows. "Yes, even by me." Veronica gestured for him to sit across from her. "If we intend to pull off this charade—"

"You're right," Joe said, sitting down. "You're absolutely right. We need to go the full distance or the shooters will smell that something's not right." He smiled wryly. "It's just, after years of 'Hey, you!' or 'Yo, paesan!' 'Your Majesty' is a little disconcerting."

Veronica's eyebrows moved upward a fraction of an inch. It figured she'd be surprised. She probably thought he didn't know any four-syllable words.

Damn, what *was* it about her? She wasn't pretty, but...at the same time, she *was*. Her hair was gorgeous—the kind of soft curls he loved to run his fingers through. Joe found his eyes drawn to her face, to her delicate, almost-pointed nose, and her beautifully shaped lips. And those eyes...

His gaze slid lower, to the dark blue blazer that covered her shoulders, tapering down to her slender waist. She wore a matching navy skirt that ended a few inches above her knees, yet still managed to scream of propriety. Her politely crossed legs were something else entirely. Not even the sturdy pumps she wore on her feet could hide the fact that her legs were long and graceful and sexy as hell—the kind of legs a man dreams about. *This* man, anyway.

Joe knew that she was well aware he was studying her. But she had turned away, pretending to look for something in her briefcase, purposely ignoring the attraction he knew was mutual.

And then the phone rang—a sudden shrill noise that broke the quiet.

"Excuse me for a moment, please," Veronica said, gracefully standing and crossing the room to answer it.

"Hello?" she said, glancing back at Joe. As she watched, he leaned his head back and closed his eyes.

Thank goodness. He couldn't undress her any further with eyes that were closed. And with his eyes closed, she didn't have to be afraid that the warmth that spread throughout her entire body at his unmasked interest would somehow show. Heaven help her if this man got the idea that he could make her heart beat harder with a single look. She had enough to worry about without having to fight off some sailor's amorous advances.

"The tailor has arrived," one of Tedric's aides told her. "May I ask how much longer you'll be?"

"We'll be up shortly," Veronica said. "Please arrange to have coffee available. And something to eat. Doughnuts. Chocolate ones." Lt. Joe Catalanotto looked the chocolate-doughnut type. They could all certainly use some extra sugar to keep them awake.

She hung up the phone and crossed back to Joe. His head was still back, and his eyes were closed. He'd slumped down in the chair as if he had no bones in his entire body.

He was totally, absolutely and quite soundly asleep.

Veronica sat down across from him and leaned forward, studying his face. He'd shaved and somehow managed to get all of the grease and dirt off in the shower. Even his hands were free of grime. His hair was clean and now, with the extensions, quite long. To the average eye, he might have looked quite a bit like Prince Tedric, but Veronica knew better.

Tedric had never been—and never would be—this handsome.

There was an edge to Joe Catalanotto's good looks. A sharpness, a definition, an *honesty* that Tedric didn't have. There was something vibrant about Joe. He was so very alive, so vital, as if he took each moment and lived it to its very fullest. Veronica had never met anyone quite like him before.

Imagine taking a squad of seven men deep behind enemy lines, she thought, with bombs falling, no less. Imagine having the courage and the confidence to risk not just one's own life, but six other lives, as well. And then imagine actually *enjoying* the danger.

Veronica thought of the men she knew, the men she was used to working with. They tended to be so very…careful. Not that they weren't risk takers—oftentimes they were. But the risks they took were financial or psychological, never physical. Not a single one would ever put himself into any real physical danger. A paper cut was the worst they could expect, and *that* usually required a great deal of hand-holding.

Most men looked softer, less imposing when asleep, but not Joe. His body may have been relaxed, but his jaw was tightly clenched, his lips pulled back in what was almost a snarl. Underneath his lids, his eyes jerked back and forth in REM sleep.

He slept ferociously, almost as if these five minutes of rest were all he'd get for the next few days.

It was strange. It was very strange. And it was stranger still when Veronica sighed.

It wasn't a particularly weighty sigh, just a little one, really. Not even very loud.

Still, Joe's eyes flew open and he sat up straight. He was instantly alert, without a hint of fatigue on his lean face.

He took a sip directly from a can of soda that was sitting on the glass-topped end table and looked at Veronica steadily, as if he hadn't been fast asleep mere seconds earlier. "Time for the tailor?" he said.

She was fascinated. "How do you do that?" she asked, leaning forward slightly, searching his eyes for any sign of grogginess. "Wake up so quickly, I mean."

Joe blinked and then smiled, clearly surprised at her interest. His smile was genuine, reaching his eyes and making the

laugh lines around them deepen. Lord, he was even more attractive when he smiled that way. Veronica found herself smiling back, hypnotized by the warmth of his eyes.

"Training." He leaned back in his chair and watched her.
"SEALs take classes to study sleep patterns. We learn to catch
catnaps whenever we can."

"Really?" Joe could see the amusement in her eyes, the
barely restrained laughter curving the corners of her mouth.
Her natural expression was a smile, he realized. But she'd
taught herself to put on that serious, businesslike facade she
wore most of the time. "Classes to learn how to sleep and wake
up?" she asked, letting a laugh slip out.

Was she laughing *at* him or *with* him? He honestly couldn't
tell, and he felt his own smile fade. Damn, what was it about
this particular girl that he found so intimidating? With any
other woman, he'd assume the joke was shared, and he'd feel
glad that he was making her smile. But *this* one . . .

There was attraction in her eyes, all right. Genuine animal
attraction. He saw it there every time she glanced in his direction. But there was also wariness. Maybe even fear. She didn't
want to be attracted to him.

She probably didn't think he was good enough for her.

Damn it, he was a Navy SEAL. There was nobody better. If
she wanted to ignore the fire that was ready to ignite between
them, then so be it. Her loss.

He would find plenty of women to distract him during this
way-too-simple operation, and—

With a hiss of silk, she crossed her long legs. Joe had to look
away.

Her loss. It was her loss. Except every cell in his body was
screaming that the loss was *his*.

Okay. So he'd seduce her. He'd ply her with wine—no, make
that expensive champagne—and he'd wait until the heat he saw
in her eyes started to burn out of control. It would be that easy.
And then . . . Oh, baby. It didn't take much to imagine his hands
in her soft red hair, then sweeping up underneath the delicate
silk of her blouse, finding the soft, sweet fullness of her breasts.
He could picture one of those sexy legs wrapped around one of
his legs, as she pressed herself tightly against him, her fingers

reaching for the buckle of his belt as he plundered her beautiful mouth with his tongue and . . .

Sure, it might be that easy.

But then again, it might not.

He had no reason on earth to believe that a woman like this one would want anything to do with him. From the way she dressed and acted, Joe was willing to bet big bucks that she wouldn't want any kind of permanent thing with a guy like him.

Veronica St. John—"Sinjin," she pronounced it with that richer-than-God accent—could probably trace her bloodline back to Henry the Eighth. And Joe, he didn't even know who the hell his father was. And wouldn't *that* just make dicey dinner conversation. *"Catalanotto . . . Italian name, isn't it? Where exactly is your father from, Lieutenant?"*

"Well, gee, I don't know, Ronnie." He wondered if anyone had ever called her Ronnie, probably not. *"Mom says he was some sailor in port for a day or two. Catalanotto is her name. And where she came from is anyone's guess. So is it really any wonder Mom drank as much as she did?"*

Yeah, that would go over *real* well.

But he wasn't talking about marriage here. He wasn't talking about much more than quenching that sharp thirst he felt whenever he looked into Veronica St. John's eyes. He was talking about one night, maybe two or three or four, depending on how long this operation lasted. He was talking short-term fling, hot affair—not a lot of conversation required.

It was true, he didn't have a lot of experience with debutantes, but hell, her money and power were only on the surface. Peel the outer trappings away, and Veronica St. John was a woman. And Joe knew women. He knew what they liked, how to catch their eye, how to make them smile.

Usually women came to him. It had been a long while since he'd actively pursued one.

This could be fun.

"We trained to learn how to drop instantly into rapid-eye-movement sleep," Joe said, evenly meeting the crystal blueness of Veronica's eyes. "It comes in handy in a combat situation, or a covert op where there may be only brief stretches of time safe enough to catch some rest. It's kept more than one SEAL alive on more than one occasion."

"What else do SEALs learn how to do?" Veronica asked.

Oh, baby, what you don't know...

"You name it, honey," Joe said, "we can do it."

"My name," she declared in her cool English accent, sitting back in her chair and gazing at him steadily, "is Veronica St. John. Not honey. Not babe. Veronica. St. John. Please refrain from using terms of endearment. I don't care for them."

She was trying to look as chilly as her words sounded, but Joe saw heat when he looked into her eyes. She was trying to hide it, but it was back there. He knew, with a sudden odd certainty, that when they made love, it was going to be a near religious experience. Not *if* they made love, *When*. It *was* going to happen.

"It's a habit that's gonna be hard to break," he said.

Veronica stood, briefcase in hand. "I'm sure you have a number of habits that will be a challenge to break," she said. "So I suggest we not keep the tailor waiting a minute longer. We have plenty of work to do before we can get some sleep."

But Joe didn't move. "So what am I supposed to call you?" he asked. "Ronnie?"

Veronica looked up to find a glint of mischief in his dark eyes. He knew perfectly well that calling her "Ronnie" would not suit. He was smiling, and she was struck by the even whiteness of his teeth. He may have chipped one at one time, but the others were straight and well taken care of.

"I think Ms. St. John will do quite well, thank you," she said. "That *is* how the prince addresses me."

"I see," Joe murmured, clearly amused.

"Shall we?" she prompted.

"Oh, yes, please," Joe said overenthusiastically, then tried to look disappointed. "Oh...you mean shall we *leave?* I thought you meant..." But he was only pretending that he misunderstood. He couldn't keep a smile from slipping out.

Veronica shook her head in exasperation. "Two days, Lieutenant," she said. "We have two days to create a miracle, and you're wasting time with sophomoric humor."

Joe stood, stretching his arms above his head. His feet and legs were bare underneath his robe. So was the rest of him, but Veronica was determined not to think about that.

"I thought you were going to call me 'Your Majesty.'"

"Two days, *Your Majesty,*" Veronica repeated.

"Two days is a breeze, Ronnie," he said. "And I've decided if I'm the prince I can call you whatever I want, and I want to call you Ronnie."

"No, you most certainly will not!"

"Why the hell not? I'm the prince," Joe said. "It's your choice—Ronnie or Honey. I don't care."

"My Lord, you're almost as incorrigible as Tedric," Veronica sputtered.

"'My Lord,'" Joe mused. "Yeah, you can call me that. Although I prefer 'Your All-Powerful Mightiness.' Hey, while I'm making royal decrees, why don't you go ahead and give the serfs a day off."

He was laughing at her. He was teasing her, and enjoying watching her squirm.

"You know, this is going to be a vacation for me, Ron," he added. "Two days of prep is a cakewalk."

Veronica laughed in disbelief. How *dare* he...? "Two days," she said. "You're going to have to completely relearn how to walk and talk and stand and sit and *eat.* Not to mention memorizing all the names and faces of the aides and ambassadors and government officials that the prince is acquainted with. And don't forget all the rules and protocols you'll have to learn, all of the Ustanzian customs and traditions..."

Joe spread his hands and shrugged. "How hard could it be? Give me a videotape of Tedric and half an hour, and you'll think I'm the same guy," he said. "I've gone on far tougher missions with way less prep time. Two days—forty-eight hours—is a luxury, sweetheart."

How could he think that? Veronica was so stressed out by the rapidly approaching deadline she could barely breathe.

"*Less* than forty-eight hours," she told him sharply. "You have to sleep some of that time."

"Sleep?" Joe smiled. "I just did."

Chapter 5

"And never, *ever* open the door yourself," Veronica said. "Always wait for someone—a servant—to do it for you."

Joe gazed at her across the top of his mug as he sat on the other side of the conference table in Tedric's royal suite. "Never?" he said. He took a sip of coffee, still watching her, his dark eyes mysterious, unreadable. "Old Ted never opens the door for anyone?"

"If he were with a king or a queen, he might open the door," Veronica said, glancing down at her notes. And away from those eyes. "But I doubt you'll be running into any such personages on *this* tour."

"What does Ted do when he's all alone?" Joe started to put his mug down on the richly polished oak tabletop, but stopped as if he were afraid to mar the wood. He pulled one of Veronica's file folders closer and set his mug down on top of the stiff manila. "Just stand there until a servant comes along to open the door? That could be a real drag if he's in a rush to use the head." He rested his chin in the palm of his hand, elbow on the table, as he continued to gaze at her.

"Your Highness, an Ustanzian prince never rests his elbows on the top of a table," Veronica said with forced patience.

Joe smiled and didn't move. He just watched her with half-closed bedroom eyes that exuded sexuality. They'd been working together all night, and not once had he let her forget that she was a woman and he was a man. "I'm not a Ustanzian prince," he said. "Yet."

Veronica folded her hands neatly on top of her notes. "And it's not called a 'head,'" she said. "Not john, not toilet, not bathroom. It's a water closet. W.C. We went through this already, remember, Your Majesty?"

"How about I call it the Little Prince's Room?" Joe asked.

Veronica laughed despite her growing sense of doom. Or maybe because of it. What was she going to do about Joe Catalanotto's thick New Jersey accent? And what was she going to do about the fact that this man didn't, for even one single second, take *any*thing they were doing seriously?

And to further frustrate her, she was ready to drop from exhaustion, while he looked ready to run laps.

"My mother's name is Maria. She was an Italian countess before she met my father. My father is King Derrick the Fourth, *his* father was Derrick the Third," Joe recited. "I was born in the capital city on January 7, 1961.... You know, this would be a whole lot easier on both of us if you would just hand me your file on this guy, and give me a videotape so I can see first-hand the way he walks and stands and..."

"Excuse me, Lieutenant." A FInCOM agent by the name of West stood politely to one side.

Joe looked up, an instant Naval Officer. He sat straighter and even looked as if he was paying attention. Now, why couldn't Veronica get him to take *her* that seriously?

"At Admiral Forrest's request, Mr. Laughton requires your consultation, sir, in planning the scheduling of the tour, and the strategy for your protection," West continued. "That is, if you wish to have any input."

Joe stood. "Damn straight I do," he said. "Your security stinks. Fortunately those terrorists took the night off, or I'd already be dead."

West stiffened. "The security we've provided has been top level—"

"What I'm saying is your so-called top-level security isn't good enough, pal," Joe countered. He looked back at Veronica. "What do you say you go take a nap, Ronnie, and we meet back at . . ." He glanced at his watch. "How's eleven-hundred hours? Just over two hours."

But Veronica stood, shaking her head. She wanted desperately to sleep, but unless she attended this meeting, the visit to Saint Mary's would be removed from the tour schedule. She spoke directly to the FInCOM agent. "I'd like to have some input in this meeting, too, Mr. West," she said coolly. "I'm sure Mr. Laughton—or Admiral Forrest—won't mind if I sit in."

Joe shrugged. "Suit yourself."

"Princes don't shrug, Your Highness," Veronica reminded him as they followed West out into the corridor and toward the conference room.

Joe rolled his eyes.

"And princes don't roll their eyes," she said.

"Sheesh," he muttered.

"They don't swear, either, Your Majesty," Veronica told him. "Not even those thinly veiled words you Americans use in place of the truly nasty ones."

"So you're *not* an American," Joe said, walking backward so he could look at her. "Mac Forrest must've been mistaken. He told me, despite your fancy accent, that you were."

Joe had talked about her with Admiral Forrest. Veronica felt a warm flash of pleasure that she instantly tried to squelch. So what if Joe had talked with the admiral about her. *She'd* talked to the admiral about Joe, simply to get some perspective on whom she'd be dealing with, who she'd be working closely with for the next few weeks.

"Oh, I'm American," Veronica said. "I even say a full variety of those aforementioned nasty words upon occasion."

Joe laughed. He had a nice laugh, rich and full. It made her want to smile. "That I won't believe until I hear it."

"Well, you won't hear it, Your Majesty. It wouldn't be polite or proper."

Her shoe caught in the thick carpeting, and she stumbled slightly. Joe caught and held her arm, stopping to make sure she had her balance.

Veronica looked really beat. She looked ready to fall on her face—which she just about did. Joe could feel the warmth of her arm, even through the sleeve of her jacket and blouse. He didn't want to let her go, so he didn't. They stood there in the hotel corridor, and FInCOM Agent West waited impatiently nearby.

Joe was playing with fire. He knew that he was playing with fire. But, hell. He was a demolitions expert. He was used to handling materials that could blow sky-high at any time.

Veronica looked down at his hand still on her arm, then lifted enormous blue eyes to his.

"I'm quite all right, Your Royal Highness," she said in that Julie Andrews accent.

"You're tired as hell," he countered bluntly. "Go get some sleep."

"Believe it or not, I do have some information of importance to add to this scheduling meeting," she said hotly, the crystal of her eyes turning suddenly to blue flame. "I'd truly appreciate it if you'd unhand me so we could continue on our way, Your Majesty."

"Wait," Joe said. "Don't tell me. A prince never offers a helping hand, is that it? A prince lets a lady fall on her face, right?"

"A prince doesn't take advantage of a lady's misfortune," Veronica said tightly. "You helped me—thank you. Now let me go. Please. Your Excellency."

Joe laughed. This time it was a low, dangerous sound. His hand tightened on her arm and he drew her even closer to him, so that their noses almost touched, so that Veronica could feel his body heat through the thin cotton shirt and dark slacks the tailor had left him with after the early-morning fitting.

"Babe, if you think this is taking advantage, you've never been taken advantage of." He lowered his voice and dropped his head down so he was speaking directly into her ear. "If you want, I'll demonstrate the differences. With pleasure."

She could feel the warmth of his breath on her neck as he waited for her to react. He was expecting her to run, screaming, away from him. He was expecting her to be outraged, upset, angry, offended.

But all she could think about was how utterly delicious he smelled.

What would he say, what would he do if she moved her head a fraction of an inch to the right and pressed her cheek against the roughness of his chin. What would he do if she lifted her head to whisper into *his* ear, "Oh, yes"?

It wouldn't be the response he was expecting, that was certain.

But the truth was, this wasn't about sex, it was about power. Veronica had played hardball with the big boys long enough to know that.

It wasn't that he wasn't interested—he'd made that more than clear in the way he'd looked at her all night long. But Veronica was willing to bet that right now Joe was bluffing. And while she wasn't going to call his bluff, she was going to let him know that merely because he was bigger and stronger than she, didn't mean he'd automatically win.

So she lifted her head and, keeping her voice cool, almost chilly, said, "One would think that a Navy SEAL might be aware of the dangers of standing too long in a public corridor, considering someone out there wants Tedric—whom, by the way, you look quite a bit like these days—dead."

Joe laughed.

Not exactly the response *she* was expecting after her verbal attack. Another man might have been annoyed that his bluff hadn't worked. Another man might have pouted or glowered. Joe laughed.

"I don't know, Ron," he said, letting her go. His dark eyes were genuinely amused, but there was something else there, too. Could it possibly be respect? "You sound so... proper, but I don't think you really are, are you? I think it's all an act. I think you go home from work, and you take off the Margaret Thatcher costume, and let down your hair and put on some little black sequined number with stiletto heels, and you go out and mambo in some Latin nightclub until dawn."

Veronica crossed her arms. "You forgot my gigolo," she said crisply. "I go pick up my current gigolo and then *we* mambo till dawn."

"Let me know when there's an opening, honey," Joe said. "I'd love to apply for the job."

All humor had gone from his eyes. He was dead serious. Veronica turned away, afraid he'd see just from looking at her how appealing she found the thought of dancing with him until dawn, their bodies clasped together, moving to the pulsing beat of Latin drums.

"We'd best not keep Mr. Laughton waiting," she said. "Your Majesty."

"Damn," Joe said. "Margaret Thatcher's back."

"Sorry to disappoint you," Veronica murmured as they went into the secret-service agents' suite. "But she never left."

"Saint Mary's, right here in Washington," Veronica said from her seat next to Joe at the big conference table. "Someone keeps taking Saint Mary's off the schedule."

"It's unnecessary," Kevin Laughton said in his flat, almost-bored-sounding Midwestern accent.

"I disagree." Veronica spoke softly but firmly.

"Look, Ronnie," Senator McKinley said, and Veronica briefly shut her eyes. Lord, but Joe Catalanotto had all of them calling her Ronnie now. "Maybe you don't understand this, dear, but Saint Mary's doesn't do us any good. The building is too small, too well protected, and too difficult for the assassins to penetrate. Besides, it's not a public event. The assassins are going to want news coverage. They're going to want to make sure millions of people are watching when they kill the prince. Besides, there's no clear targeting area going into and out of the structure. It's a waste of our time."

"This visit's been scheduled for months," Veronica said quietly. "It's been scheduled since the Ustanzian secretary of press announced Prince Tedric's American tour. I think we can take one hour from one day to fulfill a promise the prince made."

Henri Freder, the Ustanzian ambassador to the United States, shifted in his seat. "Surely Prince Tedric can visit this Saint Mary's at the end of the tour, after the Alaskan cruise, on his way back home."

"That will be too late," Veronica said.

"Cruise?" Joe repeated. "If the assassins haven't been apprehended before the cruise to Alaska is scheduled, there's no way in hell we're getting on that loveboat." He looked around the table. "A cruise ship's too isolated. It's a natural target for tangos."

He smiled at their blank expressions. "Tangos," Joe repeated. "T's. Terrorists. The bad guys with guns."

Ah. There was understanding all around.

"Unless, of course, we're ready and waiting for 'em," Joe continued. "And maybe that's not such a bad idea. Replace the ship's personnel and passenger list with platoons of SEALs and—"

"No way," Laughton said. "FInCOM is handling this. It isn't some military operation. SEALs have no place in it."

"Terrorists are involved," Joe countered. "SEAL Team Ten has had extensive counterterrorist training. My men are prepared for—"

"War," Laughton finished for him. "Your men are prepared and trained for *war*. This is not a war, Lieutenant."

Joe pointed to the cellular phone on the table in front of Laughton. "Then you'd better call the terrorists. Call the Cloud of Death, call up Diosdado. Call him up and tell him that this is not a war. Because *he* sure as hell thinks it's one."

"Please," Veronica interjected. "Before we continue, may we all agree to keep Saint Mary's on the schedule?"

McKinley frowned down at the papers in front of him. "I see from the previous list that there weren't going to be any media present at the event at Saint Mary's."

"Not all of the events scheduled were for the benefit of the news cameras, Senator," Veronica said evenly. She glanced around the table. "Gentlemen. This rescheduling means hours and hours of extra work for all of us. I'm trying my best to cooperate, as I'm sure you are, too. But I happen to know that this appearance at Saint Mary's was of utmost importance to Prince Tedric." She widened her eyes innocently. "If necessary, I'll ring up the prince and ask for *his* input and—"

"No need to do that," Senator McKinley said hastily.

Getting self-centered Prince Tedric in on this scheduling nightmare was the last thing *any*one wanted, Veronica included. His so-called "input" would slow this process down to a crawl. But she was prepared to do whatever she had to do to keep the visit to Saint Mary's on the schedule.

McKinley looked around the table. "I think we can keep Saint Mary's on the list." There was a murmur of agreement.

Joe watched Veronica. Her red curls were up in some kind of feminine arrangement on the top of her head. With her delicate features and innocent blue eyes, she looked every inch the demure, cool English lady; and again, Joe was struck by the feeling that her outward appearance was only an act. She wasn't demure *or* cool, and if his gut feelings were right, she could probably outmanipulate the entire tableful of them. Hell, she just had. But she'd done it so subtly that no one was even aware they'd been manipulated.

"About the Alaskan cruise," Senator McKinley said.

"That's not until later in the tour." Joe leaned back in his chair. "Let's keep it off the public schedule for now. We don't want the T's—terrorists—choosing that opportunity above everything else. We want 'em to strike early on. But still, we can start making arrangements with the SEAL teams, start getting 'em prepped for a potential operation aboard ship."

"No SEALs," Kevin Laughton said tersely.

Joe gave the FInCOM agent a disbelieving look. "You *want* high casualties? Is that your goal here?"

"Of course not—"

"We're all on the same team, pal," Joe said. "We all work for the U.S. Government. Just because I'm Navy and you're Fink—"

"No SEALs." Laughton turned to an aide. "Release this schedule to the news media ASAP, keeping the cruise information off the list." He stood. "My men will start scouting each of these sites."

Joe stood up, too. "You should start right here in this hotel," he said. "If you're serious about making the royal suite secure, you're understaffed. And the sliding door to the balcony in the bedroom doesn't lock. What kind of security is that?"

Laughton stared at him. "You're on the *tenth* floor."

"Terrorists sometimes know how to climb," Joe said.

"I can assure you you're quite safe," Laughton said.

"And I can assure you that I'm not. If security stays as is, if Diosdado and his gang decide to come into this hotel to rid the world of Prince Tedric, then I'm as good as dead."

"I can understand your concern," Laughton said. "But—"

"Then you won't have any objection to bringing the rest of my Alpha Squad out here," Joe interrupted. "You're obviously undermanned, and I'd feel a whole hell of a lot better if—"

"No," Laughton said. "Absolutely not. A squad of Navy SEALs? Utter chaos. My men won't stand for it. I won't have it."

"I'm going to be standing around, wearing a damned shooting target on my chest," Joe retorted. "I want my own guys nearby, watching my back, plugging the holes in FInCOM's security net. I can tell you right now, they won't get in your boys' way."

"No," Laughton said again. "*I'm* in charge of security, and I say *no*. This meeting is adjourned."

Joe watched the FInCOM chief leave the room, then glanced up to find Veronica's eyes on him.

"I guess we're going to have to do this the hard way," he said.

The man known only as Diosdado looked up from his desk as Salustiano Vargas was shown into the room.

"Ah, old friend," Vargas greeted him with relief. "Why did your men not say it was you they were bringing me to see?"

Diosdado was silent, just looking at the other man as he thoughtfully stroked his beard.

Vargas threw himself down into a chair across from the desk and casually stretched his legs out in front of him. "It has been too long, no?" he said. "What have you been up to, man?"

"Not as much as you have, apparently." Diosdado smiled, but it was a mere shadow of his normally wide, toothy grin.

Vargas's own smile was twisted. "Eh, you heard about that, huh?" His smile turned to a scowl. "I would have drilled the bastard through the heart if that damned woman hadn't pushed him out of the way."

Diosdado stood. "You are lucky—very, *very* lucky—that your bullet missed Tedric Cortere," he said harshly.

Vargas stared at him in surprise. "But—"

"If you had kept in touch, you would have been aware of what I have spent *months* planning." Diosdado didn't raise his voice when he was angry. He lowered it. Right now, it was very, *very* quiet.

Vargas opened his mouth to speak, to protest, but he wisely shut it tightly instead.

"The Cloud of Death intended to take Cortere hostage," Diosdado said. "Intends," he corrected himself. "We still intend to take him." He began to pace—a halting, shuffling process as he dragged his bad leg behind him. "Of course, now that you have intervened, the prince's security has been strengthened. FInCOM is involved, and my contacts tell me that the U.S. Navy is even playing some part in Cortere's protection."

Vargas stared at him.

"So what," Diosdado continued, turning to face Salustiano Vargas, "do you suggest we do to bring this high level of security and protection back to where it was before you fouled things up?"

Vargas swallowed, knowing what the other man was going to tell him, and knowing that he wasn't going to like what he heard.

"They are all waiting for another assassination attempt," Diosdado said. "Until they *get* another assassination attempt, security will be too tight. Do you know what you are going to do, my old friend Salustiano?"

Vargas knew. He knew, and he didn't like it. "Diosdado," he said. "Please. We're friends. I saved your *life—*"

"You will go back," Diosdado said very, very softly, "and you will make another attempt on the prince's life. You will fail, and you will be apprehended. Dead or alive—your choice."

Vargas sat in silence as Diosdado limped, shuffling, from the room.

"Tell me what it is about Navy SEALs that makes Kevin Laughton so upset, Your Majesty," Veronica said as she and Joe were delivered safely back to Prince Tedric's hotel suite. "Why doesn't he want your Alpha Squad around?"

"He knows his guys would give him problems if my guys were brought in to do their job," Joe said. "It's a slap in the face. It implies I don't think FInCOM can get the job done."

"But obviously, you don't think they can."

Joe shook his head and sat down heavily in one of the plush easy chairs in the royal living room. "I think they're probably top-notch at mid-level protection," he said. "But my life's on the line here, and the bad guys aren't street punks or crazy people with guns. They're professionals. Diosdado runs a top-notch military organization. He's a formidable opponent. He could get through this kind of security without blinking. But he couldn't get through the Alpha Squad. I *know* my SEALs are the best of the best. SEAL Team Ten is elite, and the Alpha Squad is made up of the best men in Team Ten. I want them here, even if I have to step on some toes or offend some FInCOM agents. The end result is I stay alive. Are you following me?"

Veronica nodded, sitting down on the sofa and resting her briefcase on a long wooden coffee table.

The sofa felt so comfortable, so soft. It would be so easy to let her head fall back and her eyes close. . . .

"Maybe we should take a break," Joe said. "You can barely keep your eyes open."

"No, there's so much more you need to learn," Veronica said. She made herself sit up straight. If *he* could stay awake, she could, too. "The history of Ustanzia. The names of Ustanzian officials." She pulled a file from her briefcase and opened it. "I have fifty-seven pictures of people you will come into contact with, Your Highness. I need you to memorize these faces and names, and—Lord, if there were only another way to do this."

"Earphone," Joe said, flipping through the file.

"Excuse me?"

He looked up at her. "I wear a concealed earphone," he said. "And you have a mic. We set up a video camera so that you can see and hear everything I'm doing while you're some safe distance away—maybe even out in a surveillance truck. When someone comes up to shake my hand, you feed me his name and title and any other pertinent info I might need." He flipped through the photos and handed them back to Veronica. "Pick out the top ten and I'll look 'em over. The others I don't need to know."

Veronica fixed him with a look, suddenly feeling extremely awake. What did he mean, the others he didn't need to know?

"All fifty-seven of these people are diplomats Tedric knows quite well. You could run into any one of these people at any time during the course of this tour," she said. "The original file had over three hundred faces and names."

Joe shook his head. "I don't have time to memorize faces and names," he said. "With the high-tech equipment we have access to—"

"*You* don't have time?" Veronica repeated, eyebrows lifted. "We're *all* running out of time, Lieutenant. It's *my* task to prepare you. Let me decide what there is and isn't time for."

Joe leaned forward. "Look, Ronnie, no offense, but I'm used to preparing for an operation at my own speed," he said. "I appreciate everything you're trying to do, but in all honesty, the way that Ted walks and talks is the least of my concerns. I've got this security thing to straighten out and—"

"That's Kevin Laughton's job," she interrupted. "Not yours."

"But it's my ass that's on the line," he said flatly. "FInCOM's going to change their security plans, or this operation is not going to happen."

Veronica tapped her fingernails on the legal pad she was holding. "And if you don't look and act enough like Prince Tedric," she said tartly, "this operation is not going to happen, either."

"Get me a tape," Joe countered. "Get me a videotape and an audiotape of the guy, and I promise you, I *swear* to you, I will look and act and sound exactly like Ted."

Veronica's teeth were clenched tightly together in annoyance. "Details," she said tightly. "How will you learn the details? Assuming, of course, that you are able to miraculously transform yourself into European royalty simply by viewing a videotape?"

"Write 'em down," Joe said without hesitation. "I retain written information better, anyway." The telephone rang and he paused briefly, listening while West answered it. "Lieutenant, it's for you," the FInCOM agent said.

Joe reached for the extension. "Yo. Catalanotto here."

Yo. The man answered the phone with "Yo" and Veronica was supposed to believe he'd be able to pass himself off as the prince, with little or no instruction from her?

"Mac," Joe said into the telephone. It was Admiral Forrest on the other end. "Great. Thanks for calling me back. What's the word on getting Alpha Squad out here?"

How did a lieutenant get away with calling an admiral by his first name, anyway? Veronica had heard that Forrest had been a SEAL himself at one time in his long navy career. And from what little she knew about SEALs so far, she suspected they were unconventional in more than just their warfare tactics.

Joe's jaw was tight and the muscles in the side of his face were working as he listened to Forrest speak. He swore sharply, not bothering to try to disguise his bad language. As Veronica watched, he rubbed his forehead—the first sign he'd given all day that he was weary.

"FInCOM has raised hell before," he said. "That hasn't stopped us in the past." There was a pause and he added hotly, "Their security *is* lax, sir. Damn, you know that as well as I do." Another pause. "I was hoping I wouldn't have to do that."

Joe glanced up and into Veronica's watching eyes. She looked away, suddenly self-conscious about the fact that she was openly eavesdropping. As she shuffled through the file of photographs, she was aware of his gaze still on her.

"Before you go, sir," he said into the telephone. "I need another favor. I need audio- and videotapes of Tedric sent to my room ASAP."

Veronica looked up at that, and directly into Joe's eyes. "Thanks, Admiral," he said and hung up the phone. "He'll have 'em sent right over," he said to Veronica as he stood.

He looked as if he were about to leave, to go somewhere. But she didn't even get a chance to question him.

"FInCOM's having a briefing about the tour locations here in D.C.," Joe said. "I need to be there."

"But—"

"Why don't you take a nap?" Joe said. He looked at his watch, and Veronica automatically glanced at hers. It was nearly five o'clock in the evening. "We'll meet back here at twenty-one hundred hours."

Veronica quickly counted on her fingers. Nine o'clock. "No," she said, standing. "That's too long. I can give you an hour break, but—"

"This briefing's important," Joe said. "It'll be over at twenty-hundred, but I'll need an extra hour."

Veronica shook her head in exasperation. "Kevin Laughton doesn't even *want* you there," she said. "You'll spend the entire time arguing—"

"Damn straight, I'm going to argue," Joe said. "If FInCOM insists on assuming the tangos are going to mosey on up to the front door and ring the bell before they strike, then I've got to be there, arguing to keep the back door protected."

Joe was already heading toward the door. West and Freeman scrambled to their feet, following him.

"Put those details you were talking about in writing," Joe suggested. "I'll see you in a few hours."

Veronica all but stamped her foot. "You're supposed to be working with me," she said. "You can't just . . . leave. . . ."

But he was gone.

Veronica threw her pad and pen onto the table in frustration. Time was running out.

Chapter 6

Veronica woke up from her nap at seven-thirty, still exhausted but too worried to sleep. *How* was Joe going to learn to act like Prince Tedric if he wouldn't give her any time to properly teach him?

She'd made lists and more lists of details and information Joe had no way of knowing—things like, the prince was right-handed. That was normally not a problem, except she'd noticed that Joe was a lefty. She'd written down trivial information such as the fact that Tedric always twirled the signet ring he wore on his right hand when he was thinking.

Veronica got up from the table and started to pace, alternately worried, frustrated and angry with Joe. Who in blazes actually *cared* what Tedric did with his jewelry? Who, truly, would notice? And why was she making lists of details when basic things such as Tedric's walk and ramrod-straight posture were being ignored?

Restless, Veronica pawed through the clothes in her suitcase, searching for a pair of bike shorts and her exercise bra. It was time to try to release some of this nervous energy. She dug down farther and found her favorite tape. Smiling grimly, she crossed to the expensive stereo system built into the wall and put the tape into the tape deck. She pushed Play and music came on. She cranked the volume.

The tape contained an assorted collection of her favorite songs—loud, fast songs with pulsating beats. It was good music, familiar music, *loud* music.

Her sneakers were on the floor of the closet near the bathroom. As Veronica sat on the floor to slip them onto her feet and tie them tightly, she let the music wash over her. Already she felt better.

She scrambled up and into the center of the living room, pushing the furniture back and away, clearing the floor, giving herself some space to move.

With the furniture out of the way, Veronica started slowly, stretching out her tired muscles. When she was properly warmed up, she closed her eyes and let the music embrace her.

And then she began to dance.

Halfway through the tape, it came to her—the answer to her frustration and impotent anger. She had been hired to teach Joe to act like the prince. With his cooperation, the task was formidable. Without his cooperation, it was impossible. If he failed to cooperate, she would have to threaten to withdraw.

Yes, that was exactly what she had to do. At nine o'clock, when she went down the hall to the royal suite, she would march right up to Joe and look him in the eye and—

A man wearing all black was standing just inside her balcony doorway, leaning against the wall, watching her dance.

Veronica leaped backward, her body reacting to the unannounced presence of a large intruder before her brain registered the fact that it was Joe Catalanotto.

Heart pounding, chest heaving, she tried to catch her breath as she stared at him. How in God's name had *Joe* gotten into her room?

Joe stared, too, caught in the ocean-blueness of Veronica's eyes as the music pounded around them. She looked frightened, like a wild animal, uncertain whether to freeze or flee.

Turning suddenly, she reached for the stereo and switched the music off. The silence was abrupt and jarring.

Her red curls swung and bounced around her shoulders as she turned rapidly back to look at him again. "What are you doing here?" she asked.

"Proving a point," he replied. His voice sounded strained and hoarse to his own ears. There was no mystery as to why that was. Seeing her like this had made his blood pressure rise, as well as other things.

"I don't understand," she said, her eyes narrowing as she studied his face, searching for an answer. "How did you get in? My door was locked."

Joe gestured to the sliding door that led to the balcony. "No, it wasn't. In fact, it was open. Warm night. If you breathe deeply, you can almost smell the cherry blossoms."

Veronica was staring at him, struggling to reconcile his words with the truth as she knew it. This room was on the tenth floor. Ten stories up, off the ground. Visitors didn't simply stroll in through the balcony door.

Joe couldn't keep his gaze from sliding down her body. Man, she was one hot package. In those skintight purple-and-turquoise patterned shorts and that tight, black, racer-backed top that exposed a firm, creamy midriff, with all those beautiful red curls loose around her pale shoulders, she looked positively steamy. She was slender, but not skinny as he'd thought. Her waist was small, her stomach flat, flaring out to softly curving hips and a firm, round rear end. Her legs were incredible, but he'd already known that. Still, in those tight shorts, her shapely legs seemed to go on and on and on forever, leading his eyes to her derriere. Her breasts were full, every curve, every detail intimately outlined by the stretchy fabric of her top.

And, God, the way she'd been dancing when he'd first climbed onto the balcony had exuded a raw sensuality, a barely contained passion. He'd been right about her. She *had* been hiding something underneath those boxy, conservative suits and that cool, distant attitude. Who would have guessed she would spend her personal time dancing like some vision on MTV?

She was still breathing hard from dancing. Or maybe—and more likely—she was breathing hard from the sudden shock he'd given her. He'd actually been standing inside the balcony door for about ten minutes before she looked up. He'd been in no hurry to interrupt. He could have stayed there, quite happily, and watched her dance all night.

Well, maybe not *all* night . . .

Veronica took a step back, away from him, as if she could see his every thought in his eyes. Her own eyes were very wide and incredibly, brilliantly blue. "You came in...from the *balcony?*"

Joe nodded and held something out to her. It was a flower, Veronica realized. He was holding a rather tired and bruised purple-and-gold pansy, its petals curled up for the night. She'd seen flowers just like it growing in flower beds outside the hotel.

"First I climbed down to the ground and got this," Joe said, his husky voice soft and seductive, warmly intimate. "It's proof I was actually there."

He was still holding the flower out to her, but Veronica couldn't move, her mind barely registering the words he spoke. A black band was across his forehead, holding his long hair in place. He was wearing black pants and a long-sleeved black turtleneck, with some kind of equipment vest over it, even though the spring night *was* quite warm. Oddly enough, his feet were bare. He wasn't smiling, and his face looked harsh and unforgiving. And dangerous. Very, *very* dangerous.

Veronica gazed at him, her heart in her throat. As he stepped closer and pressed the flower into her hand, she was pulled into the depths of his eyes. The fire she saw there became molten. His mouth was hard and hungry as his gaze raked her body.

And then his meaning cut through.

He'd climbed *down* to the *ground*...? *And* back up again? Ten *stories?*

"You climbed up the outside of the hotel and no one stopped you?" Veronica looked down at the flower, hoping he wouldn't notice the trembling in her voice.

He crossed to the sliding door and pulled the curtain shut. Was that for safety's sake, or for privacy? Veronica wondered as she turned away. She was afraid he might see his unconcealed desire echoed in her own eyes.

Desire? What was wrong with her? It was true, Joe Catalanotto was outrageously good-looking. But despite his obvious physical attributes, he was rude, tactless and disrespectful, rough in his manners and appearance. In fact, he was about as far from a being a prince as any man she'd ever known. They'd barely even exchanged a civil conversation. All they did was fight. So why on earth could she think of nothing but the touch of his hands on her skin, his lips on hers, his body...?

"No one saw me climbing down *or* up," Joe said, his voice surrounding her like soft, rich velvet. "There are no guards posted on this side of the building. The FInCOM agents don't see the balcony for what it is—a back door. An accessible and obvious back door."

"It's so far from the ground," she countered in disbelief.

"It was an easy climb. Under an hour."

Under an hour. *This* is what he'd been doing with his time, Veronica realized suddenly. He should have been working with *her,* learning how to act like Tedric, and instead he was climbing up and down the outside of the hotel like some misguided superhero. Anger flooded through her.

Joe took a step forward, closing the small gap between them. The urge to touch her hair, to skim the softness of her cheek with his knuckle, was overpowering.

This was *not* the scenario he'd imagined when he'd climbed up the side of the hotel and onto her balcony. He'd expected to find Veronica hard at work, scribbling furiously away on the legal pad she always carried, or typing frantically into her laptop computer. He'd expected her to be wearing something that hid her curves and disguised her femininity. He'd expected her hair to be pinned up off her neck. He'd expected her to look up at him, gasping in startled surprise, as he walked into the room.

And, yeah, he'd expected her to be impressed when he told her he'd scaled the side of the hotel in order to prove that FInCOM's security stank.

Instead, finally over her initial shock at seeing him there, Veronica folded her arms across her delicious-looking breasts and glared at him. "I can't *believe* this," she said. "I'm supposed to be teaching you how to fool the bloody world into thinking you're Prince Tedric and you're off playing commando games and climbing ten stories up the outside of this hotel?"

"I'm not a commando, I'm a SEAL," Joe said, feeling his own temper rise. "There's a difference. And I'm not playing games. FInCOM's security stinks."

"The President of the United States hasn't had any qualms about FInCOM's ability to protect *him,*" Veronica said tersely.

"The President of the United States is followed around by fifteen Finks, ready to jump into the line of fire and take a bullet for him if necessary," Joe countered. He broke away, pulling off the headband and running his fingers through his sweat-dampened hair. "Look, Ronnie, I didn't come here to fight with you."

"Is that supposed to be an apology?"

It wasn't, and she knew it as well as he did. "No."

Veronica laughed in disbelief at his blunt candor. "No," she repeated. "Of course not. Silly me. Whatever could I have been thinking?"

"I can't apologize," Joe said tightly. "Because I haven't done anything wrong."

"You've wasted time," Veronica told him. "*My* time. Maybe you don't understand, but we now have less than twenty-four hours to make this charade work."

"I'm well aware of the time we have left," Joe said. "I've looked at those videotapes Mac Forrest sent over. This is *not* going to be hard. In fact, it's going to be a piece of cake. I can pose as the prince, no problem. You've gotta relax and trust me." He turned and picked up the telephone from one of the end tables Veronica had pushed aside to clear the living-room floor of furniture. "I need you to make a phone call for me, okay?"

Veronica took the receiver from his hand and hung the phone back up. "No," she said, icily. "I need *you* to stop being so bloody patronizing, to stop patting my hand and telling me to relax. I need *you* to take me seriously for one damned minute."

Joe laughed. He couldn't help himself. She was standing there, looking like some kind of hot, steamed-up-windows dream, yet sounding, even in anger, as if she was trying to freeze him to death.

"Ah, you find this funny, do you?" Her eyes were blue ice. "I assure you, Lieutenant, you can't do this without me, and I am very close to walking out the bloody door."

She was madder than hell, and Joe knew the one thing he *shouldn't* do was keep laughing. But damned if he couldn't stop. "Ronnie," he said, pretending he was coughing instead of laughing. Still, he couldn't hide his smile. "Ronnie, Ronnie, I *do* take you seriously, honey. Honest."

Her hands were on her hips now, her mouth slightly open in disbelief. "You are *such* a…a jerk!" she said. "Tell me, is your real intention to…to…foul this up so royally that you won't have to place yourself in danger by posing as the prince?"

Joe's smile was wiped instantly off his face, and Veronica knew with deadly certainty that she'd gone too far.

He took a step toward her, and she took a step back, away from him. He was very tall, very broad and *very* angry.

"I *volunteered* for this job, babe," he told her, biting off each word. "I'm not here for my health, or for a paycheck, or for fame and fortune or for whatever the hell *you're* here for. And I'm sure as hell *not* here to be some kind of lousy martyr. If I end up taking a bullet for Prince Tedric, it's going to be despite the fact that I've done everything humanly possible to prevent it. Not because some pencil-pushing agency like FInCOM let the ball drop on standard security procedures years ago."

Veronica was silent. What could she possibly say? He was right. If security wasn't tight enough, he could very well be killed. She couldn't fault him for wanting to be sure of his own safety. And she didn't want to feel this odd jolt of fear and worry she felt, thinking about all of the opportunities the terrorists would have to train their gunsights on Joe's head. He was brave to have volunteered for this mission—particularly since she knew he had no love for Tedric Cortere. She shouldn't have implied otherwise.

"I'm sorry," Veronica murmured. She looked down at the carpet, unable to meet his eyes.

"And as for taking you seriously…" Joe reached out and with one finger underneath her chin, he lifted her head so that she was forced to look up into his eyes. "You're wrong. I take you *very* seriously."

The connection was there between them—instant and hot. The look in Joe's eyes was mesmerizing. It erased everything, *every*thing between them—all the angry words and mistrust, all the frustration and misunderstandings—and left only this basic, almost primitive attraction, this simplest of equations. Man plus woman.

It would be so easy to simply give in. Veronica felt her body sway toward him as if pulled by the tides, ancient and unquestioning. All she had to do was let go, and there would be only desire, consuming and overpowering. It would surround them, possess them. It would take them on a flight to paradise.

But that flight was a round trip. When it ended, when they lay spent and exhausted, they'd be right here—right back where they'd started.

And then reality would return. Veronica would be embarrassed at having been intimate with a man she barely knew. Joe would no doubt be smug.

And they would have wasted yet another hour or two of their precious preparation time.

Joe was obviously thinking along the exact same lines. He ran his thumb lightly across her lips. "What do you think, Ronnie?" he asked, his voice husky. "Do you think we could stop after just one kiss?"

Veronica pulled away, her heart pounding even harder. If he kissed her, she would be lost. "Don't be foolish," she said, working hard to keep her voice from shaking.

"When I make love to you," he said, his voice low and dangerous and *very* certain, "I'm going to take my sweet time."

She turned to face him with a bravado she didn't quite feel. *"When?"* she said. "Of all the macho, he-man audacity! Not *if*, but *when* I make love to you.... Don't hold your breath, Lieutenant, because it's not going to happen."

He smiled a very small, very infuriating smile and let his eyes wander down her body. "Yes, it is."

"Ever hear the expression 'cold day in hell'?" Veronica asked sweetly. She crossed the room toward her suitcase, found a sweatshirt and pulled it over her head. She was still perspiring and was still much too warm, but she would have done damn near anything to cover herself from the heat of his gaze.

He picked up the telephone again. "Look, Ronnie, I need you to call my room and ask to speak to me."

"But you're not there."

"That's the point," he said. "The boys from FInCOM think I'm napping, nestled all snug in my bed. It's time to shake them up."

Careful to keep her distance, careful not to let their fingers touch, Veronica took the phone from Joe and dialed the number for the royal suite. West picked up the phone.

"This is Ms. St. John," she said. "I need to speak to Lieutenant Catalanotto."

"I'm sorry, ma'am," West replied. "He's asleep."

"This is urgent, Mr. West," she said, glancing up at Joe, who nodded encouragingly. "Please wake him."

"Hang on."

There was silence on the other end, and then shouting, as if from a distance. Veronica met Joe's eyes again. "I think they're shaken up," she said.

"Hang up," he said, and she dropped the receiver into the cradle.

He picked up the phone then, and dialed. "Do you have a pair of sweats or some jeans to pull on over those shorts?" he asked Veronica.

"Yes," she said. "Why?"

"Because in about thirty seconds, fifty FInCOM agents are going to be pounding on your door— Hello? Yeah. Kevin Laughton, please." Joe covered the mouthpiece with his hand and looked at Veronica who was standing, staring at him. "Better hurry." He uncovered the phone. "Yeah, I'm still here."

Veronica scrambled for her suitcase, yanking out the one pair of blue jeans she'd packed for this trip.

"He is?" she heard Joe say into the telephone. "Well, maybe you should interrupt him."

She kicked off her sneakers and pulled the jeans on, hopping into them one leg at a time.

"Why don't you tell him Joe Catalanotto's on the line. Catalanotto." He sighed in exasperation. "Just say Joe Cat, okay? He'll know who I am."

Veronica pulled the jeans up and over her hips, aware that Joe was watching her dress. She buttoned the waistband and drew up the zipper, not daring to look in his direction. *When I make love to you . . .* Not if, *when.* As if their intimate joining were already a given—indisputable and destined to take place.

"Yo, Laughton," Joe said into the telephone. "How's it going, pal?" He laughed. "Yeah, I thought I'd give you a little firsthand demonstration, and identify FInCOM's security weak spots. How do you like it so far?'' He pulled the receiver away from his ear. ''That good, huh? Yeah, I went for a little walk down in the gardens.'' He met Veronica's eyes and grinned, clearly amused. ''Yeah, I was struck by the beauty of the flowers, so I brought one with me up to Ms. St. John's room to share with her, and—''

He looked at the receiver, suddenly gone dead in his hands, and then at Veronica.

''I guess they're on their way,'' he said.

Chapter 7

"I need more coffee," Veronica said. How could Joe be so *awake*? She hadn't seen him yawn even once as they'd worked through the night. "I think my laryngitis idea might work—after all, we've been giving the news media reports that Prince Tedric is ill. You wouldn't have to speak and—"

"You know, I'm not a half-bad mimic," Joe insisted. "If I work on it more, I can do a decent imitation of Prince Tedric."

Veronica closed her eyes. "No offense, Joe, but I seriously doubt you can imitate Tedric's accent just from listening to a tape," she said. "We have better things to do with your time."

Joe stood and Veronica opened her eyes, gazing up at him.

"I'm getting you that coffee," he said. "You're slipping. You just called me 'Joe.'"

"Forgive me, Your Royal Highness," she murmured.

But he didn't smile. He just looked down at her, the expression in his eyes unreadable. "I like Joe better," he finally said.

"This isn't going to work, is it?" she asked quietly. She met his eyes steadily, ready to accept defeat.

Except he wasn't defeated. Not by any means. He'd been watching videotapes and listening to audiotapes of Prince

Tedric in all of his spare moments. It was true that he hadn't had all that many spare moments, but he was well on his way to understanding the way Tedric moved and spoke.

"I can do this," Joe said. "Hell, I look just like the guy. Every time I catch my reflection and see my hair this way, I see Ted looking back at me and it scares me to death. If it can fool *me,* it can fool everyone else. The tailor's delivering the clothes he's altered sometime tomorrow. It'll be easier for me to pretend I'm Tedric if I'm dressed for the part."

Veronica gave him a wan smile. Still, it *was* a smile. She was so tired, she could barely keep her eyes open. She'd changed out of her jeans and back into her professional clothes hours ago. Her hair was up off her shoulders once again. "We've got to work on Tedric's walk. He's got this rather peculiar, rolling gait that—"

"He walks like he's got a fireplace poker in his pants," Joe interrupted her.

Veronica's musical laughter echoed throughout the quiet room. One of the FInCOM agents glanced up from his position guarding the balcony entrance.

"Yes," she said to Joe. "You're right. He does. Although I doubt anyone's described it quite that way before."

"I can walk that way," Joe said. He stood, and as Veronica watched, he marched stiffly across the room. "See?" He turned back to look at her.

She had her face in her hands and her shoulders were shaking, and Joe was positive for one heart-stopping moment that she was crying. He started toward her, and knelt in front of her and— She was laughing. She was laughing so hard, tears were rolling down her face.

"Hey," Joe said, faintly insulted. "It wasn't *that* bad."

She tried to answer, but could get no words out. Instead, she just waved her hand futilely at him and kept on laughing.

Her laughter was infectious, and before long, Joe started to chuckle and then laugh, too.

"Do it again," she gasped, and he stood and walked, like Prince Tedric, across the room and back.

Veronica laughed even harder, doubling over on the couch.

The FInCOM agent was watching them both as if they were crazy or hysterical—which probably wasn't that far from the truth.

Veronica wiped at her face, trying to catch her breath. "Oh, Lord," she said. "Oh, God, I haven't laughed this hard in years." Her eyelashes were wet with her tears of laughter, and her eyes sparkled as, still giggling, she looked up at Joe. "I don't suppose I can talk you into doing that again?"

"No way," Joe said, grinning back at her. "I draw the line at being humiliated more than twice in a row."

"I wasn't laughing at you," she said, but her giggles intensified. "Yes, I was," she corrected herself. "I *was* laughing at you. I'm so sorry. You must think I'm frightfully rude." She covered her mouth with her hand, but still couldn't stop laughing—at least not entirely.

"I think I only looked funny because I'm not dressed like the prince," Joe argued. "I think if I were wearing some sequined suit and walking that way, you wouldn't be able to tell the two of us apart."

"And *I* think," Veronica said. "*I* think . . . I think it's hopeless. I think it's time to give up." Her eyes suddenly welled with real tears, and all traces of her laughter vanished. "Oh, *damn* . . ." She turned away, but she could neither stop nor hide her sudden flow of tears.

She heard Joe's voice, murmuring a command to the FInCOM agents, and then she felt him sit next to her on the sofa.

"Hey," he said softly. "Hey, come on, Veronica. It's not that bad."

She felt his arms go around her and she stiffened only slightly before giving in. She let him pull her back against his chest, let him tuck her head in to his shoulder. He was so warm, so solid. And he smelled so wonderfully good . . .

He just held her, rocking slightly, and let her cry. He didn't try to stop her. He just held her.

Veronica was getting his shirt wet, but she couldn't seem to stop, and he didn't seem to mind. She could feel his hand in her hair, gently stroking, calming, soothing.

When he spoke, his voice was quiet. She could hear it rumble slightly in his chest.

"You know, this guy we're after?" Joe said. "The terrorist? His name's Diosdado. One name. Kind of like Cher or Madonna, but not so much fun. Still, I bet he's as much of a celebrity in Peru, where he's from. He's the leader of an organization with a name that roughly translates as 'The Cloud of Death.' He and a friend of his—a man named Salustiano Vargas—have claimed responsibility for more than twelve hundred deaths. Diosdado's signature was on the bomb that blew up that passenger flight from London to New York three years ago. Two hundred and fifty-four people died. Remember that one?"

Veronica nodded. She most certainly did. The plane had gone down halfway across the Atlantic. There were no survivors. Her tears slowed as she listened to him talk.

"Diosdado and his pal Vargas took out an entire busload of U.S. sailors that same year," Joe said. "Thirty-two kids—the oldest was twenty-one years old." He was quiet for a moment. "Mac Forrest's son was on that bus."

Veronica closed her eyes. "Oh, God . . ."

"Johnny Forrest. He was a good kid. Smart, too. He looked like Mac. Same smile, same easygoing attitude, same tenacity. I met him when he was eight. He was the little brother I never had." Joe's voice was husky with emotion. He cleared his throat. "He was nineteen when Diosdado blew him to pieces."

Joe fell silent, just stroking Veronica's hair. He cleared his throat again, but when he spoke, his voice was still tight. "Those two bombings put Diosdado and The Cloud of Death onto the Most Wanted list. Intel dug deep and came up with a number of interesting facts. Diosdado had a last name, and it was Perez. He was born in 1951, the youngest son in a wealthy family. His name means, literally, 'God's gift.'" Joe laughed a short burst of disgusted air. "He wasn't God's gift to Mac Forrest, or any of the other families of those dead sailors. Intel also found out that the sonuvabitch had a faction of his group right here in D.C. But when the CIA went to investigate, something went wrong. It turned into a firefight, and when it was over, three agents and ten members of The Cloud of Death were dead. Seven more terrorists were taken prisoner, but Diosdado and Salustiano Vargas were gone. The two men we'd wanted the most got away. They went deep underground. Ru-

mor was Diosdado had been shot and badly hurt. He was quiet
for years—no sign of him at all—until a few days ago, when
apparently Vargas took a shot at Prince Tedric.''

Joe was quiet again for another moment. ''So there it is,'' he
said. ''The reason we can't just quit. The reason this operation *is* going to work. We're going to stop those bastards for
good, one way or another.''

Veronica wiped her face with the back of her hand. She
couldn't remember the last time she'd cried like this. It must
have been the stress getting to her. The stress and the fatigue.
Still, to burst into tears like that and . . .

She sat up, pulling away from Joe and glancing around the
room, alarmed, her cheeks flushing with embarrassment. She'd
lost it. She'd absolutely lost it—and right in front of Joe and all
those FInCOM agents. But the FInCOM agents were gone.

''They're outside the door,'' Joe said, correctly reading her
thoughts. ''I figured you'd appreciate the privacy.''

''Thank you,'' Veronica murmured.

She was blushing, and the tip of her nose was pink from
crying. She looked exhausted and fragile. Joe wanted to wrap
her back in his arms and hold her close. He wanted to hold her
as she closed her eyes and fell asleep. He wanted to keep her
warm and safe from harm, and to convince her that everything was going to be all right.

She glanced at him, embarrassment lighting her crystal blue
eyes. ''I'm sorry,'' she said. ''I didn't mean to—''

''You're tired.'' He gave her an easy excuse and a gentle
smile.

They were alone. They were alone in the room. As Joe held
her gaze, he knew she was aware of that, too.

Her hair was starting to come free from its restraints, and
strands curled around her face.

He couldn't stop himself from reaching out and lightly
brushing the last of her tears from her cheek. Her skin was so
soft and warm. She didn't flinch, didn't pull away, didn't even
move. She just gazed at him, her eyes blue and wide and so
damned innocent.

Joe couldn't remember ever wanting to kiss a woman more
in his entire life. Slowly, so slowly, he leaned forward, search-

ing her eyes for any protest, alert for any sign that he was taking this moment of truce too far.

Her eyes flickered and he saw her desire. She wanted him to kiss her, too. But he also saw doubt and a flash of fear. She was afraid.

Afraid of what? Of him? Of herself? Or maybe she was afraid that the overwhelming attraction they both felt would ignite in a violent, nearly unstoppable explosion of need.

Joe almost pulled back.

But then her lips parted slightly, and he couldn't resist. He wanted a taste—just a taste—of her sweetness.

So he kissed her. Slowly, gently pressing his lips to hers.

A rush of desire hit him low in the gut and it took every ounce of control to keep from giving in to his need and pulling her hard into his arms, kissing her savagely, and running his hands along the curves of her body. Instead, he made himself slow down.

Gently, so gently, he ran his tongue across her lips, slowly gaining passage to the softness of her mouth. He closed his eyes, forcing himself to move still more slowly, even slower now. She tasted of strawberries and coffee—an enticing combination of flavors. He caressed her tongue with his own and when she responded, when she opened her mouth to him, granting him access and deepening their kiss, he felt dizzy with pleasure.

This was, absolutely, the sweetest kiss he'd ever shared.

Slowly, still slowly, he explored the warmth of her mouth, the softness of her lips. He touched only her mouth with his, and the side of her face with the tips of his fingers. She wasn't locked in his arms, their bodies weren't pressed tightly together. Still, with this gentle, purest of kisses, she had the power to make his blood surge through his veins, to make his heart pound in a wild, frantic rhythm.

He wanted her desperately. His body was straining to become joined with hers. And yet . . .

This kiss was enough. It was exhilarating, and it made him feel incredibly happy. Happy in a way he'd never been even while making love to the other women he'd had relationships with—women he'd been attracted to and slept with, but hadn't particularly cared for.

He felt a tightness in his chest, a weight of emotion he'd never felt before as, beneath his fingers, Veronica trembled.

He pulled back then, and she looked away, unable to meet his eyes.

"Well," she said. "My word."

"Yeah," Joe agreed. He hadn't intended to whisper, but he couldn't seem to speak any louder.

"That was . . . unexpected."

He couldn't entirely agree. He'd been expecting to kiss her ever since their eyes first met and the raw attraction sparked between them. What was unexpected was this odd sense of caring, this emotional noose that had somehow curled itself around his chest. It was faintly uncomfortable, and it hadn't disappeared even when he'd ended their kiss.

She glanced at him. "Maybe we should get back to work."

Joe shook his head. "No," he said. "I need a break, and you do, too." He stood, holding out his hand to her. "Come on, I'll walk you to your room. You can take a nap. I'll meet you back here in a few hours."

Veronica didn't take his hand. She simply gazed up at him.

"Come on," he said again. "Cut yourself some slack."

But she shook her head. "There's no time."

He gently touched her hair. "Yes, there is. There's definitely time for an hour of shut-eye," he said. "Trust me, Ronnie, you're gonna need it to concentrate."

Joe could see indecision on her face. "How about forty minutes?" he added. "Forty winks. You can crash right here on the couch. I'll order some coffee and wake you up at—" he glanced at his watch "—oh-six-twenty."

Slowly she nodded. "All right."

He bent down and briefly brushed her lips with his. "Sleep tight," he said.

She stopped him, touching the side of his face. "You're so sweet," she said, surprise in her voice.

He had to laugh. He'd been called a lot of things in his life, and "sweet" wasn't one of them. "Oh, no, I'm not."

Veronica's lips curved into a smile. "I didn't mean that to be an insult." Her smile faded and she looked away, suddenly awkward. "Joe, I have to be honest with you," she said quietly. "I think that kiss . . . was a mistake. I'm so tired, and I wasn't thinking clearly and, well, I hope you don't think that I... Well, right now it's not... We're not... It's a *mistake*. Don't you think?''

Joe straightened. The noose around his chest was so damn tight he could hardly breathe. A mistake. Veronica thought kissing him had been a mistake. He shook his head slowly, hiding his disappointment behind a tight smile. "No, and I'm sorry *you* think that," he replied. "I thought maybe we had something there."

"Something?" Veronica echoed, glancing up at him.

This time it was Joe who looked away. He sat down next to her on the couch, suddenly tired. How could he explain what he meant, when he didn't even know himself? Damn, he'd already said too much. What if she thought by "something" he meant he was falling in love with her?

He pushed his hair back with one hand and glanced at Veronica.

Yeah, she wanted him to fall in love with her about as much as she wanted a hole in the head. In the space of a heartbeat, he could picture her dismay, picture her imagining the restraining order she'd have to get to keep him away from her. He was rough and uncultured, blue-collar through and through. *She* hung out with royalty. It would be embarrassing and inconvenient for her to have some crazy, rough-edged, lovesick sailor following her around.

Gazing into her eyes, he could see her trepidation.

So he gave her a cocky smile and prayed that she couldn't somehow sense the tightness in his chest. "I thought we had something great between us," he said, leaning forward and putting his hand on her thigh.

Veronica moved back on the couch, away from him. His hand fell aside.

"Ah, yes," she said. "Sex. Exactly what I thought you m ant."

Joe stood. "Too bad."

She glanced at him but didn't meet his gaze for more than a fraction of a second. "Yes, it is."

He turned away, heading for the bedroom and his bed. Maybe some sleep would make this pressure in his chest lighten up or—please, God—even make it go away.

"Please, don't forget to wake me," Veronica called.

"Right," he said shortly and closed the door behind him.

The knock on the door came quickly, no less than five minutes after Joe had called for coffee from room service. Man, he
thought, people really hopped to it when they thought a guy
had blue blood.

West and the other FInCOM agent, Freeman, both drew
their guns, motioning for Joe to move away from the door. It
was an odd sensation. He was the one who usually did the protecting.

The door opened, and it was the room-service waiter. West
and Freeman handed Joe two steaming mugs of fragrant coffee. Joe carried them to the coffee table and set them down.

Veronica was still asleep. She'd slid down on the couch so
that her head was resting on the seat cushion. She clutched a
legal pad to her chest.

She looked incredibly beautiful. Her skin was so smooth and
soft looking, it was all he could do not to reach out with one
knuckle to touch her cheek.

Veronica St. John.

Who would have guessed he would have a thing for a prim-
and-proper society girl named Veronica St. John? "Sinjin," for
Pete's sake.

But she wasn't interested in him. That incredible, perfect kiss
they'd shared had been "a mistake."

Like *hell* it had.

Joe had had to force himself to fall asleep. Only his extensive training had kept him from lying on the bed, staring at the
ceiling and expending his energy by playing their kiss over and
over and over again in his mind. He'd spent enough time doing that while he was in the shower, after he woke up. Each time
he played that kiss over in his head, he tried to figure out what
he'd done wrong, and each time, he came up blank. Finally
he'd had to admit it—he'd done nothing wrong. That kiss had
been perfect, not a mistake.

Now all he had to do was convince Veronica of that fact.

Yeah, right. She was stubborn as hell. He'd have a better
chance of convincing the Mississippi River to flow north.

The hell of it was, Joe found himself actually *liking* the girl, trying to make her smile. He wanted to get another look behind her so-very-proper British facade. Except he wasn't sure exactly where the facade ended and the real girl began. So far, he'd seen two very conflicting images— Veronica in her prim-and-proper work clothes, and Veronica dressed down to dance. He was willing to bet that the real woman was hidden somewhere in the middle. He was also willing to bet that she would never willingly reveal her true self. Especially not to *him*.

Joe had more than just a suspicion that Veronica considered him substandard. He was the son of a servant, while she was a daughter of the ruling class. If she had a relationship with him, it would be a lark, a kick. She'd be slumming.

Slumming.

God, it was an ugly word. But, so what? So she'd be slumming. Big deal. What was he going to do if she approached him? Was he going to turn her down? Yeah, right. Like hell he'd turn her down.

He could just picture the scenario.

Veronica knocks on his door in the middle of the night and he says, "Sorry, babe, I'm not into being used by curious debutantes who want a peek at the way the lower half lives and loves."

Yeah, right.

If she knocked on his door, he'd fling it open wide. Let her go slumming. Just let him be the one she was slumming with.

Veronica stirred slightly, shifting to get more comfortable on the couch, and the legal pad she'd been holding fell out of her arms. Joe moved quickly and caught it before it hit the floor.

Her hair was starting to come undone, and soft red wisps curled around her face. Her lips were slightly parted. They were so soft and delicate and delicious. He knew that firsthand.

It didn't take much to imagine her lifting those exquisite lips to his for another perfect kiss—for a deep, demanding, soulful kiss that would rapidly escalate into more. *Way* more.

And then what?

Then they'd be lovers until she got tired of him, or he got tired of her. It would be no different from any of the other relationships he'd had.

But so far, everything about this *was* different. Veronica St. John wasn't some woman he'd met in a bar. She hadn't approached him, handed him the keys to her car or her motel room and asked if he was busy for the next twenty-four hours. She hadn't even approached him at all.

She wasn't his type. She was too high-strung, too uptight.

But something he'd seen in her eyes promised a paradise the likes of which he'd never known. Hell, it was a paradise he was probably better off never knowing.

Because what if he never got tired of her?

There it was. Right out in the open. The big, ugly question he'd been trying to avoid. What if this noose that had tightened around his chest never went away?

But that would never happen, right?

He couldn't let Veronica's wealth and high-class manners throw him off. She was just a woman. All those differences he'd imagined were just that—imagined.

So how come he was standing there like an idiot, staring at the girl? Why was he too damned chicken to touch her, to wake her up, to see her sleepy blue eyes gazing up at him?

The answer was clear—because even if the impossible happened, and Joe actually did something as idiotically stupid as fall in love with Veronica St. John, she would never, not in a million years, fall in love with him. Sure, she might find him amusing for a few weeks or even months, but eventually she'd come to her senses and trade him in for a more expensive model.

And somehow the thought of that stung. Even now. Even though there was absolutely nothing between them. Nothing, that is, but one perfect kiss and its promise of paradise.

"Yo, Ronnie," Joe said, hoping she'd wake up without him touching her. But she didn't stir.

He bent down and spoke directly into her ear. "Coffee's here. Time to wake up."

Nothing.

He touched her shoulder, shaking her very slightly.

Nothing.

He shook her harder, and she stirred, but her eyes stayed tightly shut.

"Go away," she mumbled.

Joe pulled her up into a sitting position. Her head lolled against the back of the couch. "Come on, babe," he said. "If I don't wake you up, you're going to be madder than hell at me." He gently touched the side of her face. "Come on, Ronnie. Look at me. Open your eyes."

She opened them. They were astonishingly blue and very sleepy. "Be a dear, Jules, and ring the office. Tell them I'll be a few hours late. I'm bushed. Out too late last night." She smiled and blew a kiss into the air near his face. "Thanks, luv." Then she tucked her perfect knees primly up underneath her skirt, put her head back down on the seat cushions and tightly closed her eyes.

Jules?

Who the hell was Jules?

"Come on, Veronica," Joe said almost desperately. He had no right to want to hog-tie this Jules, whoever the hell he was. No right at all. "You wanted me to wake you up. Besides, you can't sleep on the couch. You'll wake up with one hell of a backache."

She didn't open her eyes again, didn't sigh, didn't move.

She was fast asleep, and not likely to wake up until she was good and ready.

Gritting his teeth, Joe picked Veronica up and carried her into the bedroom. He set her gently down on the bed, trying to ignore the way she fit so perfectly in his arms. For half a second, he actually considered climbing in under the covers next to her. But he didn't have time. He had work to do. Besides, when he got in bed with Veronica St. John, it was going to be at her invitation.

Joe took off her remaining shoe and put it on the floor, then covered her with the blankets.

She didn't move, didn't wake up again. He didn't give in to the desire to smooth her hair back from her face. He just stared down at her for another brief moment, knowing that the smart thing to do would be to stay far, far away from this woman. He knew that she was trouble, the likes of which he'd never known.

He turned away, needing a stiff drink. He settled for black coffee and set to work.

Chapter 8

Veronica sat bolt upright in the bed.

Dear Lord in heaven, she wasn't supposed to be asleep, she was supposed to be working and—

What time was it?

Her watch read twelve twenty-four. Oh, no, she'd lost the entire morning. But she must have been exhausted. She couldn't even remember coming back here to her own room and—

Oh, Lord! She realized she wasn't in her own room. She was in the prince's bedroom, in the prince's bed. No, not the prince's. *Joe's. Joe's* bed.

With a dizzying flash, Veronica remembered Joe pulling her into his arms and kissing her so slowly, so sensuously that every bone in her body seemed to melt. He had rid them of their clothes like a seasoned professional and . . .

But . . . she was still dressed. Right down to her hose, which were twisted and uncomfortable. She'd only *dreamed* about Joe Catalanotto and his seductive eyes and surprisingly gentle hands.

The kiss had been real, though; and achingly, shockingly tender. It figured. Joe would know exactly how to kiss her to make her the most vulnerable, to affect her in the strongest possible way.

She'd expected him to kiss her almost roughly—an echo of the sexual hunger she'd seen in his eyes. She could have handled that. She would have known what to say and do.

Instead, Joe had given her a kiss that was more gentle than passionate, although the passion had been there, indeed. But Veronica was still surprised by the restraint he'd shown, by the sweetness of his mouth against hers, by the slow, lingering sensuality of his lips. She could very well have kissed him that way until the end of time.

Time. Lord! She'd wasted so much *time*.

Veronica swung her legs out of bed.

She'd *told* Joe to wake her up. Obviously, he hadn't. Instead of waking her, he'd carried her here, into his bedroom.

She found one of her shoes on the floor, and searched to no avail for the other. Perfect. One shoe off and one shoe on, having slept away most of the day, her dignity in shreds, she'd have to go out into the living room where the FInCOM agents were parked. She'd have to endure their knowing smirks.

She was a wimp. She'd fallen asleep—and stayed asleep for *hours*—while on the job.

And Joe . . . Joe hadn't kept his promise to wake her up.

She'd been starting to . . . like him. She'd been attracted from the start, but this was different. She actually, genuinely *liked* him, despite the fact that he came from an entirely different world, despite the fact that they seemed to argue almost constantly. She even liked him despite the fact that he clearly wanted to make their relationship sexual. Despite all that, she'd thought he had been starting to like her, too.

Her disappointment flashed quickly into anger. How *dare* he just let her sleep the day away? The *bastard* . . .

Veronica fumed as she tucked her blouse back into the top of her skirt and straightened her jacket, thankful her suit was permanent-press and wrinkle-proof.

Her hair wasn't quite so easy to fix, but she was determined not to emerge from the bedroom with it down and flowing around her shoulders. It was bad enough that she'd been sleeping in Joe's bed. She didn't want it to look as if he'd been in there with her.

Finally, she took a deep breath and, single shoe in her hand and head held high, she went into the living room.

If the FInCOM agents smirked condescendingly, Veronica refused to notice. All she knew was, Joe was not in the room. Good thing, or she might have lost even more of her dignity by throwing her shoe directly at his head.

"Good afternoon, gentlemen," she said briskly to West and Freeman as she gathered up her briefcase. Ah, good. There was her missing shoe, on the floor in front of the sofa. She slipped them both onto her feet. "Might I ask where the lieutenant has gone?"

"He's up in the exercise room," one of them answered.

"Thanks so very much," Veronica said and breezed out the door.

Joe had already run seven miles on the treadmill when Veronica walked into the hotel's luxuriously equipped exercise room. She looked a whole lot better. She'd showered and changed her clothes. But glory hallelujah, instead of putting on another of those Margaret Thatcher suits, she was wearing a plain blue dress. It was nothing fancy, obviously designed to deemphasize her femininity, yet somehow, on Veronica, it hugged her slender figure and made her look like a million bucks. Her shoes were still on the clunky side, but oh, baby, those legs . . .

Joe wiped a trickle of sweat that ran down the side of his face. When had it gotten so hot in here?

But her greeting to him was anything but warm.

"I'd like to have a word with you," Veronica said icily, without even a hello to start. "At your convenience, of course."

"Did you have a good nap?" Joe asked.

"Will you be much longer?" she asked, staring somewhere off to his left.

That good, huh? Something had ticked her off, and Joe was willing to bet that that something was him. He'd let her sleep. Correction—he'd been unable to wake her up. It wasn't his fault, but now he was going to pay.

"Can you give me five more minutes?" he countered. "I like to do ten miles without stopping."

Joe wasn't even out of breath. Veronica could see from the computerized numbers lit up on the treadmill's controls, that he'd already run eight miles. But he didn't sound winded.

He was sweating, though. His shorts were soaking wet. He wasn't wearing a shirt, and his smooth, tanned skin was slick as his muscles worked. And, dear Lord, he had so *many* muscles. Beautifully sculpted, perfect muscles. He was gorgeous.

He was watching her in the floor-to-ceiling mirrors that covered the walls of the exercise room. Veronica leaned against the wall near the door and tried not to look at Joe, but everywhere she turned, she saw his reflection. She found herself staring in fascination at the rippling muscles in his back and thighs and arms, and then she started thinking about their kiss. Their fabulous, heart-stoppingly romantic kiss. Despite his nonchalant attitude, that kiss had been laced with tenderness and laden with emotion. It was unlike any kiss she'd experienced *ever* before.

Veronica had been well aware that Joe had been holding back when he kissed her that way. She'd felt his restraint and the power of his control. She had seen the heat of desire in his eyes and known he wanted more than just a simple, gentle kiss.

Veronica couldn't forget how he'd searched her eyes as he'd leaned toward her and . . .

Excellent. Here she was, standing there reliving Joe's kiss while staring at his perfect buttocks. Veronica glanced up to find his amused dark eyes watching her watch his rear end. No doubt he could read her mind. Of course the fact that she'd been nearly drooling made it all the easier for him to know what she'd been thinking.

She might as well give in, Veronica admitted to herself. She might as well sleep with the man and get it over with. After all, he was so bloody positive that it was going to happen. And after their kiss, despite her best intentions, all Veronica could think about was "When was he going to kiss her again?" Except he hadn't woken her up, which meant that he probably didn't even *like* her, and now *she* was mad as hell at him. Yes, kissing him *had* been a royal mistake. Although at the time, when she'd said those words, she'd meant another kind of mistake entirely. She'd meant their timing had been wrong.

She'd meant it had been a mistake to add a romantic distraction to all of the other distractions already driving her half mad.

Then, of course, he'd said what *he'd* said, and . . .

The fact that Joe saw their growing relationship as one based purely on sex only added to Veronica's confusion. She knew that a man like Joe Catalanotto, a man accustomed to intrigue and high adventure, would never have any kind of long-term interest in a woman who worked her hardest to be steady and responsible and, well, quite frankly, *boring*. And even if that wasn't the case, even if by some miracle Joe fell madly and permanently in love with her, how on earth would she handle his leaving on dangerous, top-secret missions? How could she simply wave goodbye, knowing she might never again see him alive?

No, thank you very much.

So maybe this pure sex thing didn't add to her confusion. Maybe it simplified things. Maybe it took it all down to the simplest, most basic level.

Lord knew, she *was* wildly attracted to him. And so what if she was watching him?

Veronica met Joe's gaze almost defiantly, her chin held high. One couldn't have a body like that and expect people *not* to look. And watching Joe run was like watching a dancer. He was graceful and surefooted, his motion fluid and effortless. She wondered if he could dance. She wondered—not for the first time—what it would feel like to be held in his arms, dancing with him.

As Veronica watched, Joe focused on his running, increasing his speed, his arms and legs churning, pumping. The treadmill was starting to whine, and just when Veronica was sure Joe was going to start to slow, when she was positive he couldn't keep up the pace a moment longer, he went even faster.

His teeth were clenched, his face a picture of concentration and stamina. He looked like something savage, something wild. An untamed man-creature from the distant past. A ferocious, barbaric warrior come to shake up the civility of Veronica's carefully polite twentieth-century world.

"Hoo-yah!" someone called out, and Joe's face broke into a wide smile as he looked up at three men, standing near the weight machine in the corner of the room. As quickly as his smile appeared, the barbarian was gone.

Odd, Veronica hadn't noticed the other men before this. She'd been aware of the FInCOM agents lurking near her, but not these three men dressed in workout clothes. They seemed to know Joe. SEALs, Veronica guessed. They had to be the men Joe had asked Admiral Forrest to send.

Joe slowed at last, returning the treadmill to a walking speed as he caught his breath. He stepped off and grabbed a towel, using it to mop his face as he came toward Veronica.

"What's up?"

Joe was steaming. There was literally visible heat rising from his smooth, powerful shoulders. He stopped about six feet away from her, clearly not wanting to offend her by standing too close.

His friends came and surrounded him, and Veronica was momentarily silenced by three additional pairs of eyes appraising her with frank male appreciation. Joe's eyes alone were difficult enough to handle.

Joe glanced at the other men. "Get lost," he said. "This is a private conversation."

"Not anymore," said one of them with a Western twang. He was almost as tall as Joe, but probably weighed forty pounds less. He held out his hand to Veronica. "I'm Cowboy, ma'am."

She shook Cowboy's hand, and he held on to hers far longer than necessary, until Joe gave him a dark look.

"All right, quick introductions," Joe said. "Lieutenant McCoy, my XO—executive officer—and Ensigns Becker and Jones. Also known as Blue, Harvard and Cowboy. Miss Veronica St. John. For you illiterates, it's spelled Saint and John, two words, but pronounced *Sinjin*. She's Prince Tedric's media consultant, and she's on the scheduling team for this op."

Lt. Blue McCoy looked to be about Joe's age—somewhere in his early thirties. He was shorter and smaller than the other men, with the build of a long-distance runner and the blue eyes, wavy, thick blond hair and handsome face of a Hollywood star.

Harvard—Ensign Becker—was a large black man with steady, intelligent brown eyes and a smoothly shaven head. Cowboy's hair was even longer than Blue McCoy's, and he wore it pulled back into a ponytail at the nape of his neck. His eyes were green and sparkling, and his smile boyishly winsome. He looked like Kevin Costner's younger brother, and he knew it. He kept winking at her.

"Pleased to meet you," Veronica said, shaking hands with both Blue and Harvard. She was afraid if she offered Cowboy her hand again, she might never get it back.

"The pleasure's all ours, ma'am," Cowboy said. "I love what you've done with the captain's hair."

"Captain?" Veronica looked at Joe. "I thought you were a Lieutenant."

"It's a term of endearment, ma'am," Blue said. He, too, had a thick accent, but his was from the Deep South. "Cat's in command, so sometimes he gets called Captain."

"It's better than some of the other things they call me," Joe said.

Cat.

Admiral Forrest had also called Joe by that nickname. Cat. It fit. As Joe ran on the treadmill, he looked like a giant cat, so graceful and fluid. The nickname, while really just a shortened form of Catalanotto, wasn't too far off.

"Okay, great," Joe said. "We've made nice. Now you boys get lost. Finish your PT, and let the grown-ups talk."

Lt. McCoy took the other two men by the arms and pulled them toward weight-lifting equipment. Harvard began to bench-press heavy-looking weights while Cowboy spotted him, one eye still on Joe and Veronica.

"Now let's try this one more time," Joe said with a smile. "What's up? You look like you want to court-martial me."

"Only if the punishment for mutiny is still execution," Veronica said, smiling tightly.

Joe looped his towel around his neck. "Mutiny," he said. "That's a serious charge—especially considering I did my damnedest to wake you up."

Veronica crossed her arms. "Oh, and I suppose your 'damnedest' included putting me in a nice soft bed, where I'd be sure to sleep away most of the day?" she said. She glanced around, at both the FInCOM agents and the other SEALs, and lowered her voice. "I might *also* point out that it was hardly proper for *me* to sleep in *your* bed. It surely looked bad, and it implied . . . certain things."

"Whoa, Ronnie." Joe shook his head. "That wasn't my intention. I thought you'd be more comfortable, that's all. I wasn't trying to—"

"I'm an unmarried woman, Lieutenant," Veronica interrupted. "Regardless of what you intended, it is not in my best interests to take a nap in any man's bed."

Joe laughed. "I think maybe you're overreacting just a *teeny* little bit. This isn't the 1890s. I don't see how your reputation could be tarnished simply from napping in my bed. If I were in there with you, it'd be an entirely different matter. But if you want to know the truth, I'd be willing to bet no one even noticed where you were sleeping this morning, or even that you were asleep. And if they did, that's their problem."

"No, it's *my* problem," Veronica said sharply, her temper flaring. "Tell me, Lieutenant, are there many women in the SEALs?"

"No," Joe said. "There're none. We don't allow women in the units."

"Aha," Veronica retorted. "In other words, you're not familiar with sexual discrimination, because your organization is based on sexual discrimination. That's just perfect."

"Look, if you want to preach feminism, fine," Joe said, his patience disintegrating, "but do me a favor—hand me a pamphlet to read on the subject and be done with it. Right now, I'm going to take a shower."

By now they had the full, unconcealed attention of the three other SEALs and the FInCOM agents, but Veronica was long past caring. She was angry—angry that he had let her sleep, angry that he was so macho, angry that he had kissed her—and particularly angry that she had liked his kiss so damn much.

She blocked Joe's way, stabbing at his broad chest with one finger. "Don't you *dare* run away from me, Lieutenant," she said, her voice rising with each word. "You're operating in *my* world now, and I will not have you jeopardizing my career through your own *stupid* ignorance."

He flinched as if she'd slapped him in the face and turned away, but not before she saw the flash of hurt in his eyes. Hurt that was rapidly replaced by anger.

"Jesus, Mary and Joseph," Joe said through clenched teeth. "I was only trying to be nice. I thought sleeping on the couch would screw up your back, but forget it. From now on, I won't bother, okay? From now on, we'll go by the book."

He pushed past her and went into the locker room. The FInCOM agents and the three other SEALs followed, leaving Veronica alone in the exercise room. Her reflection gazed back at her from all angles.

Perfect. She'd handled that just perfectly.

Veronica had come down here to find out why he'd let her sleep so long, and wound up in a fierce argument about sexual discrimination and her pristine reputation. That wasn't the real issue at all. It had just been something to shout about, because Lord knew she couldn't walk up to him and shout that his kiss had turned her entire world upside down and now she was totally, utterly and quite thoroughly off-balance.

Instead, she had called him names. *Stupid. Ignorant.* Words that had clearly cut deep, despite the fact that he was anything but stupid and far from ignorant.

What Veronica had done was take out all her anger and frustration on the man.

But if anyone was to blame here, it was herself. After all, she was the one foolish enough to have fallen asleep in the first place.

"Hey, Cat!" Cowboy called loudly as he showered in the locker room. "Tell me more about fair Veronica 'Sinjin.' "

"There's nothing to tell," Joe answered evenly. He glanced up to find Blue watching him.

Damn. Blue could read his mind. Joe's connection to Blue was so tight, there were few thoughts that appeared in Joe's head that Blue wasn't instantly aware of. But what would Blue make of the thoughts Joe was having right now? What would he make of the sick, nauseous feeling Joe had in the pit of his stomach?

Stupid. Ignorant.

Well, that about summed it all up, didn't it? Joe certainly knew now exactly what Veronica St. John thought of him, didn't he? He certainly knew why she'd thought that kiss was a mistake.

Cowboy shut off the water. Dripping, he came out of the stall and into the room. "You sure there's nothing you can tell us about Veronica, Cat? Oh, come on, buddy, I can think of a thing or two," he said, taking a towel from a pile of clean ones and giving himself a perfunctory swipe. "Like, are you and she doing the nightly naked two-step?"

"No," Joe replied flatly, pulling on his pants.

"You planning on it?" Cowboy asked. He slipped into one of the plush hotel robes that were hanging on the wall.

"Back off, Jones," Blue said warningly.

"No." Joe answered Cowboy tersely as he yanked his T-shirt over his head and thrust his arms into the sleeves of his shirt.

"Cool," Cowboy said. "Then you don't mind if I give her a try—"

Joe spun and grabbed the younger man by the lapels of his robe, slamming him up against a row of metal lockers with a crash. "Stay the hell away from her," he snapped. He let go of Cowboy, and turned to include Blue and Harvard in his glare. "All of you. Is that clear?"

He didn't wait for an answer. He turned and stalked out of the room, slamming the door behind him.

The noise echoed as Cowboy stared at Harvard and Blue.

"Shoot," he finally said. "Anybody have any idea what the hell's going on?"

Chapter 9

Room service arrived at the royal suite before Joe did.

"Set it out on the table, please," Veronica instructed the waiter.

She'd ordered a full-course meal, from appetizers to dessert, complete with three different wines.

This afternoon's lesson was food—or more precisely, *eating* food. There was a hundred-dollar-a-plate charity luncheon in Boston, Massachusetts, that had been left on the prince's tour schedule. Both the location and the visibility of the event were right for a possible assassination attempt, but it was more than a hi-and-bye appearance. It would involve more than Joe's ability to stand and wave as if he were Prince Tedric.

The hotel-suite door opened, and Joe came inside, followed by three FInCOM agents. His shirt was unbuttoned, revealing his T-shirt underneath, and he met Veronica's eyes only briefly before turning to the laden dining table. It was quite clear that he was still upset with her.

"What's this?" he asked.

"This is practice for the Boston charity luncheon," Veronica replied. "I hope you're hungry."

Joe stared at the table. It was loaded with dishes covered with plate-warmers. It was set for two, with a full array of cutlery and three different wineglasses at each setting. What, didn't Miss High-and-Mighty think he knew how to eat with a fork? Didn't she know he dined with admirals and four-star generals at the Officers' Club?

Stupid. Ignorant.

Joe nodded slowly, wishing he was still pissed off, wishing he was still nursing the slow burn he'd felt upstairs in the exercise room. But he wasn't. He was too tired to be angry now. He was too tired to feel anything but disappointment and hurt. Damn, it made him feel so vulnerable.

The room-service waiter was standing next to the table, looking down his snotty nose at Joe's unbuttoned shirt. Gee, maybe the waiter and Veronica had had a good laugh about Joe before he'd arrived.

"This is unnecessary," he said, turning back to look at Veronica. Man, she looked pretty in that blue dress. Her hair was tied back with some kind of ribbon, and— Forget about her, he told himself harshly. She was just some rich girl who'd made it more than clear that they lived in two different worlds, and there was no crossing the border. He was stupid and ignorant, and kissing him had been a mistake. "Believe it or not, I already know which fork is for the salad and which fork is for the dessert. It might come as a shock to you, but I also know how to use a napkin and drink from a glass."

Veronica actually looked surprised, her blue eyes growing even wider. "Oh," she said. "No. No, I knew that. That's not what this is." She let a nervous laugh escape. "You actually thought *I* thought I'd need to teach you how to eat?"

Joe was not amused. "Yeah."

My God, he was serious. He was standing there, his powerful arms folded across his broad chest, staring at her with those mystifying dark eyes. Veronica remembered that flash of hurt in Joe's eyes when they'd argued in the exercise room. What had she said? She'd called him stupid and ignorant. Oh, Lord. She *still* couldn't believe those words had come out of her mouth.

"I'm so sorry," she said.

Prince Joe

His eyes narrowed slightly, as if he couldn't believe what he was hearing.

"I owe you an apology," Veronica explained. "I was very angry this afternoon, and I said some things I didn't mean. The truth is, I was frustrated and angry with myself. *I* was the one who fell asleep. It was all my fault, and I tried to take it out on you. I shouldn't have. I *am* sorry."

Joe looked at the waiter and then at the FInCOM agents who were sitting on the sofa, listening to every word. He crossed to the door and opened it invitingly. "You guys mind stepping outside for a sec?"

The FInCOM agents looked at each other and shrugged. Rising to their feet, they crossed to the door and filed out into the corridor. Joe turned to the waiter. "You, too, pal." He gestured toward the open door. "Take a hike."

He waited until the waiter was outside, then closed the door tightly and crossed back to Veronica. "You know, these guys *will* give you privacy if you ask for it," he said.

She nodded. "I know," she said. She lifted her chin slightly, steadily meeting his gaze. "It's just...I was rude to you in public, I felt I should apologize to you in public, too."

Joe nodded, too. "Okay," he said. "Yeah. That sounds fair." He looked at her, and there was something very close to admiration in his eyes. "That sounds really fair."

Veronica felt her own eyes flood with tears. Oh, damn, she was going to cry. If she started to cry, she was going to feel once more just how gentle Joe's hard-as-steel arms could be. And Lord, she didn't want to be reminded of that. "I *am* sorry," she said, blinking back the tears.

Oh, *damn,* Veronica was going to cry, Joe thought as he took a step toward her, then stopped himself. No, she was trying hard to hide it. It was better if he played along, if he pretended he didn't notice. But, man, the sight of those blue eyes swimming in tears made his chest ache, reminding him of this morning, when he'd held her in his arms. Reminding him of that unbelievable kiss...

Veronica forced a smile and held out her hand to him. "Still friends?" she asked.

Friends, huh? Joe had never had a friend before that he wanted to pull into his arms and kiss the living daylights out of.

As he gazed into her eyes, the attraction between them seemed to crackle and snap, like some living thing.

Veronica was okay. She was a decent person—the fact that she'd apologized proved that. But she came from miles on the other side of the railroad tracks. If their relationship became intimate, she'd still be slumming. And *he'd* be ...

He'd be dreaming about her every night for the rest of his life.

Joe let go of Veronica's hand as if he'd been stung. Jesus, Mary and Joseph, where had *that* thought come from ... ?

"Are you all right?" The concern in her eyes was genuine.

Joe stuffed his hands in his pockets. "Yeah. Sorry. I guess I'm ... After we do this dining thing, I'm going to take another short nap."

"A three-minute nap this time?" Veronica asked. "Or maybe you'll splurge, and sleep for five whole minutes ... ?"

Joe smiled, and she gave him an answering smile. Their gazes met and held. And held and held and held.

With another woman, Joe would have closed the gap between them. With another woman, Joe would have taken two short steps and brought them face to face. He would have brushed those stray flame-colored curls from the side of her beautiful face, then lifted her chin and lowered his mouth to meet hers.

He had tasted her lips before. He knew how amazing kissing Veronica could be.

But she wasn't another woman. She was Veronica St. John. And she'd already made it clear that sex wasn't on their agenda. Hell, if a kiss was a mistake, then making love would be an error of unbelievable magnitude. And the truth was, Joe didn't want to face that kind of rejection.

So Joe didn't move. He just gazed at her.

"Well," she said, slightly breathlessly, "perhaps we should get to work."

But she didn't cross toward the dining table, she just gazed up at him, as if she, too, were caught in some kind of force field and unable to move.

Veronica was beautiful. And rich. And smart. But more than just book smart. She was people smart, too. Joe had seen her manipulate a tableful of high-ranking officials. She couldn't have done that on an Ivy League diploma alone.

He didn't know the first thing about her, Joe realized. He didn't know where she came from, or how she'd gotten here, to Washington, D.C. He didn't know how she'd come to work for the crown prince of Ustanzia. He didn't know why she'd remained, even after the assassination attempt, when most civilians would have headed for the hills and safety.

"What's your angle?" Joe asked.

Veronica blinked. "Excuse me?"

He reworded the question. "Why are you here? I mean, I'm here to help catch Diosdado, but what are *you* getting out of this?"

She looked out the window at the afternoon view of the capital city. When she glanced back at Joe, her smile was rueful. "Beats me," she said. "I'm not getting paid nearly half enough, although it could be argued that working for royalty is a solid career boost. Of course, it all depends on whether we can successfully pass you off as Prince Tedric."

She sank down onto the couch and looked up at him, elbow on her knee, chin in her hand. "We have less than six hours before the committee makes a decision." She shook her head and laughed humorlessly. "Instead of becoming more like Tedric, you seem more different from him than when we started. I look at you, Joe, and you don't even *look* like the prince anymore."

Joe smiled as he sat next to her on the couch. "Lucky for us, most people won't look beneath the surface. They'll expect to see Ted, so...they'll see Ted."

"I *need* this thing to work," Veronica said, smoothing her skirt over her knees. "If this doesn't work..."

"Why?" Joe asked. "Mortgage payment coming due on the castle?"

Veronica turned and looked at him. "Very funny."

"Sorry."

"You don't really want to hear this."

Joe was watching her, studying her face. His dark eyes were fathomless, and as mysterious as the deepest ocean. "Yes, I do."

"Tedric's sister has been my best friend since boarding school," Veronica said. "Even though Tedric is unconcerned with Ustanzia's financial state, Wila has been working hard to make her country more solvent. It matters to her—so it matters to me." She smiled. "When oil was discovered, Wila actually did cartwheels right across the Capital lawn. I thought poor Jules was going to have a heart attack. But then she found out how much it would cost to drill. She's counting on getting U.S. aid."

Jules.

Be a dear, Jules, and ring the office. Veronica had murmured those words in her sleep, and since then, Joe had been wondering, not without a sliver of jealousy, exactly who this Jules was.

"Who's Jules?" Joe asked.

"Jules," Veronica repeated. "My brother. He conveniently married my best friend. It's quite cozy, really, and very sweet. They're expecting a baby any moment."

Her brother. Jules was her brother. Why did that make Joe feel so damned good? He and Veronica were going to be friends, nothing more, so why should *he* care whether Jules was her brother or her lover or her pet monkey?

But he *did* care, damn it.

Joe leaned forward. "So that's why Wila didn't come on this tour instead of Brain-dead Ted? Because she's pregnant?"

Veronica tried not to smile, but failed. "Don't call Prince Tedric that," she said.

He smiled at her, struck by the way her eyes were the exact shade of blue as her dress. "You know, you look pretty in blue."

Her smile vanished and she stood. "We should really get started," she said, crossing to the dining table. "The food's getting cold."

Joe didn't move. "So where did you and Jules grow up? London?"

Veronica turned to look back at him. "No," she replied. "At first we traveled with our parents, and when we were old enough, we went away to school. The closest thing we had to a permanent home was Huntsgate Manor, where our Great-Aunt Rosamond lived."

"Huntsgate Manor," Joe mused. "It sounds like something out of a fairy tale."

Veronica's eyes grew dreamy and out of focus as she gazed out the window. "It was so wonderful. This big, old, moldy, ancient house with gardens and grounds that went on forever and ever and ever." She looked up at Joe with a spark of humor in her eyes. "Not really," she added. "I think the property is only about four or five acres, but when we were little, it seemed to go to the edge of the world and back."

Night and day, Joe thought. Their two upbringings were as different as night and day. He wondered what she would do, how she would react if she knew about the rock he'd crawled out from under.

Veronica laughed, embarrassed. "I don't know why I just told you all that," she said. "It's hardly interesting."

But it *was* interesting. It was fascinating. As fascinating as those gigantic houses he'd gone into with his mother, the houses that she'd cleaned when he was a kid. Veronica's words were another porthole to that same world of "Look but don't touch." It was fascinating. And depressing as hell. Veronica had been raised like a little princess. No doubt she'd only be content to spend her life "happily ever after," with a prince.

And he sure as hell didn't fit *that* bill.

Except, what was he doing, thinking about things like happily ever after?

"How about you, Joe?" she asked, interrupting his thoughts. "Where did you grow up?"

"Near New York City. We really should get to work," he said, half hoping she'd let the subject of his childhood drop— and half hoping that she wouldn't.

She wouldn't. "New York City," she said. "I've never lived there, I've only visited. I remember the first time I was there as a child. It all seemed to be lights and music and Broadway plays and marvelous food and . . . *people,* people everywhere."

"I didn't see any plays on Broadway," Joe said dryly. "Although when I was ten, I snuck out of the house at night and hung around the theater district, trying to spot celebrities. I'd get their autograph and then sell it, make a quick buck."

"Your parents probably *loved* that," Veronica said. "A ten-year-old, all alone in New York City . . . ?"

"My mother was usually too drunk to notice I was gone," Joe said. "And even if she had, she wouldn't have given a damn."

Veronica looked away from him, down at the floor. "Oh," she said.

"Yeah," Joe said. "Oh."

She fiddled with her hair for a moment, and then she surprised him. She looked up and directly into his eyes and smiled—a smile not without sorrow for the boy he'd once been. "I guess that's where you learned to be so self-reliant. And self-confident."

"Self-reliant, maybe. But I grew up with everyone always telling me I wasn't good enough," Joe said. "No, that's not true. Not everyone. Not Frank O'Riley." He shook his head and laughed. "He was this mean old guy who lived in this grungy basement apartment in one of the tenements over by the river. He had a wooden leg and a glass eye and his arms were covered with tattoos and all the kids were scared sh— Scared to death of him. Except me, because I was the toughest, coolest kid in the neighborhood—at least among the under-twelve set.

"O'Riley had this garden—really just a patch of land. It couldn't have been more than twelve by four feet. He always had something growing—flowers, vegetables—it was always something. So I went in there, over his rusty fence, just to prove I wasn't scared of the old man.

"I'd been planning to trample his flowers, but once I got into the garden, I couldn't do it," Joe said. "They were just too damn pretty. All those colors. Shades I'd never even imagined. Instead, I sat down and just looked at them.

"Old Frank came out and told me he'd loaded his gun and was ready to shoot me in my sorry butt, but since I was obviously another nature lover, he'd brought me a glass of lemonade instead."

Why was he telling her this? Blue was the only person he'd ever mentioned Frank O'Riley to, and never in such detail. Joe's friendship with Old Man O'Riley was the single good memory he carried from his childhood. Chief Frank O'Riley, U.S.N., retired, and his barely habitable basement apartment had been Joe's refuge, his escape when life at home became unbearable.

And suddenly he knew why he was telling Veronica about Frank, his one childhood friend, his single positive role model. He wanted this woman to know where he came from, who he really was. And he wanted to see her reaction; see whether she would recognize the importance old Frank had played in his life, or whether she would shrug it off, uncaring, uninterested.

"Frank was a sailor," Joe told Veronica. "Tough as nails, and with one hell of a foul mouth. He could swear like no one I've ever known. He fought in the Pacific in World War Two, as a frogman, one of the early members of the UDTs, the underwater demolition teams that later became the SEALs. He was rough and crude, but he never turned me away from his door. I helped him pull weeds in his garden in return for the stories he told."

Veronica was listening intently, so he went on.

"When everyone else I knew told me I was going to end up in jail or worse, Frank O'Riley told me I was destined to become a Navy SEAL—because both they and I were the best of the best."

"He was right," Veronica murmured. "He must be very, *very* proud of you."

"He's dead," Joe said. He watched her eyes fill with compassion, and the noose around his chest grew tighter. He was in big trouble here. "He died when I was fifteen."

"Oh, no," she whispered.

"Frank had one hell of a powerful spirit," Joe continued, resisting the urge to pull her into his arms and comfort her because *his* friend had died more than fifteen years ago. "Wherever I went and whatever I did for the three years after he died, he was there, whispering into my ear, keeping me in line, reminding me about those Navy SEALs that he'd admired so much. On the day I turned eighteen, I walked into that navy recruitment office and I could almost feel his sigh of relief."

He smiled at her and Veronica smiled back, gazing into his eyes. Again, time seemed to stand totally still. Again, it was the perfect opportunity to kiss her, and again, Joe didn't allow himself to move.

"I'm glad you've forgiven me, Joe," she said quietly.

"Hey, what happened to 'Your Highness'?" Joe asked, trying desperately to return to a more lighthearted, teasing tone.

She was getting serious on him. Serious meant being honest, and in all honesty, Joe did *not* want to be friends with this woman. He wanted to be lovers. He was *dying* to be her lover. He wanted to touch her in ways she'd never been touched before. He wanted to hear her cry out his name and—

Veronica looked surprised. "I've forgotten to call you that, haven't I?"

"You've been calling me Joe lately," he said. "Which is fine—I like it better. I was just curious."

"You're nothing like the real prince," she said honestly.

"I'm not sure if that's a compliment or an insult."

She smiled. "Believe me, it's a compliment."

"Yeah, that's what I thought" Joe said. "But I wasn't sure exactly where *you* stood."

"Prince Tedric . . . isn't very nice," Veronica said diplomatically.

"He's a coward and a flaming idiot," Joe stated flatly.

"I guess you don't like him very much, either."

"Understatement of the year, Ronnie. If I end up taking a bullet for him, I'm gonna be really upset." He smiled grimly. "That is, if you can be upset and dead at the same time."

Veronica stared at Joe. If he ended up taking a bullet . . .

For the first time, the reality of what Joe was doing hit her squarely in the stomach. He was risking his life to catch a terrorist. While Tedric spent the next few weeks in the comfort of a safe house, Joe would be out in public. Joe would be the target of the terrorists' guns.

What if something went wrong? What if the terrorists succeeded, and killed Joe? After all, they'd already managed to kill hundreds and hundreds of people.

Joe suddenly looked so tired. Were his thoughts following the same path? Was he afraid he'd be killed, too? But then he glanced up at Veronica and tried to smile.

"Mind if we skip lunch?" he asked. "Or just postpone it for a half hour?"

Veronica nodded. "We can postpone it," she said.

Joe stood, heading toward the bedroom. "Great, I've gotta crash. I'll see you in about thirty minutes, okay?"

"Do you want me to wake you?" she asked.

Joe shook his head, no. "Thanks, but . . ."

Oh, baby, he could just imagine her coming into his darkened bedroom to wake him up. He could just imagine coming out of a deep REM sleep to see that face, those eyes looking down at him. He could imagine reaching for her, pulling her down on top of him, covering her mouth with his. . . .

"No, thanks," he said again, reaching up with one hand to loosen the tight muscles in his neck and shoulders. "I'll set the alarm."

Veronica watched as he closed the bedroom door behind him.

They were running out of time. Despite his reassurances, Veronica didn't believe that Joe could pull it off.

But those weren't the only doubts she was having.

Posing as Prince Tedric could very easily get Joe killed.

Were they doing the right thing? Was catching these terrorists worth risking a man's life? Was it fair to ask Joe to take those risks when Tedric so very clearly wouldn't?

But out of all those doubts, Veronica knew one thing for certain. She did not want Lieutenant Joe Catalanotto to die.

Chapter 10

Veronica was ready nearly thirty minutes before the meeting was set to start.

She checked herself in the mirror for the seven thousandth time. Her jacket and skirt were a dark olive green. Her silk blouse was the same color, but a subtle shade lighter. The color was a perfect contrast for her flaming-red hair, but the suit was boxy and the jacket cut to hide her curves.

Joe would call it a Margaret Thatcher suit. And he was right. It made her look no-nonsense and reliable, dependable and businesslike.

So, all right, it wasn't the height of fashion. But she was sending out a clear message to the world. *Veronica St. John could get the job done.*

Except, in a few minutes, Veronica was going to have to walk out the hotel-room door and head down the corridor to the private conference room attached to Senator McKinley's suite. She was going to go into the meeting and sit down at the table without the slightest clue whether or not she had actually gotten this particular job done.

She honestly didn't know whether or not she'd been able to pull off the task of turning Joe Catalanotto into a dead ringer for Prince Tedric.

Dead ringer. What a horrible expression. And if the security team of FInCOM agents didn't protect Joe, that's exactly what he'd be. Dead. Joe, with his dancing eyes and wide, infectious smile... All it would take was one bullet and he would be a thing of the past, a memory.

Veronica turned from the mirror and began to pace.

She'd worked with Joe all afternoon, going over and over rules and protocols and Ustanzian history. She had shown him the strange way Prince Tedric held a spoon and the odd habit the prince had of leaving behind at least one bite of every food on his plate when eating.

She had tried to show Joe again how to walk, how to stand, how to hold his head at a royal angle. Just when she thought that maybe, just *maybe* he might be getting it, he'd slouch or shrug or lean against the wall. Or make a joke and flash her one of those five-thousand-watt smiles that were so different from any facial expression Prince Tedric had ever worn.

"Don't worry, Ronnie. This is not a problem," he'd said in his atrocious New Jersey accent. "I'll get it. When the time comes, I'll do it right."

But Veronica wasn't sure what she should be worrying about. Was she worried Joe wouldn't be able to pass for Prince Tedric, or was she worried that he *would?*

If Joe looked and acted like the prince, then he'd be at risk. And damn it, why should Joe have to risk his life? Why not let the prince risk his *own* life? After all, Prince Tedric was the one the terrorists wanted to kill.

Veronica had actually brought up her concerns to Joe before they'd parted to get ready for this meeting. He'd laughed when she'd said she thought it might be for the best if he couldn't pass for Tedric—it was too dangerous.

"I've been in dangerous situations before," Joe had told her. "And this one doesn't even come close." He'd told her about the plans and preparations he was arranging with both Kevin Laughton's FInCOM agents and the SEALs from his Alpha Squad. He'd told her he'd wear a bulletproof vest at all times. He'd told her that wherever he went, there would be shielded areas where he could easily drop to cover. He'd reminded her that this operation had minuscule risks compared to most other ops he'd been on.

All Veronica knew was, the better she came to know Joe, the more she worried about his safety. Frankly, this situation scared her to death. And if this *wasn't* dangerous, she didn't want to know what dangerous meant.

But danger was part of Joe's life. Danger was what he did best. No wonder he wasn't married. What kind of woman would put up with a husband who risked his life as a matter of course?

Not Veronica, that was for sure.

Although it wasn't as if Joe Catalanotto had dropped to his knees and begged her to marry him, was it? And he wasn't likely to, either. Despite the incredible kiss they'd shared, a man like Joe, a man used to living on the edge, wasn't very likely to be interested in anything long-term or permanent. *Permanent* probably wasn't even in his vocabulary.

Veronica shook her head, amazed at the course her thoughts had taken. *Permanent* wasn't in *her* vocabulary, either. At least not right now. And certainly not when attached to the words *relationship* and *Joe Catalanotto*. At least fifty percent of the time, the man *infuriated* her. Of course, the rest of the time he made her laugh, or he touched her with his gentle sweetness, or he burned her with that look in his eyes that promised a sexual experience the likes of which she'd never known before.

Either Veronica was fighting with Joe, or fighting the urge to throw herself into his arms.

There'd been one or two...or three or so times—certainly no more than six or eight, at any rate—this afternoon, when Veronica had found herself smiling foolishly into Joe's deep brown eyes, marveling at the length of his eyelashes, and finding her gaze drawn to his straight, white teeth and his rather elegantly shaped lips.

In all honesty, once or twice, Veronica had actually thought about kissing Joe again. Well, maybe more than once or twice.

So, all right, she admitted to herself. He *was* rather unbearably handsome. And funny. Yes, he was undeniably funny. He always knew exactly what to say to make her damn near choke with laughter on her tea. He was blunt and to the point. Often

tactless at times—most of the time. But he was always honest.
It was refreshing. And despite his rough language and unre-
fined speech, Joe was clearly intelligent. He hadn't had the best
of educations, that much was true, but he seemed well-read and
certainly able to think on his own, which was more than Veronica could say for Prince Tedric.

So, okay. Maybe now that she and Joe had had a chance to
really talk, maybe now he didn't infuriate her fifty percent of
the time. Maybe he only infuriated her, say, twenty percent of
the time. But spending twenty percent of her time angry or annoyed or worrying about him was still too much—even for the
kind of casual, sexual relationship Joe wanted.

Obviously, Veronica had to continue to keep her distance.
Squaring her shoulders, she resolved to do precisely that. She'd
stay far, far away from Joe Catalanotto. No more kisses. No
more lingering looks. No more long talks about her personal
life. From now on, her relationship with Joe would be strictly
business.

Still a few minutes early, Veronica took her purse and briefcase and locked her hotel room door behind her. Down at the
end of the corridor, she could see FInCOM agents standing
outside the royal suite where Joe was getting dressed. More
agents were farther down the hall, outside the conference room.

The conference-room door was ajar, so Veronica went in.

This was it. Tonight they would decide whether or not they
could successfully pass a Navy SEAL off on the American
public as Prince Tedric of Ustanzia.

If the answer was yes, Veronica's friend Wila would be one
step closer to getting her American funding, and Joe would be
one step closer to catching Diosdado, the terrorist.

She sat down at the empty oval conference table and crossed
her legs.

If the answer was no, Joe would return to wherever it was
Navy SEALs went between missions, and Veronica would sleep
easier at night, knowing that assassins weren't trying to end his
life.

Except, if Joe wasn't on *this* mission, he'd probably be on
some other, what he considered *truly* dangerous mission. So
really, whatever happened, Veronica was going to end up worrying, wasn't she?

Veronica frowned. She was certainly expending a bit of energy thinking about a man she had decided most definitely to stay away from.

Besides, after this meeting, she probably wasn't ever going to see Joe Catalanotto again. And the pang of remorse she felt was *surely* only because she'd failed at her assignment. It wouldn't be long before Veronica had trouble remembering Joe's name. And he certainly wouldn't give *her* a second thought.

Senator McKinley came into the room, followed by his aides and the Ustanzian ambassador and *his* aides. Both men nodded a greeting, but Veronica's attention was pulled away by a young woman taking orders for coffee or tea.

"Earl Grey," Veronica murmured, smiling her thanks.

When she looked up, Kevin Laughton and some of his FInCOM security team had come into the room, along with Admiral Forrest.

The older man caught Veronica's eye and winked a hello. He came around the oval table and pulled out the seat next to hers. "Where's Joe?" he asked.

Veronica shook her head, glancing around the room again. Even in a crowd like this, Joe would have stood out. He was bigger than most men, taller and broader. Unless he was crawling across the rug on his hands and knees, he hadn't yet arrived.

"Still getting changed, I guess," she said to Mac Forrest.

"How's the transformation going?" Forrest asked. "You got him eating lady fingers with his pinky sticking out yet?"

Veronica snorted and gave him a disbelieving look.

"It's going *that* well, huh? Hmm." The admiral didn't seem disappointed. In fact, he gave her a downright cheerful smile. "He'll get it. Did he tell you, he's a pretty darn good mimic? He's got a real ear for language, Joe Cat does."

An ear for language? With his thick accent? Oh, come on.... Veronica didn't want to offend the admiral by rolling her eyes—at least not outwardly.

"Joe's a good man," Forrest told her. "A little too intense sometimes, but that's what makes him a good commander. You win his loyalty, and he'll be loyal to the end. He demands loyalty in return—and gets it. His men would follow him to hell and back." He chuckled. "And they have, on more than one occasion."

Veronica turned toward him. "Joe doesn't think this operation is dangerous," she said. "If that's true, what exactly *is* dangerous?"

"To a SEAL?" Forrest mused. "Let's see. . . . Breaking into a hostile high-security military installation to track down a pilfered nuclear warhead might be considered dangerous."

"*Might* be?"

"Depends on the location of the military installation, and how well-trained that hostile military organization actually is," he said. "Another dangerous op might be to make a HAHO jump from a plane—"

"A what?"

"HAHO," Forrest repeated. "A high-altitude high-opening parachute jump. It's when you get the green light to jump from the plane at about thirty thousand feet—way up high where the bad guys can't hear the sound of your airplane approaching. You yank the cord, the chute opens and you and your squad parasail silently to the landing zone. And maybe, when you get there, you rescue fifteen hostages—all children—from a bunch of tangos who wouldn't bat an eye over spilling the blood of innocent kids. And maybe before you can pull the kids out of there, the op goes from covert to full firefight. So you rock and roll with your HK, knowing that your body is the only thing shielding a nine-year-old from the enemy's bullets."

Veronica frowned. "Would you mind repeating that last bit in English? Before you can pull the kids out of there...what?"

Forrest grinned, a twinkle in his blue eyes. "The terrorists become aware of your presence and open fire. You've got an instant battlefield—a full firefight. You return fire with your HK—your submachine gun—scared to death because there's a tiny little girl standing directly behind you."

Veronica nodded. "I thought that was what you said." She studied Admiral Forrest's weathered face. "Are these actual operations you're describing or merely hypothetical scenarios?"

"That's classified information," the old man said. "Of course, you're a smart girl. You can probably figure out they wouldn't be classified if they were hypothetical, right?"

Veronica was silent, digesting all he had said.

"Heads up, missy," Forrest whispered. "Looks like this meeting's about to start."

"Let's get this show on the road," Senator McKinley said, his voice cutting above the other conversations from his seat at the head of the table. "Where the hell is Catalanotto?"

McKinley was looking directly at Veronica, as were most of the other people at the table. They honestly expected her to provide them with an answer.

"He said he'd be here," she said calmly. "He'll be here." She glanced at her watch. "He's only a few minutes late."

Just then, West, one of the FInCOM agents, stepped through the door. "Crown Prince Tedric of Ustanzia," he announced.

Aha. *That* was why Joe was late. He was coming to this meeting dressed in the prince's clothes. The tailor had dropped off several large garment bags late this afternoon. No doubt Joe had wanted to wear one of the resplendent suits to make him look more like Tedric.

Any minute now he'd saunter into the room, wearing a garish sequined jacket and a sheepish grin.

But West stepped back and a figure appeared in the doorway.

He was dressed in gleaming white pants and a short white jacket that clung to his broad shoulders and ended at his waist. There were no sequins in sight, but plenty of medals covered his chest, along with a row of golden buttons decorated with the royal Ustanzian shield. The shield also glittered from the bejeweled ring he wore on his right hand. His gleaming black hair was combed directly back from his face.

It was Joe. It had to be Joe, didn't it?

Veronica searched his eyes, looking for the now quite-familiar differences between Joe's and Prince Tedric's faces. But with his shoulders back, his head held at that haughty angle, and no sign of a smile curving his lips, Veronica wasn't sure exactly *who* was standing in the doorway.

And then he spoke. "I greet you with the timeless honor and tradition of the Ustanzian flag," he said in the prince's unmistakable faintly British, faintly French accent, "which is woven, as well, into my heart."

Chapter 11

Nobody moved.

Everyone stared at Prince Tedric. It *was* Prince Tedric, not Joe. That voice, that accent... Except, what was the real prince doing here, away from the safety of his secure room on the other side of town? It didn't make sense. And his shoulders seemed so broad....

As Veronica watched, the prince took several steps into the room with his peculiar, stiff royal gait. He walked like he had a fireplace poker in his pants, as Joe had so inelegantly described. Veronica fought the urge to giggle. This had to be the prince, indeed. About half-a-dozen dark-suited FInCOM agents followed him inside, and one of them closed the door tightly behind them.

One royal eyebrow lifted a fraction of an inch at the people still sitting at the conference table, and the Ustanzian ambassador scrambled to his feet.

"Your Highness!" he said. "I didn't realize you'd be attending...."

McKinley stood, too. The rest of the table followed suit.

Still, as Veronica rose to her feet, she stared. This man wasn't Joe. Or was it? Tedric had never seemed so tall, so imposing.

But this couldn't be Joe. That voice had been Tedric's. And that walk. *And* that haughty look.

The prince's gaze swept around the table. His eyes passed over Veronica without the slightest hint of familiarity, without the tiniest bit of recognition or warmth. He looked through her, not at her. No, it wasn't Joe. Joe would have winked or smiled. And yet . . .

He held out a hand decorated with a huge gold and jeweled ring for the Ustanzian ambassador to bow over.

Senator McKinley cleared his throat. "Your Majesty," he said. "It was dangerous for you to come here. I should have been informed." He glanced at his chief aide and hissed, "Why wasn't I informed?"

The prince affixed the senator with a very displeased stare. "I am not used to asking permission to leave my room," he said.

He was the prince. Veronica tried to tell herself that she was now convinced of that fact, yet doubt lingered.

"But, Your Majesty," Kevin Laughton chimed in. "It's just not safe." He looked over at the FInCOM agents who had arrived with the prince. "I *must* be told of any movement." He looked more closely at the men and a funny look crossed his face. Veronica tried to follow his gaze, to see what he saw, but he quickly looked back at the prince, his face once again expressionless.

"If there was something you needed," Henri Freder, the Ustanzian ambassador, interjected, "all you had to do was ask, Your Majesty. We will provide you with all your requests, I can assure you."

"Sit, please, sit. Sit, sit," the prince said impatiently.

Everyone sat. Except the prince. He stood pointedly next to Senator McKinley's seat at the head of the table.

Rather belatedly, McKinley realized his mistake. He hastily stood and offered the prince his chair, moving around to one of the empty seats on the side of the oval table.

On the other side of the room, one of the FInCOM agents coughed. When Veronica glanced at him, he gave her a quick wink. It was Cowboy—one of the SEALs from Joe's Alpha Squad. At least, she thought it was. She did a double take, but when she looked again, he was gone.

She turned and stared at the man who was settling himself in the now vacant chair at the head of the table. "I'll need something to write on and a pen," he announced to no one in particular. "And a glass of water."

Had she imagined Cowboy standing there? Was this really Joe, or was it Prince Tedric? Veronica honestly did not know.

Around her, all of the aides and assistants were scrambling. One of them provided the prince with a smooth white pad of paper, another with a plastic ballpoint pen that the prince simply looked at in disdain. Yes, he had to be the real prince. No one could possibly imitate that disgusted look, could they? Another assistant produced a gold-plated fountain pen, which the prince took with a nod, and yet another presented him with a tall, ice-filled glass of water.

"Thank you," he said, and Veronica sat up.

Thank you? Those words weren't in Tedric's vocabulary. At least, Veronica had never heard him say them before.

Senator McKinley was giving the prince a detailed report on all that had been done over the past several days, and on the changes to the scheduled tour.

Veronica stared down the table at the man now sitting at its head. Prince Tedric never said thank-you. This man was Joe. It *had* to be Joe. But . . . he didn't look or act or sound *any-thing* like the Joe she was starting to know so well.

The prince took a sip of his water, removed the cap from his pen.

This would prove it. Joe was left-handed; the prince only used his right.

The prince took the pen in his right hand and jotted a quick note on his pad of paper.

Oh, my God, it wasn't Joe. It was the prince. Unless . . .

As the senator continued to talk, the prince tore the piece of paper from the pad and folded it neatly in half. He glanced over his shoulder and one of the aides was instantly behind him. He handed the aide the piece of paper and whispered a few words into the young man's ear before turning back to Senator McKinley.

Veronica watched as the aide came around the table, directly toward her. The young man handed her the folded piece of paper.

"From Prince Tedric," the aide whispered almost soundlessly in her ear.

She glanced down the table toward the prince, but he wasn't paying her the slightest attention. He was absently twisting his ring as he listened to McKinley.

Why would Prince Tedric write *her* a note?

Hardly daring to breathe, she unfolded the paper.

"Hey, Ronnie," she read, printed in big, childish block letters. "How'm I doing? Love, Prince Joe."

Veronica laughed. Aloud. McKinley stopped talking midsentence. The entire table turned and looked at her. Including Joe, who gave her a withering look, identical to those she'd received from Prince Tedric in the past. "It's Joe," she said.

Nobody understood. They all just stared at her as if she'd gone mad—except Kevin Laughton, who was nodding, a small smile on his face, and Admiral Forrest, who was rocking back in his seat and chuckling.

Veronica gestured down toward the head of the table, toward Joe. "This is not Prince Tedric," she explained. "It's Lieutenant Catalanotto. Gentlemen, he's fooled us all."

Everyone started talking all at once.

The prince's haughty expression turned into a slow, friendly smile as he gazed down the table at Veronica. His cold eyes turned warm. Oh, yes, this was definitely Joe.

"You're amazing," she mouthed to him. She knew he wouldn't be able to hear her over the din, but she had no doubt he could read her lips. She wouldn't be surprised to find there was nothing Joe Catalanotto couldn't do, and do well.

He shrugged. "I'm a SEAL," he mouthed back, as if that explained everything.

"I knew it was the lieutenant," Veronica heard Kevin Laughton say. "But only because I knew three of the men who came in with him weren't on my staff."

"I knew it was him, too," Senator McKinley's loud voice boomed. "I was waiting to see when y'all would catch on."

Still, Veronica gazed into Joe's dark eyes. "Why didn't you tell me?" she silently asked.

"I did," he answered.

And he was right. He *had* told her. "Don't worry, I'll get it," he'd said. "I'm a pretty good mimic."

Pretty good?

Veronica laughed. He was *amazing*.

Joe smiled back at her as everyone around them continued to talk at once. But they might have been alone in this room, for all the attention she paid anyone else.

That was admiration he could see in Veronica's blue eyes. Admiration and respect. She wasn't trying to hide it. She was sending him a message with her eyes as clear as the one she'd sent with her lips.

Joe could also see traces of the attraction she was never really able to conceal. It was always back there, lurking, waiting patiently for the moment when her defenses were down, waiting for her to temporarily forget that he wasn't a regular of the country-club set.

And, God, he was waiting, too.

Except she wasn't going to forget. It was only at times like this, when they were safely across the room from each other, that Veronica gazed into his eyes. It was only when she was safely out of reach that she let him drown in the swirling ocean-blueness of her eyes.

It didn't take much to imagine what being Veronica St. John's lover would be like, to see her with her red curls tumbled down her back, dressed only in the skimpiest of satin and lace, desire turning her sea-colored eyes to blue flames. As Joe gazed into her eyes, he felt himself going under for the third and final time.

He wanted her so desperately, he was nearly dizzy with desire. Somehow, some way, he was going to change her mind, break through that flimsy wall she'd thrown up between them.

Admiral Forrest raised his voice to be heard over the noise. "I think this meeting can be adjourned," he said. "We can announce to the press that Prince Tedric's tour will resume as of oh-eight-hundred hours tomorrow. Are we in agreement?"

Veronica reluctantly pulled her eyes away from the molten lava of Joe's gaze. Her heart was pounding. Good Lord, the way that man looked at her! If they had been alone, he would have kissed her again. Or if he hadn't, maybe *she* would have kissed *him!*

Lord save her from herself.

She shuffled the papers in front of her, attempting to regain her equilibrium as the room slowly cleared.

Senator McKinley shook her hand briefly, commending her on a job well-done before he rushed off to another appointment.

Veronica could feel Joe's eyes still on her as he stood and talked to Admiral Forrest. The FInCOM men tried to escort them out of the room, but Joe hung back, clearly waiting for her.

Taking a deep breath, she gathered her briefcase and went to join them.

Joe was looking down at the ring on his hand. "Did you know this ring is worth more than a new car?" he mused. "And did you know old Ted has about twenty of 'em?"

Mac Forrest grinned at Veronica, slapping Joe on the back one more time as they walked down the hotel corridor. "You couldn't tell it was Joe, could you?" Forrest asked her.

Veronica glanced up at Joe. She wasn't prepared for the jolt of warmth and energy that surrounded her as she met his dark eyes. He was smiling at her, and she found herself smiling foolishly back, until she realized the Admiral had asked her a question. She tore her eyes away.

"No, sir, I couldn't," she answered hoping that she didn't sound as breathless as she felt. "Except . . ."

"What?" Joe asked.

She looked up at him, bracing herself before meeting his hypnotizing eyes again. "You said 'Thank you,'" she replied. "Tedric wouldn't dream of thanking a servant."

"Well, maybe ol' Ted's been reading up on the American version of Miss Manners," Joe said. "Because for the next five weeks, he's going to be saying 'thank you' to all the lowly servants. And maybe even 'please,' every now and then."

"That's fine with me. I think everyone should say thank-you. I think it's rude not to," Veronica said.

"The equipment you ordered is coming in late tonight," Admiral Forrest said to Joe. "It'll be ready for tomorrow."

"We leave the hotel at oh-eight-hundred?" Joe asked.

Veronica dug into her briefcase and checked the schedule. "That's right," she said. "There're a number of public appearances—just visual things—a chance for the news reporters to get footage of you climbing in and out of limousines and waving. Tomorrow night there's an optional embassy function, if you feel up to it. There *will* be people there who know Tedric quite well, though. You'll have to be ready to recognize them."

"Can *you* recognize them?" Joe asked.

"Well, yes," Veronica said. "Of course. But—"

"Then I'm ready," he said with a grin.

"We've ordered a surveillance van," Admiral Forrest said to her. "You'll have the seat of honor at the main mike. Joe will wear an earphone and a microphone so the communication can go both ways. He'll hear you and you'll hear him. *And* we'll have miniature video cameras set up, so you'll be able to see both Joe *and* from Joe's point of view."

They stopped outside the royal suite, waiting while West went inside to make a quick security sweep. "All clear," he said, coming back out. The entire group moved into the room.

Admiral Forrest clasped Joe's hand again. "Good job, son." He nodded at Veronica. "You, too, missy." He glanced at his watch. "I've got to make some status reports." As Mac turned to leave, he shook his finger at Joe. "No more unauthorized field trips down the outside of the building," he admonished. "No more games." He turned to the other SEALs, Blue, Cowboy and Harvard, who were standing by the door with the FInCOM agents. "You're on the same side as security now," he said to them. "You make sure Lieutenant Catalanotto stays secure. Have I made myself clear?"

"I gave them liberty tonight, Admiral," Joe interjected. "I figured—"

"You figured wrong," Forrest said. "As of thirty minutes ago, this operation has started."

Cowboy clearly wasn't happy about that.

The admiral opened the door to the hallway. "As a matter of fact, I need to see this security team in the corridor, pronto."

"But, sir—" Cowboy started.

"That was an order, Ensign," Forrest barked.

Still, the three SEALs didn't move until Joe gave them an almost-imperceptible nod.

The door closed behind them and the room was suddenly silent.

"What was *that* about?" Veronica asked Joe, suddenly aware of how close they were standing, of how delicious he smelled, of how he managed to make even that ridiculous white jacket look good.

He gave her one of his familiar sheepish smiles as he sat on the arm of the sofa. "I think Mac's realized that Diosdado could get lucky and take me out," he said. "He doesn't want to lose the commanding officer of the Alpha Squad."

"He doesn't want to lose a friend," Veronica corrected him.

"He's not going to," Joe said. "I have no intention of dying." It was a fact. His quiet statement combined with the certainty in his eyes and on his face convinced Veronica that it was, indeed, a fact. He looked hard and invincible, and quite possibly immortal.

But he wasn't immortal. He was human. He was flesh and blood, and starting tomorrow morning, he was going to be a target. When he stepped out the hotel door dressed as Prince Tedric, there could be an assassin's gun trained on him.

By tomorrow at this time, Joe could very well have been shot. He could be seriously injured. Or worse. He could be dead.

Permanently dead.

Joe might be able to disregard the danger, but Veronica couldn't. He was going to be out in public with a security team that wasn't up to par. Sure, the odds were better now that the three SEALs from the Alpha Squad had joined FInCOM's team, but there were no guarantees.

Veronica was going to be safely tucked away in some surveillance vehicle where, if the terrorists *did* get through the security force, she'd have a front-row seat to watch Joe die.

He was sitting there watching her, and she was struck by his casual bravery, his unassuming heroism. He was doing this for Admiral Forrest, for the admiral's dead son, and for all of the other U.S. sailors who'd been killed at Diosdado's hands. And for all the people, sailors and civilians, who would be hurt or killed by the terrorists if they were not stopped here and now.

Yes, there was a chance that he might die. But in Joe's eyes, it was obviously a risk worth taking if it meant they'd catch these killers. But what a tremendous risk, an incredible sacrifice. He'd be risking his life, his precious, irreplaceable life. It was the most he could possibly give. And to Joe, it was also the least he could do.

"Has anyone bothered to thank you for what you're do-ing?" Veronica asked, her throat feeling unnaturally tight as she gazed into Joe's eyes.

He shrugged, a loose casual move, echoed in his easygoing smile. "If it all works out, I'll probably get the Ustanzian Medal of Honor." He glanced down at the rows of Prince Tedric's medals on his chest and made a face. "Considering Ted's got four, I'm not sure I want one," he added. "Even if I can talk 'em out of giving me one, there'll be some kind of ceremony, and I'll have to smile for the cameras and shake Ted's sweaty hand."

"And if it doesn't work out . . . ?" Her voice trembled.

He shrugged and his smile became a grin. "Then I won't have to shake Ted's hand, right?"

"Joe."

He stood up. "Ronnie," he said, mimicking her intensity. "Lighten up, all right?"

But she couldn't. How could she lighten up when tomorrow he might very well be dead? Veronica glanced around the room, aware once again that they were alone. They were alone, and she might never have another chance to hold him in her arms.

Despite her resolve to stay away from Joe, Veronica stepped toward him, closing the gap between them, slipping her arms around his waist and holding him tightly, resting her head against his shoulder.

He was shocked. She'd seen the surprise in his eyes. She still felt it in the stiffness and tension in his entire body. Never in a million years had he expected her to put her arms around him.

As she started to pull back, she lifted her head and she could see a vulnerability deep in his eyes, a flash of almost childlike wonder. But it was gone so quickly, she was left wondering if she hadn't imagined it.

He almost didn't react. *Almost* didn't. But before she pulled away, he encircled her with his arms, holding her gently but quite firmly in place. He sighed very softly as he allowed his body to relax against hers.

Joe couldn't make himself release her. Veronica was in his arms, and he was damned if he was going to let her go. She fit next to him so perfectly, they might have been made for each other. She was soft in all the right places, and firm in all the others. Holding her like this was heaven.

Veronica stared up at him, her ocean blue eyes wide.

There were few things he wanted right this moment as much as he wanted to kiss her. He wanted to plunder her soft, sweet mouth with his tongue. To kiss her deeply, savagely, until she clung to him, dizzy from desire. He wanted to sweep her into his arms and carry her into the bedroom, where he'd undress her with his teeth and kiss every inch of her smooth, supple body before driving himself into her sweet, welcoming warmth.

He felt nearly delirious just thinking about it—the sheer bliss. And it would start with one small kiss...

He slowly lowered his head to kiss her.

Veronica gazed up into his eyes, transfixed, lips slightly parted.

He was a fraction of a second from paradise, and...she turned her head.

Joe's mouth landed on her cheek as she quickly pulled free of his arms.

Frustration made every muscle in his body tighten. *Damn* it. What had just happened here? Hell, *she'd* made the first move. She was the one who'd put her arms around him. And then...

"Veronica," he said, reaching for her.

But she stepped away from him, out of reach, as the door opened and the FInCOM agents and SEALs came back inside.

"I gotta run, Cat," Admiral Forrest called out, waving briefly through the open door. "We'll talk tomorrow. Be good."

"Well," Veronica said, her voice intentionally light as she collected her briefcase. "I'll see you in the morning, Lieutenant."

That was it? She was going to not kiss him and then just walk away?

She wouldn't meet his eyes as she made a beeline for the door, and short of running after her and tackling her, there was little that Joe could do to stop her.

"Thanks again," Veronica added, and she was out the door.

"Walk her to her room," Joe ordered West, suddenly afraid for her, walking alone in the hotel corridor, even the short distance to her own room.

The man nodded and followed Veronica, closing the door behind him.

"Thanks again?" Cowboy echoed her departing words. He wiggled his eyebrows suggestively at Joe. "Something happen in here we should know about?"

Joe shot him one long look. "Stop," he said.

Cowboy started to say something else, but wisely kept his mouth shut.

Thanks again.

Veronica's words echoed in Joe's head. *Thanks again.*

She had been thanking him. Of course. When she had put her arms around him, she wasn't giving in to the attraction that simmered between them. No way. She was *thanking* him. She was being the generous aristocrat thanking the lowly servant. Damn, he was *such* a fool.

Joe had to sit down.

"Everything all right, Cat?" Blue asked softly in his gentle Southern accent.

Joe stood again and headed for the bedroom. "Fine," he answered shortly, keeping his head turned away so his friend wouldn't see the hurt he knew was showing in his eyes.

Chapter 12

When the embassy party started at nine—twenty-one-hundred hours according to Joe—Veronica was feeling an old pro at handling the equipment in the surveillance van.

She wore a lightweight wireless headset with an attached microphone positioned directly under her lips. Joe could hear every word she spoke through a miniature receiver hidden in his right ear. And Veronica could hear him quite clearly, too. His wireless mike was disguised as a pin he wore in the lapel of his jacket.

She could see Joe, too, on a TV screen built into the side panel of the van. Another screen showed a different angle—Joe's point of view. Both views were courtesy of miniaturized video cameras discreetly held by several FInCOM agents. So far, Veronica hadn't had much use for the TV screen that showed the world from Joe's eyes. It would come in handy tonight, though.

The three SEALs from Alpha Squad were also wearing microphones and earphones patched into the same frequency that Veronica and Joe were using. It was easy to tell Blue's, Cowboy's and Harvard's voices apart, and of course, she would recognize Joe's voice anywhere.

More often than not, the SEALs used some kind of abbreviated lingo, using phrases like "LZ" and "recon" and "sneak and peek." They talked about the "T's" or "tangos," which Veronica knew to mean terrorists. But for every word she recognized, they used four others whose meanings were mysterious. It was like listening to another language.

Throughout the day, Veronica had reminded Joe when to bow and when to wave, when to ignore the news cameras, and when to look directly into their lenses and smile. She'd warned him when his smile became a bit too broad—too Joe-like—and he'd adjusted instantly in order to seem more like the real prince.

The high-tech equipment made the process infinitely easier than any other job she'd ever done.

What she was never going to get used to, however, was the slightly sick feeling in the pit of her stomach as she watched Joe on the video cameras and wondered when the assassins were going to strike.

"Okay," came the word from Kevin Laughton, who was also in the surveillance van. "The limo is approaching the embassy."

"Got it," West said over the van's speakers. "I see them coming up the drive." FInCOM was using a different frequency for their radio communication. Joe's earphone had been modified to maintain a direct link with them, too. If someone—SEAL or Fink—so much as breathed a warning, he wanted to hear it.

"Check, check," Veronica heard Joe say into his mike. "Am I on?"

"We're reading you," Laughton said. "Do you copy?"

"Gotcha," Joe said. "Ronnie, you with me?"

"I'm here," Veronica said, purposely keeping her voice low and calm. Her heart was beating a mile a minute at the thought of Joe walking into the Ustanzian Embassy and actually relying on her for the information he needed to pull off his masquerade as Prince Tedric. And if *she* was on edge, he must be incredibly nervous. He not only had to think about successfully portraying Tedric, but he also had to worry about not getting killed.

"Cameras are on," a FInCOM agent's voice reported. "Surveillance van, do you have picture?"

"Roger that, FInCOM," Veronica said, and Joe laughed, just as she'd known he would.

"What, are you getting into this?" he asked her.

"Absolutely," she said smoothly. "I don't know the last time I've so looked forward to an embassy party. I get to sit out here in comfort instead of tippy-toeing around all those dignitaries and celebrities, eating overcooked hors d'oeuvres and smiling until my face hurts."

Joe leaned across the limousine, closer to the camera. "Overcooked hors d'oeuvres?" he said, making a face. *"That's* what I have to look forward to here?"

"Ready to open the limo doors," West's voice announced. "Everyone in position?"

"Joe, be careful," Veronica murmured quickly.

He touched his ear briefly, giving her the signal that he heard her. She saw something flicker in his eyes before he looked away from the video camera.

What was he thinking? Was he thinking of last night, of the way he'd almost kissed her? He *would* have kissed her again, and she probably would have kissed him, too, if she hadn't heard the hotel-room door start to open.

Probably? Definitely—despite her better judgment. She should be grateful they had been interrupted when they were. She *knew* she was grateful that she'd heard the sound of the doorknob turning. How awful would it have been to have three FInCOM agents, three SEALs and one navy admiral open the door to find her locked in Joe's embrace.

Joe had been oddly distant this morning—no doubt a direct result of her rapid flight from his hotel room last night. Veronica felt guilty about running away. But if she'd stayed, and if he'd pursued her, she would have ended up in his arms again. And, quite probably, she would have ended up in his bed.

She had thought maybe a little time and a little distance would take the edge off the attraction she felt for this man. But when she had walked out of her room this morning, Joe had been dressed in one of Tedric's least flashy dark suits and was already waiting with the FInCOM agents in the corridor. She'd looked at him, their eyes had met, and that attraction had sparked again.

No, time and distance had done nothing. She'd wanted to kiss Joe as much this morning as she had wanted to kiss him last night. Maybe even more so.

The security team had led him down the hallway to the elevators and she'd followed a step or two behind. Once downstairs, they'd gone immediately to work.

Admiral Forrest had explained the array of equipment in the van, and Joe had stared unsmiling into the cameras as the screens and relays were checked and double-checked. She'd talked to him over her headset, and although his replies had started out terse and to the point, over the course of the long day, he'd warmed up to his usual self, with his usual sardonic humor.

"Doors are opening," West announced now, and the pictures on the TV screens jumped as the agents holding the cameras scrambled out of the limo.

The paparazzi's flashbulbs went off crazily as Joe stepped out of the long white car, and Veronica held her breath. If someone was going to shoot him, it would happen now, as he was walking from the car to the embassy. Inside the building, security was very tight. He would still be in some danger, but not half as much as out here in the open.

The FInCOM agents surrounded him and hustled him inside, one of them roughly pushing Joe's head down, out of target range.

"Well, *that* was fun," Veronica heard Joe say as the embassy doors closed behind them. "Warn me next time you decide to put me in a half nelson, would you, guys?"

"We're inside," West's voice said.

On Veronica's video screen, the Ustanzian ambassador approached Joe, followed by an entourage of guests and celebrities. Joe instantly snapped into character, shoulders back, expression haughty.

"Henri Freder, Ustanzian ambassador to the United States," Veronica told Joe. "He knows who you are. He was at the meeting last night, and he's available to help you."

"Your Highness." Freder gave Joe a sweeping bow. "It is with great pleasure that I welcome you to the Ustanzian Embassy."

Joe nodded in return, just a very slight inclination of his head. Veronica smiled. Joe had Tedric's royal attitude down cold.

"The man to Freder's left is Marshall Owen," Veronica said to Joe, calling up additional background on Owen on the computer. "Owen's a businessman from . . . Atlanta, Georgia, who owns quite a bit of real estate in Europe, Ustanzia included. He's a friend of your father's. You've only met him three or four times—once in Paris. You played racketball. You won, but he probably threw the game. Shake his hand and address him as 'Mr. Owen'—Daddy owes him quite a bit of money."

On-screen, Joe shook Marshall Owen's hand. "Mr. Owen," he said in Tedric's unmistakable accent. "A pleasure to see you again, sir. Will you be in town long? Perhaps you can come to the hotel for a visit? There are racketball courts next to the weight room, I believe."

"Excellent," Veronica murmured.

With this equipment and Joe's ability to mimic, it was going to be—what was that expression of Joe's?—a piece of cake.

Joe sat on the couch in the royal suite, drinking beer from the bottle and trying to depressurize.

There was a soft knock on the hotel-room door, and West moved to answer it, opening it only slightly. The FInCOM agent opened it wider and Veronica slipped inside.

She smiled when she saw Joe. "You were great today."

He felt his face relaxing as he smiled back at her. "You weren't so shabby yourself." He started to stand, but she waved him back into his seat. "Want a beer? Or something to eat? We could order up . . . ?"

Jesus, Mary and Joseph, could he sound any more eager for her company?

She shook her head, still smiling at him. "No, thank you," she said. "I really just wanted to stop in and tell you what a good job you did."

Joe had tried to keep his distance all day long. He'd tried to act cool and disinterested. Tried. Jesus, Mary and Joseph, after last night, after he realized Veronica had only put her arms around him as a gesture of thanks, he should have had no problem staying away from her. He should have known better. Even after she'd apologized for her angry outburst, for calling him stupid and ignorant, he should have known that just because she'd apologized for saying those things, it didn't mean that she didn't think they were true.

Veronica had told him that she wanted to be friends—yeah, probably the way she would befriend a stray dog.

But all day long, he'd found himself playing to the hidden video cameras, knowing she was watching him, enjoying the sound of her voice speaking so intimately into his ear.

It didn't matter that they were dozens, sometimes even hundreds of yards apart. Veronica was his main link to the surveillance van. Hers was the voice Joe heard most often over his miniaturized earphone. He had to depend on her and trust her implicitly when she gave him information and instructions. Whether she knew it or not, their relationship *had* become an intimate one.

And Joe suspected that she knew it.

He was staring at her again, he realized. Her eyes were so blue and wide as she gazed back at him.

He looked away first. Who was he kidding? What was he trying to do? Weren't two rejections enough? What did he want, three for three?

"It's getting late," he said gruffly, wanting her either in his arms or gone.

"Well," she said, clearly flustered. "I'm sorry. I'm . . ." She shook her head and fished for a moment in her briefcase. "Here is tomorrow's schedule," she added, handing him a sheet of paper. "Good night, then." She moved gracefully toward the door.

"Saint Mary's," Joe said aloud, his eyes catching the name halfway down the schedule.

Veronica stopped and turned back toward him. "Yes, that's right," she said. "I meant to ask you to wear something . . . special."

"What? My giant chicken suit?"

She laughed. "Not exactly what I had in mind."

"Then maybe you should be more specific."

"Blue jacket, red sash, black pants," Veronica instructed. "I think of it as Tedric's Prince Charming outfit. Didn't you get fitted for something like that?"

"I did and I'll wear it tomorrow." Joe bowed. "Your wish is my command."

Chapter 13

Veronica rode to Saint Mary's in the limousine with Joe.

He was wearing the Prince Charming-like suit she'd asked him to wear, and he looked almost ridiculously handsome.

"This is going to be a difficult one," she said, doing some last-minute work on her laptop computer.

"Are you kidding?" Joe said. "No media, no fanfare—how hard could it be?"

"I'm going in with you this time," Veronica said, as if she hadn't heard him.

"Oh, no, you're not," he countered. "I don't want you within ten feet of me."

She looked up from her computer screen. "There's no danger," she said. "Saint Mary's wasn't on the schedule we released to the press."

"There's always danger," Joe insisted. "There's always a possibility that we're being followed."

Veronica looked out the rear window. Three other limos, plus the surveillance van, were trailing behind them. "Goodness gracious," she said in mock surprise. "You're right! We're being followed by three *very* suspicious-looking limousines and—"

"Knock off the comedy routine, St. John," Joe muttered. "You're not going in there, and that's final."

"You don't want me to get hurt." Veronica closed her computer and slid it back into its carrying case. "That's so sweet."

"That's me," Joe said. "Prince Sweetie-Pie."

"But I *need* to go in."

"Ronnie—"

"Saint Mary's is a hospice, Joe," Veronica said quietly. "For children with cancer."

Joe was silent.

"There's a little girl named Cindy Kaye who is staying at Saint Mary's," she continued, her voice low and even. "She wrote a letter to Tedric, asking him to stop and visit her during his tour of the United States. She'd like to meet a real prince before—well—before she dies." She cleared her throat. "Cindy has an inoperable brain tumor. She's been writing to Tedric for months—not that he bothers to read the letters. But I've read them. Every single one. She's incredibly bright and charming. And she's going to die in a matter of weeks."

Joe made a low, pain-filled sound. He rubbed his forehead with one hand, shielding his eyes from her view.

"I spoke to her mother on the phone this morning," Veronica said. "Apparently Cindy's taken a turn for the worse. She's been practicing her curtsy for months, but as of last night, she's . . ." She cleared her throat again. "The tumor's affecting more and more of her motor functions, and she's now unable to get out of bed."

Joe swore, long and loud, as the limo pulled up outside the hospice.

It was a clean, white building, with lots of windows, and beautiful flowers growing in the neatly tended gardens outside. There was a statue of the Madonna, also gleaming white, in among the flowers. It was lovely to look at, so peaceful and serene. But inside . . . Inside were children, all dying of cancer.

"What am I supposed to say to a kid who's dying?" Joe asked, his voice hoarse.

"I don't know," Veronica admitted. "I'll come with you—"

"No way." Joe shook his head.

"Joe—"

"I said, *no.* I'm *not* risking your life, goddammit!"

Veronica put her hand on his arm and waited until he looked up at her. "Some things are worth the risk."

Cindy Kaye was tiny, so skinny and frail. She looked more like a malnourished six-year-old than the ten-year-old Veronica knew her to be. Her long brown hair was clean and she wore a pink ribbon in it. She was lying on top of her bedspread, wearing a frilly pink dress with lots of flounces and lace. Her legs, covered in white tights, looked like two slender sticks. She wore white ballet slippers on her narrow feet.

The little girl's brown eyes filled with tears, tears that spilled down her cheeks, as Joe came into the room and gave her his most royal of bows.

"Milady," he said in Tedric's unmistakable accent. He approached Cindy and the vast array of tubes and IVs and medical equipment that surrounded her without the slightest hesitation. He sat on the edge of Cindy's bed and lifted her skeletal hand to his lips. "It is a great honor to meet you at last. Your letters have brought great joy and sunshine to my life."

"I wanted to curtsy for you," Cindy said. Her voice was trembling, her speech slurred.

"When my sister, the Princess Wila, was twelve," Joe said, leaning forward as if he were sharing a secret with her, "she injured her back and neck in a skiing accident, and was confined to her bed, much the way you are now. Our great-aunt, the Duchess of Milan, taught her the proper social etiquette for such a situation. The duchess taught her the 'eyelid curtsy.'"

Cindy waited silently for him to continue.

"Close your eyes," Joe commanded the little girl, "count to three, then open them."

Cindy did just that.

"Excellent," Joe said. "You must have royal blood in your veins to be able to do the eyelid curtsy so elegantly your very first time."

Cindy shook her head, the corners of her mouth finally curving upward.

"No royal blood? I don't believe it," Joe said, smiling back at her. "Your dress is very beautiful, Cindy."

"I picked it out just for you," she said.

Joe had to lean close to understand. He looked up to meet the eyes of the woman seated beside the bed—Cindy's mother. She gave him such a sweet, sorrowful, thankful smile, he had to look away. Her daughter, her precious, beautiful daughter, was dying. Joe had always believed he was a strong man, but he wasn't sure he would have the strength to sit by the bedside of his own dying child, day after day, hiding all his frustration and helplessness and deep, burning anger, offering only comforting smiles and peaceful, quiet, reassuring love.

He felt some of that frustration and rage form a tornado inside him, making his stomach churn. Somehow, he kept smiling. "I'm honored," he said to Cindy.

"Do you speak Ustanzian?" Cindy asked.

Joe shook his head. "In Ustanzia we speak French," he said.

"Je parle un peu français," Cindy said, her words almost unrecognizable.

Oh, God, thought Veronica. Now what?

"Très bien," Joe said smoothly. "Very good."

Veronica relaxed. Joe knew a bit of French, too. Thank goodness. That might have been a real disaster. Imagine the child's disappointment to find that her prince was an imposter...

"I would love to see your country," Cindy said, in her stilted schoolgirl French.

Oh, dear. Veronica stood. "Cindy, I'm sure Prince Tedric would love for you to see his country, too, but he should really practice his English, now that he's visiting America."

Joe looked up at her. "It's all right," he murmured, then turned back to Cindy. "I know a way you can see my country," Joe replied in perfect French. His accent was impeccable—he spoke like a native Parisian. "Close your eyes, and I will tell you all about my beautiful Ustanzia, and you will see it as if you are there."

Veronica's mouth was hanging open. Joe spoke *French? Joe* spoke *French?* She pulled her mouth shut and listened in silence as he described Ustanzia's mountains and valleys and plains in almost poetic language—both in French and English, as he translated the too-difficult words for the little girl.

"It sounds wonderful," Cindy said with a sigh.

"It is," Joe replied. He smiled again. "Do you know some people in my country also speak Russian?" He then repeated his question in flawless Russian.

Veronica had to sit down. Russian? What *other* languages did he speak? Or maybe she should wonder what languages *didn't* he speak . . .

"Do you speak Russian?" Joe asked the little girl.

She shook her head.

"Say '*da*,' " Joe said.

"*Da*," she said.

"That's Russian for 'yes,' " he told her, and smiled—a big, wide, warm Joe smile, not one of Tedric's pinched smiles. "Now you speak Russian."

"*Da*," she said again, with a brilliant smile in return.

A FInCOM agent appeared in the doorway. When Joe looked up, the man touched his watch.

"I have to go now," Joe said. "I'm sorry I can't stay longer."

"That's okay," Cindy said, but once again her eyes filled with tears.

Joe felt his heart clench. He'd been there, visiting Cindy, for only thirty minutes. When they'd set up the schedule for the tour, McKinley had wanted to allot only five minutes for Saint Mary's, but Veronica had been adamant that they take a full half hour. But now, even a half hour didn't seem long enough.

"I'm so glad I got to meet you," Joe said, leaning forward to kiss her on the forehead as he stood.

"Your Majesty . . . ?"

"Yes, milady?"

"I heard on the news that there are lots of kids hungry in Ustanzia right now," Cindy said, laboring over the words.

Joe nodded seriously. "Yes," he said. "That news report was right. My family is trying to fix that."

"I don't like it when kids are hungry," she said.

"I don't either," Joe said, his voice husky. The tornado inside him was growing again. How could this child think of others' troubles and pain, when her own pain was so great?

"Why don't you share your food with them?" Cindy said.

"It's not always that easy," Joe said. But she already knew that. Surely she, of all people, knew that.

"It should be," she said.

He nodded. "You're right. It should be."

She closed her eyes briefly—an eyelid curtsy.

Joe bowed. What could he say now? Stay well? That would be little more than a cruel joke. I'll see you soon? An untruth. Both he and the child knew they would never meet again. His rage and frustration swelled up into his throat, making it difficult to speak. "Goodbye, Cindy," he managed to say, then moved toward the door.

"I love you, Prince," Cindy said.

Joe stopped, and turned back to her, fighting hard to smile. "Thank you," he said. "I'll treasure this day, Cindy—always—and carry you forever in my heart."

The little girl smiled, made happy by such a small thing, such a small pleasure.

Somehow Joe kept the smile on his face until he was outside the room. Somehow he managed to walk down the hall without putting his fist through a wall. Somehow he managed to keep walking—until the burning rage in his stomach and throat and behind his eyes grew too intense, and his feet wouldn't carry him another step forward.

He turned toward the wall—the same wall he hadn't put his fist through—and leaned his arms against it, burying his face in the crook of his elbow, hoping, *praying* that the pain that was burning him would soon let up.

But why should it? The pain Cindy was in wasn't going to let up. She was going to die, probably in a matter of days. The injustice of it all was like a knee to his groin. Bile filled his mouth and he wanted to shake his fist at the sky and curse the God Who could let this happen.

"Joe."

Ronnie was there, then. Leading him down the hall, she pulled him into the semiprivacy of a tiny chapel. Warm and soft, she put her arms around him and held him tightly.

"Oh, God," he said, fighting the hot rush of tears to his eyes. "Oh, *God!*"

"I know," she said. "I know. But you were so good. You made her smile. You made her *happy.*"

Joe pulled back to look at Veronica. Light filtered in through the stained-glass windows, glowing red and blue and gold on the tile floor. "I'm not even a real prince," he said harshly. "It was all just a lie."

Veronica shook her head. "Tedric would've disappointed her horribly," she said. "You've given her something good to dream about."

Joe laughed, but it came out sounding more like a sob. He stared up at the crucifix on the wall behind the altar. "Yeah, but for how long?"

"For as long as she needs good dreams," Veronica said quietly.

Joe felt his eyes fill with tears again. He tried to blink them back, but one or two escaped, rolling down his face. He was crying. God, he hadn't cried since he was fifteen years old. Embarrassed, he wiped at his face with the back of one hand. "This is why you insisted that Saint Mary's stay on the schedule," he said gruffly. "*You're* really the one responsible for making that little girl happy."

"I think it was teamwork," Veronica said, smiling at him through her own tears.

He'd never seen her look more beautiful. Nearly everything she'd done up to this point, he realized, she'd done for the sake of one little dying girl. Sure, she wanted to help catch the terrorists. And she wanted to help her friend, the princess of Ustanzia. But what *really* had driven her to make sure Joe could pass as Prince Tedric, was the little sick kid back in that bed.

He knew that as sure as he knew his heart was beating.

The noose around Joe's chest drew so tight, for one heart-stopping moment he was sure he'd never be able to breathe again. But then something snapped—not the noose, but something in his head—and a little voice said, "You're in love with this woman, you flaming idiot," and he knew it was true.

She was wonderful. And he was *crazy* in love with her.

Her smile faded and there was only warmth in her eyes, warmth and that ever-present flame of desire. She moved back into his arms, and lifted her mouth to his and . . .

God, he was kissing her. He was actually kissing her.

He took her lips hungrily, pulling her lithe body closer to him. He wanted to inhale her, devour her, become one with her. He kissed her again and again, his tongue sweeping fiercely past any pretense of civility, as he savagely claimed her mouth.

He could feel her arms around his neck, feel her pressing herself even tighter against him as she kissed him with equal abandon.

It was so right. It was so utterly, perfectly right. This woman, his arms around her, their two hearts beating—pounding—in unison. Two souls intertwined. Two minds so different, yet alike.

Joe knew with sudden frightening clarity what he'd been fighting and denying to himself for days now.

He wanted.

Ronnie St. John.

Permanently.

As in "till death do us part."

He wanted to make love to her, to possess her, to own her heart as completely as she owned his. He wanted to see her eyes widen in pleasure, hear her cry his name as he filled her, totally, absolutely, in a perfect act of total and binding love.

For the first time in his life, Joe understood the concept of happily ever after. It was a promise he'd never allowed himself before, an impossible rank he'd never thought to achieve.

But it was right there, staring him in the face whenever Veronica walked into the room. It was in the way she stood, the way she tilted her head very slightly as she listened to him talk, the way she tried so ineffectually to tuck her wild curls back up into her bun, the way her blue eyes danced as she laughed. And it was in the way she was kissing him, as if she, too, wanted to wrap her gorgeous mile-long legs around his waist and feel him inside her forever and ever and ever and *ever.*

But then, as suddenly as the kiss had started, it stopped.

Veronica pulled away, as if she suddenly realized that they were standing in the middle of the hospice chapel, surrounded by stained glass and soothing dark wood and candles, with a FInCOM agent watching them from the doorway. A nun knelt quietly before the altar. They'd been standing there, kissing, in front of a *nun,* for crying out loud....

Veronica's cheeks flushed pink as Joe looked into her eyes, trying to see what she was thinking. Was this just another "mistake"? Or was this simply a more emotional thank-you? Or was it more than that? Please, God, he wanted it to be more. He wanted it to mean she was feeling all of the things that he felt. But they weren't alone, and he couldn't ask. He couldn't even speak. All he could do was hope.

She looked away from him, the expression in her eyes unreadable as she murmured an apology.

An apology. Mistakes and accidents required apologies.

Joe's heart sank as the FInCOM agents quickly led them both back to the waiting limos. And when Kevin Laughton hustled Veronica into a different limousine and she didn't even glance in Joe's direction before getting inside, his heart shattered.

He had his answer. That kiss had been another mistake.

Joe was quiet on the charter flight to Boston. Even his friends from the Alpha Squad knew enough to stay away from him.

Veronica slipped into the seat next to his, and he glanced up, his eyes wary.

"Are you all right?" she asked quietly.

He smiled tightly. "Why wouldn't I be all right?"

Veronica wasn't sure how to answer that question. Because you just spent time with a dying child. Because you talked to her and you didn't try to pretend that she had a future, that she wasn't dying. Because it hurts like hell to know that there's nothing you or anyone else can do for that little girl, except make her smile a few more times....

And because you kissed me as if your world were crumbling beneath your very feet, and when I pulled away, you looked at me as if I were ripping the heart from your chest....

Joe shook his head. "You know, that's the problem when big, mean guys like me show we actually have a soul," he complained. "Everyone gets all worried, like, he lost it once, now he's gonna burst into tears every time someone says 'Boo.' Well, forget about it. I'm fine."

Veronica nodded, not daring to comment, certainly not daring to mention the kiss. Not yet. They sat for a moment in silence, and then she turned back to look at him. "I had no idea you spoke French," she said, tackling a much safer subject, hoping he'd be the one to bring up the topic of the kiss they'd shared. "*And* Russian?"

Joe shrugged. "I'm a language specialist," he said, shortly. "It's no big deal."

"How many languages do you speak?"

"Eight," he said.

"Eight," Veronica repeated. The way he said it, it was nothing. She spoke English and French and a very small bit of Spanish, and *that* hadn't been nothing. In fact, it had been a great deal of work.

"Someone in the team has to be able to communicate with the locals," he said, as if that explained everything. His SEAL Team needed him to speak eight different languages, so he'd learned eight different languages.

"What else do you specialize in?" she asked.

Joe shrugged. "The usual SEAL tricks."

"Balancing beach balls on your nose and barking like a dog?"

He finally smiled. "Not quite," he said.

"I assume some kind of swimming is involved," Veronica said. "Or else you wouldn't be called SEALs."

"Yeah, swimming," he said. "And scuba diving. Skydiving. Parasailing." He started ticking the list off on his fingers. "Explosives, underwater and on land. Weapons and other high-tech war toys. Martial arts and some less conventional hand-to-hand techniques. Computers. Locks. Alarm systems. And so on."

"Admiral Forrest said you were a sharpshooter," Veronica said. "An expert marksman."

"Everyone in SEAL Team Ten is," he replied, shrugging it off.

"Besides languages, what else do *you* specialize in?" Veronica asked.

He gazed at her for several long seconds. "I know a little more than the other guys when it comes to the high-tech war toys," he finally said. "I'm also a classified expert in jungle, desert and arctic survival. You know about the languages and my...ability to mimic. Comes in handy at times. I can fly any type of aircraft, from a chopper to a Stealth." He smiled, but it lacked the wattage of his usual grins. "Hell, I could probably handle the space shuttle if I had to. And I'm an expert mechanic. I could fix it if it breaks. There's some other stuff that you don't want to know, and some that I can't tell you."

Veronica nodded slowly. Admiral Forrest had told her much of this before, but she hadn't believed it. She probably still wouldn't believe it if she hadn't heard Joe speaking perfect French. He could do all those incredible things, superhuman things, and yet it was his humanity—his compassion and kindness for a dying child—that had moved her the most. Moved her profoundly.

She looked down at her hands, folded nervously in her lap. "Joe, about this morning," she started to say.

"It's okay, Ronnie. You can forget about it," he interrupted, knowing that she was talking about their kiss. His eyes were guarded as he glanced at her again. He looked away, out the window of the jet. "It was ...something we both needed right then. But, it ... didn't mean anything, and I know you're not going to let it happen again. No more mistakes, right? So we don't need to talk about it. In fact, I'd rather *not* talk about it."

"But ..."

"Please," he said, turning to look at her again.

It didn't mean anything. His words suddenly penetrated, and Veronica stared at him, her mouth slightly open. She closed her mouth, and looked back down at her hands.

She sat there in silence, afraid to move, afraid to breathe, afraid to *think,* because she was afraid of what she'd feel.

It didn't mean anything.

That kiss had been more than a kiss. It had been an exchange of emotions, a joining of souls. It had been filled with feelings she didn't want to feel, powerful feelings for a man who scared her more than she wanted to admit. A man who specialized in making war. A man who risked his life as a matter of course. A man she'd tried to keep her distance from. Tried and failed.

She'd kissed him. In *public.* And he thought it didn't *mean* anything?

The seat-belt light flashed on, and the pilot's voice came over the loudspeaker.

"We're approaching Boston. Please return to your seats."

Joe stared out the window as if he'd never seen Boston before, as if the aerial view was infinitely more interesting than anything he could see inside the jet.

Veronica forced her voice to sound even and controlled. "We'll be arriving in Boston in a few minutes," she said. Joe lifted his head in acknowledgment, but still didn't look in her direction. "From the airport, it's only about a fifteen-minute drive downtown to the hotel where the charity luncheon is being held. Your speech will be on a TelePrompTer. It'll be brief and all you'll have to do is read it.

"This evening, there's a private party on Beacon Hill," she said, wishing she felt as cool and detached as she sounded. Wishing she didn't feel like crying. *It didn't mean anything.* "The host and hostess are friends of Wila's. And mine. So I won't be in the surveillance van tonight."

He turned and frowned at her, his dark eyes piercing. "What? Why not?"

"Ambassador Freder will be in the van," Veronica said, purposely not meeting the intensity of Joe's gaze. "I'll be attending my friends' party. There'll be virtually no risk for you. Consider this another one of Tedric's obligations that couldn't be gotten out of."

She could feel him watching her, giving her a long, measuring look. "There's never no risk," he said. "I'd feel much better if you were in the van."

"We won't stay long," she said, glancing up at him.

"Just long enough to get shot, maybe, huh?" Joe said. He forced a smile. "Relax, Ronnie, I was kidding."

"I don't think getting shot is ever funny," Veronica said tightly.

"Sorry," he said. God, she was strung as tight as he was. Probably the tension from worrying about his reaction to this morning's kiss. No doubt the relief hadn't set in yet.

Sitting next to her like this was torture. Joe jerked his thumb toward the window. "It's been a while since I've been in New England," he said. "Mind if I...?"

Veronica shook her head. "No, that's... Go right ahead and..."

He'd already turned to look out the window.

She'd been dismissed.

Rather than stare at the back of Joe's head, agonizing over his impersonal words, Veronica ignored the seat-belt sign and stood, moving toward the front of the plane where there were several empty seats.

It didn't mean anything.

Maybe not to Joe, but that kiss *had* meant something to Veronica.

It meant *she'd* been a real fool.

Chapter 14

Salustiano Vargas, the former right hand of the man known by most of the world only as Diosdado, stared at the telephone in his cheap motel room as it rang. It was hotter than hell in there and the air conditioner chugged away to no avail.

He had told no one, *no one,* where he would be staying. Still, he knew damn well who was on the other end of the line. There was nowhere he could run where Diosdado couldn't find him.

He picked it up after the seventeenth ring, unable to stand it any longer. "Yes?"

Diosdado said only one word. "When?"

"Soon," Vargas replied, closing his eyes. "You have my word."

"Good." The line was cut without a goodbye.

Vargas sat in the heat for several moments, not moving.

It truly *was* hotter than hell in this cheap room.

When he stood, it took him only a few minutes to pack up his things. He carried his suitcase to his rented car and headed across town—toward a fancy, expensive resort. He couldn't afford to stay there, but he would put it on his credit card. He wanted luxury. He wanted clean sheets, a firm bed. He wanted room service and a view of a sparkling swimming pool with young girls lounging around it. He wanted the cool, sweet, fresh air of a fancy hotel room.

He didn't want hell. He'd be there soon enough.

As the applause died down, Joe smiled in the direction of the TV news cameras. "Good afternoon," he said. "It is an honor and a pleasure to be here today."

Veronica couldn't concentrate on his words. All her attention was on Blue and Cowboy and Harvard's voices as they kept a constant lookout for danger.

This was the perfect setting for an assassination attempt. There were TV cameras here from every network, including cable news, *and* the event was political—a hundred-dollars-a-plate fund-raiser for a well-known senator's reelection campaign.

But if the terrorists were going to try to shoot the prince—Joe—they hadn't set up in any of the obvious vantage points. If they were here, they were in with the crowd, sitting in the rows of banquet tables.

FInCOM agents were everywhere. Veronica could see them on her video screens, their eyes sweeping the crowd, watchful for any sign of danger or trouble.

Please, Lord, protect Joe and keep him safe—

There was a sudden commotion at one of the tables in the back, and Veronica's heart lodged in her throat.

She could hear the SEALs shouting and see the FInCOM agents running, all converging on one table, and one man.

"I have my rights!" the man was shouting as he was wrestled to the floor. "I've done nothing wrong! I'm a Vietnam veteran and I want to know—"

Noise erupted as people tried to get away from the commotion, and the FInCOM agents tried to get the man out of the room. And Joe . . . Joe was still standing at the podium, watching. Why didn't he get down, out of harm's way?

"Joe," Veronica said into her microphone. "Take cover!"

But he didn't move.

"Joe!" she said again. "Damn it, get down!"

He wasn't listening. He was watching as the man was dragged toward the door.

"Wait," he said sharply, his commanding voice echoing over the PA system, cutting through hubbub, through the sound of eight hundred voices all talking at once. "I said, *wait!*"

Blue froze. They all froze—the FInCOM agents and their prisoner, looking up toward Joe. A hush fell over the crowd.

"Is he armed?" Joe asked, more quietly now.

Blue shook his head. "No, sir."

"I only wanted to ask a question, Your Highness," the man called out, his voice ringing clearly across the room.

Veronica sat on the edge of her seat, watching. She could see the TV cameras catching every bit of the drama.

"He only wanted to ask a question," Joe repeated mildly. He turned to Kevin Laughton, who now stood on the stage next to him. "Has it become illegal in this country to ask a question?"

"No, sir," Laughton said. "But—"

Joe turned pointedly away from Laughton. "He would like to ask a question," he said to the watching crowd, "and I would like to *hear* his question, if the rest of you don't mind...?"

Someone started to clap, and after a brief smattering of applause, Joe bowed his head to the man.

"The question I wanted to ask you, Prince Tedric," the man said in his clear voice, "and the question I want to ask *all* of you," he added, addressing the entire crowd, "is how can you sit here in good conscience, spending so much money for one meal, when right next door a homeless shelter and soup kitchen for Vietnam veterans is about to be shut down from lack of funding?"

It was so quiet in the room, a pin could have been heard falling on the floor.

Joe didn't answer at first. He let the question sit, filling the air, surrounding all the luncheon guests.

"What is your name?" Joe asked the man.

"Tony Pope, sir," the man said. "Sergeant Tony Pope, U.S. Marines, retired."

"You served in Vietnam, Sergeant?" Joe asked.

Pope nodded. "Yes, sir."

Joe looked at Blue and the FInCOM agents who were still holding Pope's arms. "I think you can release him," he said. "I think we've determined he's not out for blood."

"Thank you, sir." Pope straightened his jacket and tie.

He was a good-looking man, Veronica realized, with a neatly trimmed goatee and mustache. His suit was well-tailored, if rather worn and fraying in spots. He held himself proudly, standing tall, with his shoulders back and head high.

"Do you run this homeless shelter, Sergeant Pope?" Joe asked.

"Yes, sir," Pope replied. "The Boylston Street Shelter. For ten years, sir." His mouth tightened. "We've had some tough times, but never like this. The few grants we had left ran out, and it'll be six months before we stand a chance of getting any additional funding. And now the city says we need to make repairs to the facility by the end of the month—Friday—or our site's condemned. We barely have enough cash to feed our residents, let alone make the kind of repairs they're demanding. To be bluntly honest, sir, the Vietnam vets that live at Boylston Street Shelter are getting screwed—again."

"How many men use your facility?" Joe asked quietly.

"Daily we average around two hundred and fifty," the man replied. "These are men who have nowhere else to go—no food, no place but the street to sleep."

Joe was silent.

"Our yearly overhead cost is twenty thousand dollars," Tony Pope said. He looked around the room. "That's what two hundred of you are paying right now, for one *single* meal."

"Is the Boylston Street Shelter serving lunch today?" Joe asked.

"Today and every day," Pope said. "Until they nail our doors shut."

"Do you mind if I come take a look?" Joe asked.

If Pope was surprised, he hid it well. "I'd be honored."

"No way," Veronica heard Kevin Laughton say vehemently. "Absolutely no way."

"Joe, what are you doing?" she asked. "You can't leave the building, it's not safe."

But Joe had already jumped down, off the stage, and was striding between the tables, toward Sgt. Tony Pope, U.S.M.C., retired.

As Veronica watched, Pope led Joe—surrounded by FInCOM agents and his three SEALs—out of the room. The TV news cameras and reporters scrambled after them.

The shelter was, quite literally, right next door to the hotel. Once inside, Pope gave Joe—and the camera crews—a tour of his modest facility, from the cafeteria to the kitchen. He pointed out the holes in the roof and the other parts of the building that needed repairs. He introduced Joe to many of the longtime residents and workers.

Joe addressed them by rank, even the grungiest, rag-clad winos, and spoke to them all with the utmost respect and courtesy.

And as Joe was leaving, he slipped the jeweled ring from his finger and handed it to Tony Pope. "Fix your roof," he said.

Tears sprang to the older man's eyes. "Your Majesty," he said. "You've already given us so much." He gestured to the TV cameras. "The publicity alone is priceless."

"You need some quick cash, and I have one ring too many," Joe said. "The solution is so obvious. So simple." He smiled into the TV news cameras. "Just like my friend Cindy says."

"Oh, Joe, that ring's not yours to give away," Veronica breathed, knowing that she would pay for the ring herself, if she had to.

The final scene in the evening news report showed all of the men in the Boylston Street Shelter sharply saluting Prince Tedric as he left the building.

"Sergeant Tony Pope asks that contributions be sent directly to the Boylston Street Shelter," the news anchor said, "at 994—"

The phone rang, and Veronica pushed the Mute button as she answered it.

"Did you see it?" It was Henri Freder, the Ustanzian ambassador. "Did you see the news? It's not just a local story, it's being run nationally, *and* by the cable network."

"I saw it," Veronica said.

"Gold," Freder said. "Pure, solid gold."

"I know that ring was valuable, sir," Veronica started to say. "But—"

"Not the ring," Freder enthused. "Prince Tedric's image! Absolutely golden! He is America's newest hero. Everyone *loves* him. We couldn't have done it better if we'd tried. I've got to go, my other phone is ringing—"

Veronica stared at the disconnected telephone and slowly hung up the receiver. Everyone loved Prince Tedric—who was really a sailor named Joe, and not a real prince at all.

Or was he?

He was more of a prince than Tedric had ever been.

Now, because of Joe, everyone loved Prince Tedric. Except Veronica. She was falling in love with a prince named Joe.

Veronica had two hours to rest before the party. She lay down on the bed and stared at the ceiling, trying not to let the words Joe had spoken on the plane echo in her mind.

The kiss they'd shared. *It didn't mean anything.*

She was in love with a man who had told her, on more than one occasion, that the best she could hope for with him was a casual sexual relationship. He'd told her that the kisses they'd shared meant nothing to him.

He *did* desire her, though.

Veronica knew that from looking into his eyes. She knew it, too, from the way he'd kissed her in the chapel at Saint Mary's. If they'd been alone, it wouldn't have taken much for that one, single kiss to escalate into lovemaking.

But he didn't love her.

So now what? Was she going to just sit around loving Joe from a distance until the terrorists were caught, until he went back to SEAL Team Ten's temporary base in California? Or was she going to do something foolish, like make love to the man, stupidly hoping that the physical act would magically make him fall in love with her, too?

It would never happen. He would have all he'd ever wanted from her—sex. And she would have a broken heart.

A single tear slid down the side of her face and lodged rather uncomfortably in her ear. Perfect. She was now one-hundred-percent pitiable and pathetic.

The telephone rang, and Veronica rolled over and looked at it. She contemplated letting the front desk take a message, but after three rings, she finally picked it up. She wasn't going to get any sleep anyway.

"Veronica St. John," she said on a sigh.

"Hey."

It was Joe.

Veronica sat up, hastily wiping the moisture from her face, as if he would somehow be able to tell she'd been crying. She hadn't expected the caller to be Joe. Not in a million years. Not after their dreadful conversation on the plane.

"Are you awake?" he asked.

"I am now," she said.

"Oh, damn," he said, concern tingeing his voice. "Did I really wake you?"

"No, no," she said. "I was just . . . No."

"Well, I won't take too much of your time," Joe said. His husky voice sounded slightly stiff and unnatural. "I just wanted to tell you that if you get any flak about me giving away that ring of Tedric's—"

"It's all right," Veronica interrupted. "The ambassador called and—"

"I just wanted to let you know that I'll pay for it," Joe said. "I don't know what I was thinking—giving away something that didn't belong to me. But—"

"It's all taken care of," Veronica said.

"It is?"

"Your popularity rating is apparently through the roof," she told him. "I think the Ustanzian ambassador is considering having you knighted or perhaps made into a saint."

Joe laughed. "I can see it now. Joe, the patron saint of celebrity impersonators."

"Don't you mean, the patron saint of dying children and struggling causes?" Veronica said softly. "You know, Joe, you never fail to surprise me."

"That makes two of us," he muttered.

"What?"

"Nothing. I should go—"

"You really are softhearted, aren't you?" Veronica asked.

"Honey, I'm not soft anywhere." She could almost see him bristle.

"I didn't mean that as an insult," she said.

"Look, I just have a problem with the way this country treats war veterans, all right?" he said. "I'm tired of seeing good men, soldiers and sailors who risked their lives fighting for this country, being forced to live in the lousy gutter."

Veronica pushed her hair from her face, suddenly understanding. This was personal. This had something to do with that old sailor Joe had known when he was a child. What was his name...? "Frank O'Riley," she said, hardly realizing she'd spoken aloud.

Joe was silent for several long seconds. "Yeah," he finally said. "Old Man O'Riley went on a binge and lost his job. Got himself evicted. It damn near killed him to think of losing his garden, and he sobered up, but it was too late. No one helped him. He was a war hero, and he was out on the street in the goddammed middle of the goddammed winter."

"And because of that, he died," Veronica guessed correctly.

"He caught pneumonia." Joe's voice was curiously flat, and she knew by his lack of inflection and emotion that Frank O'Riley's death *still* hurt him deeply.

"I'm sorry," Veronica murmured.

Joe was quiet again for a moment. Then he sighed. "What I don't get, is how the hell our armed forces can send our guys to fight a war without really preparing them. And if we *are* going to send out these . . . *kids,* then we shouldn't be so damned surprised when they come home and fall apart. And then—and this is *real* genius—we try to sweep the pieces under the rug so no one will see. Nice move, huh?"

"Those are pretty tough words for someone who specializes in making war," Veronica said.

"I'm not suggesting we demilitarize," Joe said. "I think that would be a mistake. No, I just think the government should take responsibility for the veterans."

"But if there were no wars, there'd be no veterans. If we spent money on diplomatic relations rather than guns and—"

"Right," Joe said. "But there are enough bad guys in the world that wouldn't hesitate to step forward and kick some butt if our country couldn't defend itself. I mean, sure we could hand out flowers and love beads, but we'd get back a round of machine-gun fire in our gut. There are some mean bastards out there, Ronnie, and they don't want to play nice. We need to be as tough and as mean as they are.''

"And that's where *you* come in," Veronica said. "Mr. Tough and Mean. Ready to fight whatever war pops up.''

"I'm a fighter," Joe stated quietly. "I've been prepared for war my entire life." He laughed softly, his voice suddenly so intimate and low in her ear. "It's the other surprises in life that knock me over.''

"You are so utterly un-knock-overable." Veronica wished the same were true of herself.

"You're wrong," Joe countered. "The past few days, I can barely remember what solid ground feels like.''

Veronica was quiet. She could hear Joe breathing on the other end of the phone line, three doors down the hotel corridor. "Cindy?" she asked softly. He didn't say a word. "I'm sorry," she added. "I should have prepared you more for—''

"Not Cindy," he said. "I mean, going to see her *was* tough, but . . . I was talking about you.''

Veronica felt all the air leave her lungs. "Me?" She couldn't speak in more than a whisper.

"God, would you look at the time? I gotta go.''

"Joe, what—''

"No, Ronnie, I don't know why I said that. I'm just asking for trouble and—'' He broke off, swearing softly.

"But—''

"Do yourself a favor tonight, babe," Joe said brusquely. "Stay the hell away from me, okay?''

The phone line was disconnected with a click.

Veronica sat on the bed for a long time, holding the receiver against her chest. Was it possible . . . ? Could it be . . . ? Did Joe think *she* was the one who didn't want any kind of relationship?

What was it that he'd said on the plane . . . ? About the kiss they'd shared . . . *It didn't mean anything, and I know you're not going to let it happen again.*

You're *not going to let it happen again.*

Not *we*. *You*. Meaning Veronica. Meaning...what? That she was the one who was preventing their relationship from growing?

The telephone began to emit a series of piercing tones, and Veronica quickly dropped the receiver into the cradle.

If Joe really thought she didn't want a relationship with him, then she was going to have to set him straight.

Veronica stood and crossed to the closet, her nap forgotten. She looked quickly through her clothes, glancing only briefly at the rather staid dress she'd intended to wear to the party tonight. That dress wouldn't do. It wouldn't do at all....

Chapter 15

Joe stood in the marble-tiled front hallway of Armand and Talandra Perrault's enormous Beacon Hill town house, chatting easily in French with the couple who were the host and hostess of tonight's party.

Armand Perrault was a charming and gracious silver-haired Frenchman who'd retired a millionaire from his import-export business. His wife, Talandra, was a tall, beautiful young black woman with a rich, infectious laugh.

Talandra had known Veronica from college. Apparently they'd been roommates and good friends. They'd even gone on vacations together—that was how Talandra had met Wila Cortere, Joe's supposed sister.

God, at times like this, Joe felt like such a liar.

"Where *is* Véronique, Your Highness?" Talandra asked him.

He fought the temptation to shrug. "She wasn't ready to leave the hotel when I was," he said instead in Tedric's royal accent. "I'm sure she'll be here soon."

Ambassador Freder was in the surveillance van, sitting in Veronica's seat, ready to provide names and facts and any other information Joe might need.

Damn, how he wished it was Veronica whispering in his ear. Even though this party was not public and therefore technically a low risk, Joe was on edge. He *liked* knowing that Veronica was safely tucked away in the van, out of danger. Tonight, he was going to spend all of his time wondering where she was, and praying that she was safe.

Damn, he hated not knowing where she was. Where *was* that other limousine?

"May I get you another glass of champagne?" Talandra asked.

Joe shook his head. "No, thank you."

He could feel Talandra's dark brown eyes studying him. "You're not as Wila and Véronique described you," she said.

"No?" Joe's gaze strayed back to the front door as several FInCOM agents pulled it open.

Please, God, let it be her . . .

The woman who came in the door was a redhead, but there was no way on God's earth it could be Veronica, wearing a dress that exposed so much skin and—

Hot *damn!*

It *was* her. It *was* Veronica.

Over his earphone, Joe could hear Cowboy. "Whoo-ee, boss, babe alert at eleven o'clock!"

Sweet God! Veronica looked . . . out of this world. The dress she was wearing was black and long, made of a soft silky fabric that clung to her every curve. Two triangles of black barely covered her breasts, and were held up by two thin strips of fabric that crossed her shoulders and met between her shoulder blades, at the cutaway back of the dress. There was a slit up the side of the skirt, all the way up to the top of her thigh, that revealed flashes of her incredible legs. Her shoes were black, with high, narrow heels that were a polar opposite to the clunky-heeled pumps she normally wore.

She was wearing her hair up, piled almost haphazardly on top of her head, with stray curls exploding around her face.

"Tell me, Your Majesty, does Véronique know how you feel?" Talandra whispered into his ear.

Startled, he glanced at her. "Excuse me?"

She just smiled knowingly and crossed the room toward Veronica.

"Yeah, Your Majesty," Harvard said over Joe's earphone as Joe watched Veronica greet her old friend with a warm hug and kiss. "You might want to keep that royal tongue *inside* your royal mouth, do you copy that?"

Joe couldn't see Cowboy or Harvard, but he knew that wherever they were, they could see him. But what exactly did they see? And what had Talandra seen in his face that made her make that very personal comment?

Was he *that* transparent? Or was this just the way being in love was? Was it impossible to hide? And if so, could Veronica see it just as easily? If so, he was in big trouble here.

Veronica turned her head, about to glance in his direction, and he abruptly turned away. He'd have to stay far, far away from her. He'd already revealed way too much this afternoon, when he'd talked to her on the phone. And damn it, he was trying hard *not* to be in love with her. How tough could it be? After all, he'd spent nearly his entire life not in love with Veronica. It shouldn't be too difficult to get back to that state.

What was love, anyway, but a mutated form of lust? And he'd easily walked away from women he'd lusted after before. Why, then, did his legs feel as if they were caught in molasses when he tried to walk away from Veronica?

Because love *wasn't* lust, and love *wasn't* something a man could turn off and on like a faucet. *And* he was crazy in love with this woman, no matter that he tried to convince himself otherwise.

And God, if she found out, her gentle pity would kill him.

"Hell, boss," Cowboy said. "She's heading straight toward you, and you're running *away?*"

"You've got it backward, Cat," Harvard chimed in. "A woman like that walks in your direction, you stand very, *very* still."

Blue's south-of-the-Mason-Dixon-Line accent made his voice sound gentle over Joe's earphone, but his words were anything but. "You boys gonna enjoy explaining to Admiral Forrest how you got Joe Cat killed while you were watchin' women instead of watchin' for T's?"

Cowboy and Harvard were noticeably silent as Joe moved around the corner into an enormous room with a hardwood floor.

It was the ballroom—not that he'd ever been in a ballroom in a private house before. But it was pretty damn unmistakable. A jazz trio was playing in one corner, the furniture was placed around the edges of the room and people were out in the middle of the floor, dancing. This had to be the ballroom. It sure as hell wasn't the bathroom or the kitchen.

Joe headed for a small bar set up in the far corner, across from the band. The bartender greeted him with a bow.

"Your Highness," the young man said. "What can I get for you?"

Whiskey, straight up. "Better make it a ginger ale," Joe said instead. "Easy on the ice."

"I'll have the same," said a familiar voice behind him. It was Veronica.

Joe didn't want to turn around. Looking at her from a distance had been hard enough. Up close, that dress just might have the power to do him in.

He closed his eyes briefly, imagining himself falling to his knees in front of her, begging her to...what? To marry him? Yeah, right. Dream on, Catalanotto.

He forced a smile and made himself turn. "Ms. St. John," he said, greeting her formally.

She smiled up at him. Light gleamed off her reddish gold hair, and her eyes seemed to sparkle and dance. She was unbelievably beautiful. Joe couldn't imagine that at one time he'd thought her less than gorgeous.

She lifted her hand, and he took it automatically, bringing it halfway to his lips before he realized what he was doing. God Almighty, all those hands he'd pretended to kiss over the past few days... But this time, he wasn't going to have to pretend. He brought Veronica's hand to his mouth and brushed his lips lightly across her delicate knuckles.

He heard her soft intake of breath, and when he glanced up, he could see that her smile had faded. Her blue eyes were enormous, but she didn't pull her hand away.

Joe stood there, like an idiot, staring into eyes the color of the Caribbean Sea. Her gaze flickered down to his lips and then farther, to the pin he wore in his lapel—the pin that concealed the microphone that would broadcast everything they said to the surveillance truck, the FInCOM agents and the SEALs.

Joe heard only silence over his earphone, and he knew they were all listening. All of them. Listening intently.

"How are you, Your Majesty?" Veronica asked, her voice cool and controlled.

Joe found his own voice. "I'm well, thanks," he said. Damn, he sounded hoarse, and not an awful lot like Prince Tedric. He cleared his throat, then moistened his dry lips, and realized that Veronica's eyes followed the movement of his tongue. God, was it possible that she wanted to kiss him . . . ?

Her eyes met his, and something flamed—something hot, something molten, something that seared him to his very soul, something that made his already dry mouth turn into something resembling the floor of Death Valley.

Veronica gently disengaged her hand from his and reached to take one of the glasses of ginger ale from the bar. "Have you met my friend Talandra?" she asked him.

"Yeah," Joe said, catching himself and correcting himself by saying, "Yes. Yes, I have." He concentrated on doing the Ustanzian accent. But as he watched, she took a delicate sip of her soda and all he could think about were her lips. And the soft curves of her creamy skin, and of her breasts, exposed by the fabulous design of that dress. "She seems . . . nice."

Their eyes met, and again, he was hit by a wave of heat so powerful it nearly knocked him over.

Veronica nodded politely. "Yes, she is."

What kind of game was this?

She turned to watch the dancers, and her arm brushed against his. She smiled an apology and moved slightly away. But when it happened again, Joe knew damn well it was no accident. At least he hoped it was no accident. His pulse began to race with the implications.

"I love to dance," she said, glancing at him.

Oh yeah, he knew that. He'd seen her dance. It hadn't been like this—all stiff and polite and formal. When she'd danced, she'd moved with a sensuality and abandon that would've shocked the hell out of half of the people in this room.

Veronica tucked her hand into the crook of his elbow, and Joe's heart began to pound.

She was coming on to him.

Not in any way that the video cameras and microphones could pick up, but she *was* coming on to him. It all made sense. The dress, the shoes, the fire she was letting him see in her eyes . . .

He couldn't figure out why the sudden change of heart.

Joe opened his mouth to speak, but quickly shut it. What could he ask her? What could he say? Certainly nothing that he wanted broadcast over the entire security network.

Instead, he put his hand over hers, covering her cool fingers with his. He gently stroked her smooth skin with his thumb.

Veronica turned to look up at him, and Joe could see her desire in her eyes. No doubt about it—she was letting him see it. She wanted him, and she wanted him to know it.

She smiled then—a beautiful, tremulous smile that brought his heart up into his throat. He wanted to kiss her so badly, he had to clench his teeth to keep from leaning toward her and caressing her lips with his own.

"Your Majesty," she said very softly, as if she couldn't find the air to do more than whisper, "may I have this dance?"

He could have her in his arms, right here, right now. Damn, wouldn't that be heaven?

But then, from across the room, came an earsplitting crash.

Joe reacted, pulling Veronica into his arms and shielding her with his body. What the hell was he thinking? What was he doing, standing here next to her like this, as if he weren't the target of assassins? She was close enough so that bullets meant for him could end her life in the beat of a heart.

"It's all right, Cat." He heard Blue's voice over his earphone. "It's cool. Someone dropped a glass. We do not have a situation. Repeat, there is *no* situation."

Joe pulled Veronica in even closer for a second, closing his eyes and pressing her tightly against him before he released her. Adrenaline was flooding his system and his entire body seemed to vibrate. Jesus, Mary and Joseph, he'd never been so scared. . . .

Veronica touched his arm. "I guess we're all on edge," she said with a small smile. "Are you all right?"

Joe looked wound tighter than a drum. There was a wildness in his eyes she'd never seen before and his hand actually trembled as he pushed his hair back, off his face.

"No," he said curtly, not bothering to disguise his voice with Tedric's odd accent. "No, I'm not all right. Ronnie, I need you to stay the hell away from me."

Veronica felt her smile fade. "I thought we were going to...dance."

Joe let out a short burst of exasperated air. "No way," he said. "Absolutely not. No dancing."

She looked down at the floor. "I see."

As Joe watched, Veronica turned and started to walk away, unable to disguise the flash of hurt in her eyes. My God. She thought he was rejecting her. He tried to catch her arm, to stop her, but she was moving faster now.

"No, you *don't* see," he called after her in a low voice.

But she didn't stop walking. Joe started to follow.

Damn! Short of breaking into a sprint, there was no way he could catch her. And although shouting "Yo, Ronnie!" was something Joe Catalanotto might not have hesitated to do even at a posh society party, Prince Tedric was not prone to raising his voice in public.

When Joe rounded the corner into the front hall, Veronica was nowhere in sight. Damn! Double damn! How could he follow her if he didn't know where she went?

He headed toward the living room and the spacious kitchen beyond, hearing the unmistakable sound of Talandra's laughter from that direction.

But Talandra stood near a large stone fireplace, sipping champagne and talking with a group of elegantly dressed women—none of whom were Veronica. "Oh, here's the prince now," Talandra said, smiling at Joe.

There was nothing he could do but go and greet the group of ladies as Talandra made introductions.

"Code Red," came Cowboy's voice, loud and clear over Joe's earphone. "We have an open window on the third floor! Repeat, open window, third floor. Possible break-in. Joe, get the *hell* out of here. Double time! This is not a drill. Repeat. This is *not* a drill!"

Everything switched into slow motion.

Joe had to get out of here. He had to get away from these ladies—God help them all if a terrorist burst into the room firing a submachine gun.

"Get down!" he shouted at the women. "Get to cover!"

Talandra was the first to react. Of course, she'd probably been warned about an assassination attempt. She led the entire group of ladies down a hallway to the back of the house.

God, all it would take was one man and one gun and— Jesus, Mary and Joseph! Ronnie was somewhere in this house.

"Blue, where's Ronnie?" Joe said into his mike, heading for the kitchen door as he pulled out the gun he kept hidden under his jacket. FInCOM had ordered he remain unarmed. He'd smiled and said nothing. He was damn glad now that he'd ignored that order. If someone was going to start shooting at him, damn it, he was going to shoot back. "Blue, I need you to find Ronnie!"

"I don't see her, Cat," his XO reported, his gentle drawl replaced by a staccato stream of nearly accentless words. "But I'm looking. Get your own butt under cover!"

"Not till I know she's safe," Joe retorted as he burst through the kitchen door. A man in a chef's hat looked up at him in shock, his eyes glued to the gun. "Get down," Joe ordered him. "Or get out. We've got trouble."

The chef scurried for the back door.

A new voice came over the earphone. It was Kevin Laughton, the FInCOM chief. "Veronica St. John's already in a limo, heading back to the hotel. Proceed to the emergency escape vehicle, Lieutenant," he ordered.

"Double-check that info, Alpha Squad," Joe said as he pushed open the pantry door, hard, and went inside, gun first. The small storage room was empty.

"Information verified," Harvard's calm voice reported. "Ronnie has left the building. Suggest you do the same, Cat."

Joe was filled with relief. Ronnie was safe. The relief mingled with adrenaline and made him almost light-headed.

"Kitchen's empty and clear," he announced over his mike.

"Move it out, Cat," Cowboy said. "We got this situation under control."

"Are you kidding?" Joe said into his microphone, pushing the door to the living room open an inch. "And leave all the fun to you guys?"

Joe could see about ten FInCOM agents heading toward him. He swore under his breath and stepped back as they came through the door. They surrounded him instantly. West and Freeman were on either side of him, shielding him with their own bodies as they moved him toward the back door.

There was a car idling outside the kitchen, waiting for exactly this type of emergency. The car door was thrown open, and West climbed into the back seat first, pulling Joe behind him. Freeman followed, and before the door was even closed, the driver took off, peeling out down the narrow alleyway and onto the dark city streets.

West and Freeman were breathing hard as they both holstered their weapons. They watched without much surprise as Joe rested his own gun on his lap.

"You're not supposed to be carrying," West commented.

"Kevin Laughton would throw a hissy fit if he knew," Freeman said. "'Course, he doesn't have to know."

"Imagine Kevin's shock," Joe said, "if he knew that I've got another gun in my boot and a knife hidden in my belt."

"And probably another weapon hidden somewhere else that you're not telling us about," West said blandly.

"Probably," Joe agreed.

The car was moving faster now, catching green lights at all of the intersections as it headed downtown. Joe took out his earphone—they were out of range. He leaned forward and asked the driver, "Any word on the radio? What's happening back there? Any action?" He hated running away from his squad like this.

The driver shook his head. "The word is it's mostly all clear," he said. "It's an alleged false alarm. One of the party guests claims she opened the window in the third-floor bathroom because she was feeling faint."

Joe sat back in his seat. False alarm. He took a deep breath, trying to clear the nervous energy from his system. His guys were safe. Ronnie was safe. *He* was safe. He holstered his gun and looked from Freeman to West. "You know, I had no idea you guys were willing to lay it on the line for me."

West looked out one window, Freeman looked out the other. "Just doing our job, sir," West said, sounding bored.

Joe knew better. It was odd, sitting here between two relative strangers—strangers who would have died for him today if they'd had to. It was odd, knowing that they cared.

With a sudden flash, Joe remembered a pair of crystal blue eyes looking at him with enough heat to ignite a rocket engine.

West and Freeman weren't the only ones who cared.

Veronica St. John cared, too.

Chapter 16

Veronica stood at the window, looking out over downtown Boston. With all the city lights reflected in the Charles River, it was lovely. She could see the Esplanade and the Hatch Shell, where the Boston Pops played free concerts in the summer. She could see Back Bay and the Boston Common. And somewhere, down there, hidden by the trees of the common was Beacon Hill, where Talandra lived, and where there was a party going on right this very moment—without her.

She took another sip of her rum and cola, feeling the sweet warmth of the rum spreading through her.

Well, *she'd* certainly made a fool of herself tonight. Again. Veronica could see her wavery reflection in the window. She looked like someone else in this dress. Someone seductive and sexy. Someone who could snap her fingers and have dozens of men come running. Someone who wouldn't give a damn if some sailor didn't want her near him.

She laughed aloud at her foolishness, but her laughter sounded harsh in the empty hotel suite. She'd gone to this party with every intention of seducing Joe Catalanotto. She'd planned it so perfectly. She'd wear this incredible dress. He would be stunned. They'd dance. She'd dance really close. He would be even more stunned. He would follow her back to the hotel. She'd ask him into her room under the pretense of briefing him for tomorrow. But he'd know better. He'd ask the FInCOM agents to wait outside, and once the hotel-room door closed, he would pull her into his arms and . . .

It was perfect—except that she'd forgotten one small detail. Her plan would work only if Joe wanted her, too.

She had thought she'd seen desire in his eyes when he looked at her tonight, but obviously, she'd been mistaken.

Veronica took another sip of her drink and turned from the window, unable to bear the silence another minute.

There was a radio attached to the television, and she turned it on. It was set to a soft-rock station—not her favorite kind of music, but she didn't care. Just as long as there was *some*thing to fill the deadly silence.

She knew she ought to change out of her dress. It was only helping to remind her what a total imbecile she'd been. She looked at herself again in the mirror that hung on the hotel-room wall. The dress was practically indecent. The silky fabric clung to her breasts, broadcasting the fact that she was wearing no bra, and the cut of the dress showed off all kinds of cleavage and skin and curves. Good grief, she might as well have gone topless. *Whatever had possessed her to buy this dress, anyway?* It was like wearing a nightgown in public.

Veronica stared at herself in the mirror. She knew why she had bought the dress. It was to be an unspoken message to Joe. *Here I am. I'm all yours. Come and sweep me off my feet.*

To which he'd responded quite clearly. *Stay the hell away from me.*

She sighed, fighting the tears ready to spring into her eyes. She should change into something more sensible—her flannel nightie, perhaps—instead of standing here, feeling sorry for herself. She wasn't here, in Boston, to be either sexy or romantic. She was here to do her job. She wasn't looking for sex or romance or even friendship, with Joe Catalanotto. She was simply looking to get a job done well. Period, the end.

"You are such a bloody liar," Veronica said aloud to her reflection, her voice thick with disgust.

"You're not talking to me, I hope."

Veronica spun around, nearly spilling her rum and cola down the front of her dress.

Joe.

He was standing no more than three feet away from her, leaning against the wall next to the mirror. He stepped forward and took the drink from her hand.

Veronica's heart was pounding. "What are you doing here?" she gasped. "How did you get in?"

There was no balcony this time. And she was *positive* that the room's single door had been securely locked. But of course, he *had* told her he was an expert at picking locks.

Joe just smiled.

He was still wearing his party clothes. He wore a navy blue military-style jacket that buttoned up both sides of his chest and ended at his trim waist. His pants were made of a khaki-colored fabric that looked soft to the touch. They fit him like a second skin, clinging to his muscular thighs and perfect derriere. They were tucked into a pair of shiny black, knee-high boots. He wore a red sash around his waist, and the splash of color completed the princely picture.

He looked devastatingly, heart-breakingly handsome. Veronica's stomach flip-flopped. Lord, the way he was smiling at her... But whatever he was doing here, it wasn't personal, she told herself. Joe had made it clear at the party that he wanted her to stay away from him.

As she watched, he set her drink down on the end table next to the sofa and crossed to the windows. He pulled the curtains shut. "I've been wearing my bull's-eye long enough for one day," he said.

Veronica glanced at her watch. It was only nine-thirty. "The Perraults' party was supposed to last until midnight or one o'clock," she said, unable to keep her surprise from sounding in her voice. "You were supposed to stay until at *least* eleven."

Joe shrugged. "We had a little incident."

Veronica took an involuntary step forward, fear propelling her toward him. An *incident?* "Are you all right?"

"It was a false alarm," he said with another of his easy smiles.

He was standing in front of her, relaxed and smiling, absolutely at ease—or so he wanted her to believe. But she knew better. Beneath his feigned calm, he was tense and tight and ready to burst at the seams. He was upset—or he'd been upset.

"Tell me what happened," she said quietly.

He shook his head, no. "I came to get my dance."

She didn't understand. His words didn't seem to make sense. "Your...what?" She looked around the room. This was the first time he'd been in her room at the Boston hotel—how could he have left something behind?

"You asked me to dance," Joe said.

All at once, Veronica understood. He'd come here, to her room, to *dance* with her. She felt her face flush with embarrassment. "You don't have to do this," she said tightly. "I suppose I got a little silly, and—"

"When I told you to stay away from me—"

"It's okay that you didn't want—"

"I didn't want to dance with you, because you're not wearing a bulletproof vest under that dress," Joe said.

Veronica glanced down at her barely covered chest and felt her blush grow even stronger. "Well," she said, trying to sound brisk and businesslike. "Obviously not."

Joe laughed, and she looked up, startled, into the warmth of his eyes.

"God, Ron," he said, holding her gaze. "I didn't even get a chance to tell you how...perfect you look tonight." The warmth turned to pure fire. "You're *gorgeous*," he whispered, moving closer to her, one step at a time.

Veronica closed her eyes. She didn't have the strength to back away. "Don't, Joe," she said quietly.

"You think I didn't *want* to dance with you at that party?" Joe asked. He didn't give her a chance to answer. He touched her, gently cupping her shoulders, and her eyes opened. He slid his hands down to her elbows in the sweetest of caresses. "Lady, tonight I would have sold my soul for one kiss, let alone a chance to hold you in my arms." Gently, he pulled her even closer, clasping her hand in a dance hold. "Like this."

Slowly, he began to dance with her, moving in time to the soft ballad playing over the radio.

Veronica was trapped. She was caught both by his powerful arms and by the heat in his eyes. Her heart was pounding. She'd wanted him to touch her, to hold her, to dance with her, but not this way. Not because he pitied her...

"But I would've sold *my* soul. Not yours." Joe's voice was a husky whisper in her ear as he pulled her even closer. "Never yours, baby. I wasn't about to risk your life for a dance."

Veronica felt her pounding heart miss a beat. What was he saying? She pulled back to look into his eyes, searching for answers.

"You were in danger just standing next to me," Joe explained. "I should've told you to get lost the minute you walked into that room."

Was he saying that he hadn't wanted to dance with her because he feared for her safety? Dear Lord, if so, then she'd misunderstood his sharp words of warning for a brush-off, for a rejection. When in reality...

"I don't know what I was thinking," Joe said, then shook his head.

In reality, maybe he'd wanted her as badly as she'd wanted him. Veronica felt a burst of hope and happiness so intense, she almost laughed out loud.

"Hell, I *wasn't* thinking," Joe added. "I was... I don't know what I was."

"Stunned?" Veronica supplied. She could smile again, and she smiled almost shyly up at him.

Joe's slow smile turned into a grin. "Yeah. You bet. 'Stunned' about says it all. When you walked into the party, I was totally blown away. And I was thinking with a part of my anatomy that has nothing to do with my brain."

Veronica had to laugh at that. "Oh, really?"

"Yeah," Joe said. His smile grew softer, his eyes gentler. "My heart."

And then he kissed her.

She saw it coming. She saw him lean toward her, felt him lift her chin to meet his mouth. She knew he was going to kiss her. She expected it—she wanted it. But still, the softness of his lips took her by surprise, and the sweetness of his mouth on hers took her breath away.

It was dizzying. The earth seemed to lose all its gravity as he pulled her even closer to him, as he slowly, sensuously, languidly explored her lips with his, as she opened her mouth to him, deepening the kiss.

And still they danced, the thin wool covering his thighs brushing the silk of her dress. The softness of her stomach pressed intimately against the hardness of his unmistakable desire. Her breasts were tight against his powerful chest.

It was heaven. Giving in to her passion, giving up trying to fight it was such an enormous relief. Maybe this was a mistake, but Veronica wasn't going to think about it anymore. At least not right now, not tonight. She was simply going to kiss Joe Catalanotto, and dance with him, and savor every last moment. Every delicious, wonderful, magnificent second.

"Yo, Ronnie?" Joe whispered, breaking the kiss.

"Yo, Joe?" she said, still breathless.

He laughed. And kissed her again.

This time it was hotter, harder, stronger. It was still as sweet, but it was laced with a volcanic heat. Veronica knew without a doubt that tonight she was in for the time of her life.

Joe pulled back, breathing hard. "Whoa," he said, freeing one hand to push his hair back, out of his face. He closed his eyes briefly, took in a deep breath then forced it quickly out. "Ronnie, if you want me to leave, I should go now, because if—"

"I don't want you to leave."

He looked into her eyes. *Really* looked. As if he were searching for the answers to the mysteries of the universe.

Veronica could see his sharp intelligence, his raw, almost brutal strength, and his gentle tenderness all mixed together in his beautiful deep brown eyes.

"Are you sure?" he asked, his voice a ragged whisper.

Veronica smiled. And kissed him. Lord knew, she'd found the answers to all of her questions in *his* eyes.

"Unh," he said, as she swept her tongue fiercely into his mouth. And then his hands were in her hair, on her throat, on her breasts. He was touching her everywhere, as if he wanted to feel all of her at once and didn't know where to start. But then his hands slid down her back to her derriere, pressing her hips tightly against him, holding her in place as he slanted his head and kissed her even harder.

She opened her legs, taking advantage of the slit up the side of her dress, and she rubbed the inside of her thigh against his. His hand caught her leg, and he pressed her still closer to him.

Joe's mouth slid down to her neck as his hand cupped her breast. The roughness of his callused fingers rasped against the silk as he stroked the hard bud of her nipple.

"Oh, man," Joe breathed between kisses, as he slipped his hand under the fabric of her top, and touched her, really touched her, with nothing between his fingers and her flesh. "For how many days have I been *dying* to touch you like this?"

Veronica's fingers fumbled with the buttons of his jacket. "Probably the same number of days *I've* been dying for you to touch me like that."

He lifted his head, looking into her eyes. "Really?" His gaze was so intense, so serious. "Maybe it was love at first sight, huh?"

Veronica felt her own smile fade as her pulse kicked into overtime. "Love?" she whispered, hardly daring to hope that this incredible man could possibly love her, too.

Joe looked away, down at his hand still cupping her breast. "Love...lust... Whatever." He shrugged and kissed her again.

Veronica tried to hide her disappointment. *Whatever.* Well, all right. "Whatever" was better than not being desired. "Whatever" was what she'd been expecting—what he'd told her to expect from him right from the start.

But she didn't want to think about that now. She didn't want to think about anything but the way he was making her feel as he kissed and caressed her.

Joe pulled back then, and looked into her eyes. Slowly he slid the dress's narrow strap off her right shoulder. As it fell away, the silk covering her breast fell away, too.

And still he gazed into her eyes.

Veronica felt the coolness of the air as it touched her skin. And then she felt Joe, as he lightly ran one finger across the tip of her breast. She felt her body tighten, felt her nipples grow more taut, even more fully aroused.

He held her gaze longer than she would have believed possible before his eyes dropped down to caress the bareness of her breast.

"God," he breathed, moistening his lips with the tip of his tongue. "You're so beautiful."

They were frozen in place as if time had somehow stopped. But time hadn't stopped. Her heart was still beating, and with every beat, every surge of blood through her veins, Veronica wanted him even more.

But still he didn't touch her; at least, no more than another of those light-as-a-feather brushes with one finger. And she wanted him to touch her. She wanted him, so very badly, to touch her.

"If you don't touch me, I'm going to *scream,*" she said from between clenched teeth.

Joe's smile turned hot. "Is that a threat or a promise?" he asked.

"Both," she said, lost in the heat of his eyes. She was begging now. "Touch me."

"Where?" he asked, his voice hoarse. "How?"

"My breast, your mouth," she said. "Now. *Please.*"

He didn't hesitate. He brought his mouth to her breast and swept his tongue across her sensitive nipple. Veronica cried out, and he drew her into his mouth, pulling hard.

She reached for him, pushing his jacket off his shoulders. The buttons on his shirt were so tiny, so difficult to unfasten. But she wanted his shirt off. She wanted to run her hands against all those incredible muscles in his chest and shoulders and arms. She wanted to feel the satiny smoothness of his skin beneath her fingers.

She could hear her voice moaning her pleasure as Joe suckled and kissed her again and again.

But then he lifted his head and, stopping only to kiss her deeply on the mouth, he gazed into her eyes again. "What else do you want?" he demanded. "Tell me what you want."

"I want this bloody shirt off you," she said, still worrying the buttons.

He reached up with both hands and pulled. Buttons flew everywhere, but the shirt was open. He yanked it off his arms.

Veronica touched his smooth, tanned muscles with the palms of her hands, closing her eyes at the sensation, running her fingers through the curly dark hair on his chest. Oh, yes. He was so beautiful, so solid.

"Tell me what you want," Joe said again. "Come on, Ronnie, tell me where you want me to touch you."

She opened her eyes. "I want you to touch every single inch of me with every single inch of you. I want you and me on that bed in the other room. I want to feel you between my legs, Joe—"

Joe picked her up. He simply swept her effortlessly into his arms and carried her into the bedroom.

Veronica had her hands on the button of his pants before he yanked back the bedcover and laid her on the clean white sheets.

As she unfastened his sash, he found the zipper in the back of her dress. As he peeled her dress down toward her hips, she unzipped his pants and pushed them over his incredible rear end.

Her dress landed with a hiss of silk on the carpet and Joe pulled back, nearly burning her with his eyes as he took her in, lying propped up on her elbows on the bed, wearing only her black lace panties and a pair of thigh-high stockings. Lord, when he looked at her like that, with that fire in his eyes, she felt like the sexiest woman in the world.

She sat up, taking the last of the pins from her hair.

Slowly, he pushed off his shoes and stepped out of his trousers, still watching her.

Veronica was watching him, too. She rolled first one and then the other stocking from her legs as she let herself look at Joe. He was wearing only a pair of white briefs. She'd seen him in running shorts before, shorts that were nearly as brief, that exposed almost as much of his magnificent body. But this time she really let herself look.

His shoulders were broad and solid as rock. His arms were powerful and so very big. She couldn't have even begun to span his biceps with both of her hands, although she wanted rather desperately to try. His chest was wide and covered with thick dark hair. His muscles were clearly defined, and they rippled sensually when he so much as breathed. His stomach was a washboard of ridges and valleys, his hips narrow, his legs as strong as steel.

Yes, when she'd seen him run, although she'd tried not to look, she'd managed to memorize his body in amazing, precise detail, down to the scars on his shoulder and left leg, and the anchor tattoo on his arm.

But tonight there *were* some differences. She let her eyes linger on the enormous bulge straining the front of his briefs.

Veronica looked up to find Joe watching her, a small smile playing across his lips.

"Part of me wants to stand here and just look at you all night," he said.

She glanced down at his arousal, then smiled into his eyes. "Another part of you won't be very happy if you do that."

"Damn straight," he said with a laugh.

"Do I really have to beg you to come over here?" Veronica asked.

"No."

And then he was next to her on the bed and she was in his arms, and Lord, he was kissing her, touching her, running his hands across her body, filling her mouth with his tongue, tangling her legs with his.

It was ecstasy. Veronica had never felt anything remotely like it before. It was the sweetest, purest, most powerful passion she had ever known.

This was love, she thought. This incredible whirlwind of emotions and heightened sensations was love. It carried her higher, to an intellectual and emotional plane she'd never before imagined, and at the same time, it stripped her bare of every ounce of civility she had, leaving her ruled by ferocious passion, enslaved by the burning needs of her body.

She touched him, reaching down between their bodies to press the palm of her hand against his hardness, and when he cried out, she heard herself answer—the primitive call and response between a savage animal and his equally savage mate.

His hands were everywhere and his mouth was everywhere else. His fingers dipped down inside the lace of her panties, and he moaned as he felt her wet heat.

"Yes," Veronica said. It was the only word she seemed able to form with her lips. "Yes."

She tugged at his briefs, pulling him free from their confines, moaning her pleasure at the sensation of him in her hands. He was silky smooth and so hard, and oh . . .

He sat up, pulling away from her to slide her panties down and off. She sat up, too, following him, kneeling next to him on the bed, reaching for him, unwilling to let him go.

Joe groaned. "Ronnie, baby, I got to get a condom on."

He turned to reach for his pants, now crumpled on the floor, but Veronica was faster. She opened the drawer of the bedside table and took out a small foil package—one of the condoms she'd bought just hours ago when she'd bought the dress. She'd put them in the drawer in hopes of using them precisely this way with precisely this man.

"Whoa," Joe said as she pressed it into his hand. He was surprised that she was prepared. "I guess it's stupid *not* to be ready for anything these days, huh?"

He was just holding the little package, looking at her.

Good Lord, did he actually think she kept these things on hand all the time? Was he imagining a steady stream of male visitors to her room? Veronica took it from him and tore it open. "I bought it for you. For you and me," she said, somehow finding her voice in her need to explain. "I was hoping we'd make love tonight."

She saw the understanding in his eyes. She'd bought it because she'd wanted to make love—to *him*.

Veronica touched him, covering him with her fingers, gazing from that most intimate part of him, to the small ring of latex in her hand. "I'm not sure exactly how this is supposed to work," she said. "It doesn't really look as if it's going to fit, does it?"

She gazed into the heat of his eyes as he took the condom from her. "It'll fit," he said.

"Are you sure?" she asked, her smile turning devilish. "Maybe I should have bought the extra-large Navy SEAL size."

Joe laughed as he quickly and rather expertly sheathed himself. "Flattery will get you *every*thing."

Veronica encircled his neck with her arms, brushing the hard tips of her breasts against his solid chest and her soft stomach against his arousal. "I don't want everything," she breathed into his ear. "I think I already told you precisely what I want."

He kissed her—a long, sweet, slow, deep kiss that made her bones melt and her muscles feel like jelly. Still kissing her, he pulled her onto his lap, so that she was straddling his thighs. Then, taking her hips in his hands, he slowly, so slowly, lifted her up, above him.

Veronica pulled back from Joe's kiss, her eyes open. He began to lower her down, on top of him, and as the very tip of him parted her most intimately, he opened his own eyes, meeting her gaze.

Slowly, impossibly slowly, a fraction of an inch at a time, he lowered her onto him, staring all the while into her eyes.

The muscles in his powerful arms were taut, but the sweat on his upper lip wasn't from physical exertion. He lifted her slowly back up, off him, and then brought her down again, so that he was barely inside her, setting a deliberate and leisurely teasing rhythm.

Veronica moaned. She wanted more. She wanted *all* of him. She tried to shift her weight, to bring herself down more fully on top of him, but his strong arms held her firmly in place. Her moan changed to a cry of pleasure as his mouth latched on to her breast, but still he didn't release her hips.

"Please," she cried, the words ripped from her throat. "Joe, please! I want more!"

He covered her mouth with his, kissing her fiercely as he arched his body up and pushed her hips down and filled her completely, absolutely, incredibly.

The sound she heard herself make was almost inhuman as he plunged into her, filling her again and again and again. The rhythm was frantic, feverish, and Veronica threw back her head, delirious from the sweet sensations exploding inside her as she found her release. Arrows of pleasure shot through her— straight to her heart.

Joe's fingers stabbed through her hair as he called out her name and she clung to his neck and shoulders. She rode his explosive release, letting his passion carry her higher, even higher, loving the way he held her as if he were never going to let her go.

And then it was over. Joe sank back on the bed, pulling her down along with him.

Veronica could feel his heart beating, hear him breathing, feel his arms still tightly around her. She waited, hoping he would be the first to speak.

But he didn't speak. The silence stretched on and on and on, and through it, Veronica died a thousand times. He was regretting their lovemaking. He was trying to figure out a way to get out of her room with the least amount of embarrassment. He was worrying about the rest of the tour, wondering if she was going to chase after him like a lovesick fool and . . .

He sighed. And stretched. And nuzzled the side of her face. Veronica turned toward him and he met her lips in a slow, lingering kiss.

"When can we do this again?" he asked, his voice husky in the quiet. He brushed her hair back so he could see her face.

His eyes were half-closed, but she could see traces of the ever-present flame still burning.

He *didn't* regret what they'd just done. How could he, if he already wanted to know when they'd make love again? She smiled, suddenly feeling ridiculously, foolishly happy. His answering smile was sleepy, and very, *very* content.

"You gonna answer my question?" he asked. His eyes opened slightly wider for a second. "Or is that smile my answer?"

Veronica slowly trailed her fingers down his arm, watching as they followed the contours of his muscles. "Are you in any hurry to leave?" she asked.

His arms tightened around her. "Nope."

"Good."

"Yeah."

Veronica glanced up at him and saw he was watching her. He smiled again, laughing softly as she met his eyes.

"What?" she asked.

"You really want to know?"

She nodded, making a face at him. "Of course. You look at me and laugh. I should say I'd want to know what you were thinking."

"Well, I was thinking, who would've guessed that proper Ms. Veronica St. John is a real screamer in bed."

Veronica laughed, feeling her cheeks heat. "But I'm not," she protested. "I mean, I *don't* . . . I mean, I never have before. . . . Made all that . . . noise, I mean."

"I loved it," Joe said. "And I love it even more, knowing that I'm the only one who makes you do it." His words were teasing, but his eyes were serious. "It's an incredible turn-on, baby." His voice got lower, softer, more intense. "*You're* an incredible turn-on."

"You're embarrassing me," she admitted, pressing her warm cheeks against his shoulder.

"Perfect," he replied, with his wonderful, husky laugh. "I also love it when you blush."

Veronica closed her eyes. He loved what she did, he loved when she blushed. What she would have given to hear him say that he loved *her*.

"You know what would absolutely kill me?" Joe asked, his voice still low and very, very sexy.

Oh, dear Lord, she could feel him growing inside her. She felt her body respond, felt her pulse start to quicken.

"If you danced for me," Joe said, answering his own question.

Veronica closed her eyes, imagining the nuclear heat that would be generated in the room if she danced for Joe—and only for Joe. She could imagine discarding various articles of clothing until she moved in time to music clad only in the tiniest black panties and the fire from his eyes....

Veronica blushed again. Could she really dance for him that way? Without laughing or feeling foolish?

Joe hugged her tighter. "No pressure," he said quietly. "I only want you to dance for me if you want to. It's just a fantasy, that's all. I thought I'd share it with you. No big deal. Two out of three's not bad."

Veronica lifted her head. "Two out of three . . . ?"

"Fantasies that have come true," Joe said. He smiled. "The first one was making love to you. The second one was making love to you twice in the same night."

"But . . ."

Joe kissed her sweetly. Then he made his second fantasy come true.

Chapter 17

Chicago, Dallas and Houston were a blur. During the day and sometimes in the evening, Veronica sat in the surveillance van, feeding information to Joe via his earphone, praying that the man she loved wasn't about to be killed in front of her very eyes.

Joe would look into the hidden, miniaturized video cameras and smile—a sweet, hot, secret smile meant only for her.

At night, Joe came to her room. How he got out from under the watchful eyes of the FInCOM agents, Veronica never knew. How he got into her room was also a mystery. She never heard him. She would just look up, and he'd be there, smiling at her, heat in his eyes.

In Dallas, he came carrying barbecued chicken, corn on the cob, and a six-pack of beer. He was wearing jeans and T-shirt and an old baseball cap backward on his head. He wouldn't tell her where he got the food and beer, but she had the feeling he'd climbed down the outside of the building to the street below and walked a few blocks over to a restaurant.

They had a picnic on her living-room floor, and made love before they'd finished eating, right there on the rug in front of the sofa.

He always stayed until dawn, holding her close. They sometimes talked all night, sometimes slept, always woke up to make love again. But as the sun began to rise, he would vanish.

Then in Albuquerque, there was another "incident," as Joe called them. Veronica sat in the van, her heart in her throat after one of the FInCOM agents thought he saw a man with a concealed weapon in the crowd outside the TV station where "Tedric" had been interviewed.

The SEALs and the FInCOM agents had leapt into action, ready to protect Joe. They'd hustled him into the limousine and to safety, but Veronica was shaken.

She sat in her hotel room, fighting tears, praying Joe would arrive soon, praying his quicksilver smile would make her forget about the danger he was in, day in and day out, as he stood in for the real prince. But she had to remember that he was no stranger to dangerous situations. His entire life was filled with danger and risk. Even if he survived these particular assassins, it would only be a matter of time before he'd be facing some new danger, some other perhaps-even-more-deadly risk.

How could she let herself love a man who could die—violently—at any given moment?

"Yo, Ronnie."

Veronica turned around.

Joe. There he was, still dressed in his shiny white jacket and dark blue pants, his hair slicked back from his face. He looked tired, but he smiled at her, and she burst into tears.

He came across the room so quickly, she didn't see him move. Pulling her into his arms, he held her tightly.

"Hey," he said. "Hey."

Embarrassed, she tried to pull away, but he wouldn't let her go.

"I'm sorry," she said. "Joe, I'm sorry. I just . . ."

Joe lifted her chin and kissed her gently on the mouth.

"I'm all right," he told her, knowing, the way he always did, exactly what she was thinking. "I'm fine. Everything's okay."

"For right now," she said, looking up into the mysterious midnight depths of his eyes, wiping the tears from her face with the heel of her hand.

"Yeah," he said, catching a tear that hung on her eyelashes with one finger. "For right now."

"And tomorrow?" she asked. "What about tomorrow?" She knew she shouldn't say the words, but they were right on the tip of her tongue and she couldn't hold them back.

He gently ran his hand through her hair again and again as he gazed down into her eyes. "You really that worried about me?" he asked, as if he couldn't quite believe her concern.

"I was scared today," Veronica admitted. She felt her eyes well with tears again and she tried to blink them back.

"Don't be scared," Joe told her. "Blue and the other guys aren't going to let anything happen to me."

Nice words and a nice thought, but Blue and Cowboy and Harvard weren't superhuman. They were human, and there was no guarantee one of them wouldn't make a very human mistake.

Tomorrow at this time, Joe could very well be dead.

Tomorrow, or next week or next year...

Reaching up, Veronica pulled his head down and kissed him. She kissed him hard, almost savagely, and he responded instantly, pulling her against his body, lowering his hands to press her hips closer to him.

She found the buckle of his belt and started to unfasten it, and he lifted her up and carried her into the bedroom.

Veronica pulled him tightly to her and closed her eyes, trying to shut out her fears. With the touch of his hands, with his mouth and his body against hers, tomorrow didn't exist. There was only here and only now. Only ecstasy.

But when morning dawned, and Joe crept out of bed trying not to wake her, Veronica still hadn't slept. She watched him dress, then closed her eyes as he kissed her gently on the lips.

And then he was gone.

It was not beyond the realm of possibility that he could be gone forever.

Phoenix, Arizona.

The April sunshine was blazing hot, reflecting off the streets, heating the air and making it difficult to breathe.

Inside the protection of the limousine parked on the street in front of the brand-new Arizona Theatre and Center for the Arts building, Joe was cool and comfortable.

But he was glad for the sunglasses he wore. Even with them on, even with the tinted glass of the limo, Joe squinted in the brightness as he sat up to get a better look at the morning's location.

A broad set of shallow steps led to a central courtyard. It was flat and wide and surrounded by a series of marble benches placed strategically in the shade of flowering trees. The lobby of the theater was directly behind the courtyard, and the Center for the Arts offices surrounded it on the other two sides.

There was a stage in the courtyard, set up in the shade of the theater. That was where Joe—as Tedric—would go for the theater's dedication ceremony.

People were already milling around, trying to stay cool in the shade, fanning themselves with copies of the arts center's events schedule.

Joe could hear Veronica over his earphone as she sat in the surveillance van.

"Please test your microphones, Alpha Squad," she said.

Blue, Cowboy and Harvard all checked in.

"Lieutenant Catalanotto?" she said, her voice brisk and businesslike.

"Yo, Ronnie, and how are you this fine morning?" Joe said, even though he'd spent the night with her, even though he'd left her room mere hours earlier and knew *exactly* how well she was.

"A simple check would be sufficient," she murmured. "Cameras?"

Joe grinned into the miniaturized video camera that the FInCOM agent sitting across from him was carrying. God forbid someone should find out about the incredible steamy nights they spent together—the high-class media consultant and the sailor from a lousy part of New Jersey. Veronica always played it so cool in public, often addressing him as "Lieutenant Catalanotto," or "Your Majesty."

Actually, they'd never talked about whether or not she wanted their relationship to go public. Joe had just assumed she didn't, and had taken precautions to protect her.

Of course, Blue and Cowboy and Harvard knew where Joe went every night. They had to know. Without their help, it would have been too damned hard to get out from under the

FInCOM agents' eyes. But aside from the ribbing he endured when the four SEALs were alone, Joe knew his three friends would never tell a soul. They were SEALs. They knew how to keep a secret.

And as far as Joe was concerned, Veronica St. John was the best-kept secret *he'd* ever known.

She'd been upset last night. That incident in Albuquerque had really shaken her up. She'd actually *cried* because she'd been so afraid for him. For *him*. And the way she'd made love to him...as if the world were coming to an end. Oh, man. That had been powerful.

Joe had thought at first that maybe, just maybe, the impossible had happened and Veronica had fallen in love with him. Why else would she have been so upset? But even though he'd tried to bring up the subject of her concerns for his safety later in the night, she hadn't wanted to talk.

All she'd wanted was for him to hold her. And then make love to her again.

Joe smiled at the irony. He falls in love for the first time in his life, and for the first time in his life, *he's* the one who wants to talk. Yeah, it was true. He had been in bed with a gorgeous, incredibly sexy woman, and what he wanted desperately was to *talk* after they made love. But all *she* wanted was more high-energy sex.

Of course, Joe reminded himself, he sure had suffered, making Veronica happy last night. Oh, yeah. Life should *always* be so tough.

Joe closed his eyes briefly, remembering the smoothness of her skin, the softness of her breasts, the sweetness of surrounding himself in her heat, the hot pleasure in her beautiful, bluer-than-the-ocean eyes, the curve of her lips as she smiled up at him, the sound of her ragged cry as he took her with him, over the edge...

Joe opened his eyes, taking a deep breath and letting it quickly out. Oh, *yeah*. He was going out in public in about thirty seconds. Somehow he seriously doubted that old Ted would appreciate Joe pretending to be the prince with a raging and quite obvious royal hard-on for all the world to see. And he had a job to do, to boot. It was time to go.

Joe climbed from the limo and felt the sudden rush of heat. It was like opening an oven door. Welcome to Phoenix, Arizona.

As the FInCOM agents hustled him across the courtyard, Joe tried to bring himself back to the business at hand. Daydreaming about his lover was good and fine and—

Lover.

Veronica St. John was his lover.

For the past four amazing days and incredible nights, Veronica St. John had been his *lover.*

The word conjured up her mysterious smile, the devilish light in her eyes that promised pleasures the likes of which he'd never known before, the softness of her sighs, the feel of her fingers in his hair, their legs intertwined, bodies slippery with soap as they kissed in the hotel's oversize bathtub....

But...

Did she think of him as her lover? Did she ever even consider the word *love* when she thought about him?

God, what he would give to hear her say that she loved him.

Damn, he was distracted today. He forced himself to look again at the buildings. *Pay attention,* he ordered himself. *Hell of a lot of good it'll do you to realize you're in love with this woman and then get yourself killed.*

Joe looked around him. The roofs of the office buildings were lower than the theater roof. They were the perfect height and distance from the stage—perfect, that is, for a sniper to shoot from. Of course, the office windows—if they could be opened—wouldn't be a bad choice for a shooter, either.

Joe snapped instantly alert, instantly on the job.

Damn, the Arizona Theatre and Center for the Arts dedication ceremony was the ideal setup for an assassination attempt. The crowd. The TV news cameras. The three buildings, forming a square U, with the courtyard between them. The glare from the sun. The heat making everyone tired and lazy.

"This is it," Joe murmured.

"You bet, Cat," Blue's voice came over his earphone. "If I were a tango, I'd pick this one."

"What?" Veronica asked from her seat in the surveillance truck. "What was that you said?"

The FInCOM agents were hurrying Joe to the relative safety of the theater lobby. Once inside, he couldn't answer Veronica, because the governor of Arizona was shaking his hand.

"It's a real honor, Your Majesty," the governor said with his trademark big, wide, white-toothed smile. "I can't tell you how much it means to the people of Arizona to have you here, at the dedication of this very important theater and arts center."

"Dear Lord," Joe heard Veronica say over his earphone. Then there was silence. When she spoke again, her voice was deceptively calm. Joe knew damn well that her calm was only an act. "Joe, you think that the terrorists are going to be here, don't you? Today. Right now."

Joe couldn't answer. Ronnie had to know that he couldn't answer. She could see him on her video screen. He was standing in a crowd of government officials. She could hear the governor still talking.

Joe smiled at something the lieutenant governor said, but his mind was focused on the voices of his men from the Alpha Squad—and the woman—his lover—sitting inside the surveillance van.

"Damn it, Joe," Veronica said, her voice breaking and her calm cracked. "Shake your head. Yes or no. Is there going to be an assassination attempt here this afternoon?"

Inside the surveillance van, Veronica held her breath, her eyes riveted to the video monitor in front of her. Joe looked directly into the camera, his dark eyes intense—and filled with excitement. He nodded once. Yes.

Dear God. Veronica took a deep breath, trying to steady herself. As she watched, the governor of Arizona said something, and the entire group of men and women surrounding Joe laughed—Joe included.

Dear God. She'd actually seen *excitement* in Joe's eyes. He was excited because something was finally going to happen. He was ready. And willing. Willing to risk his *life* . . .

Her mouth felt dry. She tried to moisten her lips with her tongue, but it didn't help.

Dear God, don't let him die. "Joe," she said, but then couldn't speak.

He touched his ear, the sign that he had heard her.

She could hear Blue's unmistakable accent, and the voices of Cowboy and Harvard as the three men tried to outguess the assassin.

Cowboy was on the roof of the theater with high-powered binoculars and a long-range, high-powered rifle of his own. He did a visual sweep of the two lower roofs, reporting in continuously. No one was up there. No one was *still* up there.

"Windows in the offices don't open," Kevin Laughton said, from his seat next to Veronica. "Repeat, windows do *not* open."

"I'm watching 'em anyway," Cowboy said.

"You're wasting time," Laughton said. "And manpower. We could use you down in the crowd."

"The hell I'm wasting time," Cowboy muttered. "And if you think this shooter's going to be standing in the crowd, you're dumber than the average Fink."

On-screen, Joe was still talking to the governor and his aides. "The theater and these arts buildings are very beautiful," he said. "All these windows—it's quite impressive, really. Do they open?"

"The windows?" the governor asked. "Oh, no. No, these buildings are all climate controlled, of course."

"Ah," Joe said in Tedric's funny accent. "So if someone inside absolutely needed some fresh air, they'd have to have a glass cutter, yes?"

The governor looked slightly taken aback, but then he laughed. "Well, yes," he said. "I suppose so."

"Roger that, Mr. Cat," Cowboy said. "My thoughts exactly. Court-martial me if you have to, FInCOM, but I'm watching those windows."

"Okay," Veronica heard Blue say. "They're coming out to the stage. Let's be ready. You, too, Cat."

"Shall we go to the stage?" the governor asked Joe.

Joe nodded. "I'm ready," he said with a smile.

He was so calm. He was walking out there to be a target, and he was *smiling*. Veronica could barely breathe.

Two of the FInCOM agents opened the doors that led to the courtyard. Outside, a band began to play.

"Joe," Veronica said again. Dear Lord, if she didn't tell him now, she might never get another chance. . . .

He touched his ear again. He heard her.

"Joe, I have to tell you . . . I love you."

Joe stepped outside into the sunshine, and the heat and brightness exploded around him. But it wasn't all from the sun. In fact, most of it was coming from inside him, from the center of his chest, from his very heart.

She loved him. Ronnie *loved* him.

He laughed. Ronnie loved *him*. And she'd just announced it to everyone who was working on this operation.

"Hell, Ronnie, don't go telling him that *now*," Blue's scolding voice sounded over Joe's earphone. "Cat's gotta concentrate. Come on, Joe, keep your eyes open."

"I'm sorry," Veronica said. She sounded so small, so lost.

Joe touched his ear, trying to tell her that he'd heard her, wishing there was a way he could say he loved her, too. He touched his chest, his heart, with one hand, hoping that she'd see and understand his silent message.

And then he climbed the stairs to the stage.

"Come on, Cat," Blue's voice said. "Stop grinning like a damn fool and get to work."

Work.

His training clicked in, and Joe was instantly focused. Damn, with this warm sensation in his heart, he was better than focused. Veronica loved him, and he was damn near superhuman.

He checked the stage to make sure the cover zones were where FInCOM had said they would be.

The podium was reinforced, and it would act as a shield—provided, of course, that the shooter didn't have armor-piercing bullets. Down behind the back of the stage was also shielded. There was a flimsy metal railing to keep people from falling off the platform, but that could be jumped over easily. The stage was only about eight feet from the ground.

Joe scanned the crowd. About six hundred people. Five different TV cameras, some of them rolling live for the twelve o'clock news. He knew with an uncanny certainty that the assassin wouldn't fire until he stepped up to the podium.

"Roof is *still* clear," Cowboy announced. "No movement at the windows. Shoot, FInCOM, maybe you better keep watching that crowd. I got nothing yet."

Joe sat in a folding chair as the governor approached the podium.

"We're going to make this dedication ceremony as quick as possible," the governor said, "so we can get inside that air-conditioned lobby and have some lemonade."

The crowd applauded.

Veronica's heart was in her throat. Joe was sitting there, just *sitting* there, as if there weren't any threat to his life.

"Without further ado," the governor continued, "I'd like to introduce our special guest, Crown Prince Tedric of Ustanzia."

The sound of the crowd's applause masked the continuous comments of the SEALs and the FInCOM agents. On Veronica's video screen, Joe stood, raising both hands to quiet the crowd.

"Thank you," he said into the microphone. "Thank you very much. It's an honor to be here today."

"I still got zip on either roof," Cowboy said. "No movement near the windows, either. I'm starting to think these tangos don't know a good setup when they see—"

A shot rang out.

One of the big glass windows in the front of the theater shattered into a million pieces.

The crowd screamed and scattered.

"Joe!" Veronica gripped the table in front of her, leaning closer to the screen, praying harder than she'd ever prayed in her life.

He was gone, she couldn't see him. Had he ducked behind the podium, or fallen, struck by the bullet?

On her headphones, she could hear all three SEALs reporting in, all talking at once. The roofs were still clear, no shooter visible at the windows.

Beside her, Kevin Laughton had rocketed out of his seat. "What do you mean, you don't know where that came from?" he was shouting over the chaos. "A shot was fired—it had to come from *some*where!"

"Do we need an ambulance?" another voice asked. "Repeat, is medical assistance needed?"

Another shot, another broken window.

"God damn," Laughton said. "Where the *hell* is he shooting from?"

Joe heard the second shot, felt the impact of the bullet as it hit the stage, and knew. The assassin was *behind* him. Inside the theater. And with all of the shielding facing out, away from the theater, Joe was a damn sitting duck. It was amazing he was still alive. That second shot should have killed him.

It should have, but it hadn't. The son of a bitch had missed.

Joe dove off the stage headfirst, gun drawn, shouting instructions to his men and to the FInCOM agents who were surrounding him. Cowboy was on the roof of the theater, for God's sake. They could cut the shooter off, nail the bastard.

Inside the surveillance van, the video monitors went blank. Power was gone. Lord, what was happening out there? Veronica had heard Joe's voice. He was alive, thank God. He hadn't been killed. Yet.

The gunman was inside the theater. Upper balcony, above the lobby, came the reports. The back door was surrounded, they had the assassin cornered.

Veronica stood, pushing past Kevin Laughton and opening the door of the van. She could see the theater, see the two shattered windows. She could see the FInCOM agents crouched near the front of the theater. She could see three figures, scaling the outside of the theater, climbing up to the roof.

God in heaven, it was Joe and two of his SEALs.

Veronica lowered her mouthpiece into place. She hadn't wanted to speak before this, afraid she'd only add to the confusion, but this . . .

"Joe, what are you doing?" she said into the microphone. "You're the *target!* You're supposed to get to safety!"

"We need radio silence," Blue's voice commanded. "Right now. Except for reports of tango's location."

"Joe!" Veronica cried.

One of the FInCOM agents leaned out the van door. "I can't cut this line," he said to Veronica, "so unless you're quiet, I'm going to have to take your headset."

Veronica shut her mouth, watching as a tiny figure—Cowboy—helped Joe and the rest of his team up onto the theater roof.

Up on the roof, Joe looked around. There was one door, leading to stairs that would take them down.

You all right? Cowboy hand-signaled to Joe.

Fine, he signaled back.

The gunman surely had a radio, and was probably monitoring their spoken conversation. From this point on, the SEALs would communicate only with hand signals and sign language. No use tipping the gunman off by letting him know they were coming.

Harvard had an extra HK submachine gun, and he handed it to Joe with a tight smile.

Another shot rang out.

"Agent down," came West's voice over Joe's earphone. "Oh, man, we need a medic!"

"T's location stable," said another voice. "Holding steady in the lobby balcony."

"Get that injured man out of the line of fire," Laughton commanded.

"He's dead," West reported, his normally dispassionate voice shaken. "Freeman's dead. The bastard plugged him through the eye. The sonuvabitch—"

Let's go, Joe signaled to his men. *I'm on point.*

Blue gestured to himself. He wanted to lead the way instead. But Joe shook his head.

Soundlessly he opened the door and started down the stairs.

Another shot.

More chaos. Another agent was hit with unerring accuracy.

"Stay down," Laughton ordered his men. "This guy's a sharpshooter and he's here for the long haul. Let's get our own shooters in position."

Silently, with deadly stealth, fingers on the triggers of their submachine guns, the SEALs moved down the stairs.

Veronica paced. She hadn't heard Joe's voice in many long minutes. She could no longer see any movement on the roof.

"One of the cameras is back on," someone said from inside the surveillance van, and she went back in to see.

Sure enough, the video camera that had been dropped and left on the stage had come back to life. It now showed a sideways and somewhat foggy picture of the theater lobby. Behind the reflections in the remaining glass windows, Veronica could see the shadowy shape of the assassin on the upper balcony.

It was quiet. No one was moving. No one was talking. Then . . .

"FInCOM shooters, hold your fire." It was Joe's voice, loud and clear, over the radio.

Veronica felt herself sway, and she groped for her seat. Joe and his SEALs were somewhere near the gunman—in range of the FInCOM agent's guns. Please, God, keep him safe, she prayed.

A door burst open. She heard it more than she saw it on the shadowy video screen.

The gunman turned, firing a machine gun rather than his rifle. But there was no one there.

Another door opened, on the other side of the balcony, but the gunman had already moved. Using some sort of rope, he swung himself over the edge and down to the first floor.

Veronica saw Joe before the gunman did.

He was standing in the lobby, gun aimed at the man scurrying down the rope. She knew it was Joe from his gleaming white jacket. The three other SEALs were dressed in dull brown.

"Hold it right there, pal," she heard Joe say over her headphones. "We can end this game one of two ways. We can either take you out of here in a body bag, or you can drop your weapons right now and we'll all live to see tomorrow."

The gunman was frozen, unmoving, halfway down the rope as he stared at Joe.

Then he moved. But he didn't drop his gun, he brought it up, fast, aimed directly toward Joe's head.

The sound of gunfire over the radio was deafening.

The gunman jumped to the ground—or did he fall? Who had been hit? And where was Joe . . . ?

"Joe!" Veronica couldn't keep silent another second as she leaned closer to the blurry screen.

"Do you need medical assistance?" a voice asked over the headphones.

"Alpha Squad, check in," Blue's voice ordered. "McCoy."

"Becker."

"Jones."

"Catalanotto," Joe's familiar, husky voice said. "We're all clear. No need of a medic, FInCOM."

Veronica closed her eyes and rested her head on her arms on the tabletop.

"This stupid sonuvabitch just made himself a martyr for the cause," Joe's voice said into her ear.

Joe was alive. It was all over, and Joe was alive.

This time.

Chapter 18

It was after nine o'clock in the evening—twenty-one hundred hours—before Veronica's phone rang.

She'd been busy all afternoon and evening with meetings and debriefings. She'd worked with Ambassador Freder and Senator McKinley, scheduling the remainder of Prince Tedric's tour. A report had come in from FInCOM that made them all breathe easier. The assassin had been ID'd as Salustiano Vargas—Diosdado's former right-hand man. *Former.* Apparently the two terrorists had parted ways, and Vargas was no longer connected with the Cloud of Death. He had been acting on his own. Why? No one seemed to know. At least not yet. At any rate, Vargas was dead. *He'd* be giving them no answers.

But now that the assassin was no longer a threat, the ambassador and senator wanted to get the tour back on track. Tedric was flying in from the District of Columbia. He would meet them all in Seattle in the morning, where they would board a cruise ship to Alaska. They would finish the tour with a flourish.

Security would return to near normal. Two or three FInCOM agents would remain, but everyone else, including the SEALs—including Joe—would go home.

At dinnertime, Veronica had searched for Joe, but was told he was in high-level security debriefings. She returned to her room to pack, but couldn't stop thinking. *What if he didn't get finished before morning?* Sometimes those meetings went on all night. What if she didn't see him before she had to leave...?

But then, at nine o'clock, the phone rang. Veronica closed her eyes, then picked it up. "Hello?"

"Yo, Ronnie."

"Joe." *Where are you? When will you be here?* She clamped her mouth tightly shut over those words. She didn't own him. She may have given her feelings away this morning when she'd told him—and the entire world—that she loved him, but she could stake no claim on his time or his life.

"Have you had dinner yet?" he asked.

"No, I was..." *Waiting for you.* "I wasn't hungry."

"Think you'll be hungry in about twenty minutes?" he asked.

"Hungry for what?" She tried to make her voice sound light, teasing, but her heart felt heavy. No matter how she approached this relationship, the conclusion she kept coming to was that it wasn't going to work out. Tomorrow they were both heading in different directions, and that would be it. All that was left was tonight. She'd been so worried earlier that she wasn't going to get to spend this final night with Joe. But now she couldn't help but think that it might be easier to simply say goodbye over the phone.

"Ow," he said, laughter in his voice. "You kill me, lady. But I meant are you hungry for *food.* Like, you and me—the real me, no disguises—going out somewhere for dinner." He paused. "In public. Like to a restaurant." He paused again, then laughed. "God, am I smooth, or what? I'm trying to ask you out to dinner, Ron. What do ya say?"

He didn't give her time to answer. "I'm still downtown," he continued, "but I can catch a cab and make it up to the hotel in about fifteen or twenty minutes. Wear that black dress, okay? We'll go up to Camelback Mountain. Mac says there's a great restaurant at the resort there. There's a band and dancing, and a terrific view of the city."

"But—"

"Oh, *yes*. There's a cab pulling up, right outside. Gotta run, babe. Get dressed—I'll be right there."

"But I don't want to go out. It's our last night—maybe forever—and I want to spend it alone with you," Veronica said to the dead phone line.

She slowly hung up the phone.

She had one more night with Joe. One more night to last the rest of her life. One more night to burn her imprint permanently into his memory.

Hmm.

Veronica picked up the phone and dialed room service. Joe wanted dinner and dancing and a view of the city? The view from this room wasn't too shabby. And the four-star restaurant in this hotel delivered food to the rooms. As for dancing...

Holding the telephone in one hand, Veronica crossed to the stereo that was attached to the entertainment center. Yes, there was a tape deck. She smiled.

For the first time, Joe actually knocked on her door rather than picking the lock and letting himself in.

With the long skirt of her black silk dress shushing about her legs, Veronica crossed to the hotel-room door and flung it open and herself into his arms. "Lord, I've waited all day to do this," she said. "You scared me to death this morning."

Having his arms around her felt so good. And when his lips met hers, she felt herself start to melt and she wrapped her own arms more tightly around his neck. Her fingers laced through his hair and—

Veronica pulled back.

His long hair was gone. Joe had cut his hair. Short. *Really* short. She looked at him, really *looked* at him for the first time since she'd opened her hotel-suite door. He was wearing a naval dress uniform. It was dark blue with rows and rows and *rows* of medals and ribbons on his left breast. He wore a white hat on his head, and he took it off, holding it almost awkwardly in his hands. His dark eyes were slightly sheepish as he watched her take in his haircut. His hair had been buzz cut around his ears and at the back. The top and front were slightly longer—just long enough so that a lock of dark hair fell forward over his forehead.

He smiled ruefully. "The barber went a little overboard," he said. "I don't usually wear it quite this short and..." He closed his eyes, shaking his head. "Damn, you hate it."

Veronica touched his arm, shaking her own head. "No," she said. "No, I don't *hate* it...." But she didn't like it, either. Not that he looked bad. In fact, he didn't. If anything, his short cut made his lean face more handsome than ever. But it also made him look harder, tougher, unforgiving—dangerous on an entirely new level. He looked like exactly what he was—a highly trained, highly competent special-forces officer. She couldn't help but be reminded that he was a man who risked his life as a matter of course. And *that* was what Veronica didn't like. "It suits you," she told him.

He searched her eyes, and whatever he saw there seemed to satisfy him. "Good."

"You look...wonderful," Veronica said honestly.

"So do you." His eyes flared with that familiar heat as he ran them down and then back up her body.

"This is the way I thought you were going to look—before we met," she said.

A brief shadow flickered across his face. "Yeah, well, I guess I oughta tell you, I can count on my fingers and toes the times I've worn this dress uniform. What you saw when we met is closer to the truth. I usually wear fatigues or jeans. And if I've been working with engines, they're usually covered with grease or dirt."

Why was he telling her this? It seemed almost like a warning. He seemed so serious, Veronica felt compelled to make things lighter. "Are you saying this because you want me to do your laundry?" she teased.

Joe gave her one of his quicksilver grins. Yes, seeing him smile that way, his teeth so very white against his lean, tanned face, Veronica could say that this new haircut definitely suited him. "You *want* to do my laundry?" he countered.

The casual question suddenly seemed to carry more meaning, as Joe watched her intently. His dark eyes were sharp, almost piercing as he waited for an answer.

Veronica laughed, trying to hide her sudden nervousness. Why were they talking about *laundry?* "I don't do my *own* laundry," she said with a shrug. "When do I have time?"

She stepped back, opening the door wider to let him in. "We're standing in the hall," she added. "Won't you come in?"

Joe hesitated. "Maybe we should just go...."

She smiled. "Think if you come inside we'll never leave?"

He touched the side of her face. "I don't just think it, baby, I *know* it."

She kissed the palm of his hand. "Would that be so terrible?" she whispered, gazing up into the midnight depths of his eyes.

"No." He stepped inside the room, closing the door behind him.

Veronica was nervous. Joe could see that she was nervous as she moved out of his grasp and into the room and—

The table was set and covered with a very grand-looking room-service dinner. And the rest of the room... Veronica had pushed all the furniture out of the center of the living room.

She'd done that before. Back in D.C. Back when he'd climbed up to the balcony and gone in her sliding-glass door and...

Joe looked up to find her watching him. She moistened her lips nervously and smiled. "Dinner and dancing," she explained. "I made room, so that we could dance."

"We?"

Veronica blushed, but she held his gaze. "So I can dance for you," she correctly herself softly. "Although, at some point you *will* dance with me, too. But maybe we should have dinner first."

The fragrant smell of gourmet food filled the air. Joe knew that he hadn't eaten since lunchtime. He also knew that dinner was the very last thing he wanted right now. Veronica was going to dance for him. She was going to dance the way he'd seen her dance when he'd climbed up to her room. Only this time, she would know right from the start that he was watching. "Maybe we should have dinner later," he said huskily.

As he watched, she crossed to the window and closed the curtains. God, his heart was pounding as if he'd just run a three-minute mile. He could feel his blood surging hotly through his veins with each pulsing beat. She was really going to do this. She knew he wanted her to—he'd asked her to dance for him. But he'd never thought she'd actually do it. He thought he'd asked for too much.

Veronica smiled at him as she crossed back to the dinner table and took a bottle of beer from a small bottle cooler. She opened it, poured it into a glass and carried it to him.

"Thanks," Joe said as she handed him both the glass and the bottle.

"Why don't you sit down?" Veronica murmured, and with a whisper of silk, she moved back to the other side of the room.

Sit down. Yeah, right. Sit down. As Joe lowered himself into a chair, Veronica crossed to the stereo and slipped a tape into the deck.

Joe knew what her dancing meant to her. She'd told him that it was private and intensely personal. It was a way to let off steam, to unwind, to really relax. And she was going to share it with him now. She was going to let her personal, private pleasure become *his* pleasure.

The fire that was shooting through his veins reached his heart and exploded. Veronica St. John had told him she loved him today. And tonight, by sharing herself with him this way, she was showing him just how much.

The music started—softly, slowly—and Ronnie stood in the middle of the room, head back, eyes closed, arms at her sides. God, she was beautiful. And she was his. All his. Forever, if he had anything to say about it. And he did. He had a lot to say about it. Hell, he could write a book on the subject.

The music changed with a sudden burst of volume, and Veronica brought her hands up sharply, into the air.

And then she began to move.

She was graceful, fluid, and her dress seemed an extension of her body, moving with her. Her eyes were still closed, but then she opened them and looked directly at Joe.

She blushed, and his heart burned even hotter. She was such a contradiction. The slightest thing could make her blush—until passion overcame her. And when that happened, she was amazingly uninhibited. Joe had never had a lover like Veronica St. John. One moment she was seemingly prim and proper, and the next she was wild, giving him pleasure in ways he'd only dreamed of, and telling him—quite specifically, in no uncertain terms—exactly what he could and should do to please her.

As Joe watched, Veronica closed her eyes again, and again the music changed, the rhythm getting stronger, faster, more insistent. Her dancing, too, became less careful, less contained. Her movements were freer, broader, more powerful.

More passionate.

She reached up with both hands and with one swift motion, removed the pins that were holding her hair. It tumbled down around her shoulders, an avalanche of red gold curls.

Joe's mouth was dry, and he took a sip of the beer she'd given him.

Veronica kicked off her high heels, and, as Joe watched, she *became* the music. She moved to the funky, bluesy instrumental piece, visually capturing every nuance, every musical phrase with her body.

Her body.

They hadn't been lovers for long, but Joe already knew every inch of Veronica's beautiful body intimately. But seeing her body in motion this way was an entirely new experience. Her dress barely restrained her breasts and they moved with and against the forces of gravity. The black silk slid across her abdomen and thighs, allowing glimpses of the firm muscles and flesh underneath when occasionally it clung for a second or two.

Veronica made a twisting, writhing motion that was pure sex, pure abandon.

The long skirt of her dress was no longer moving with her— it was getting in her way.

This time when she opened her eyes and looked at Joe, she didn't blush. She smiled—a sweet, hot, sexy smile—and reached behind her for the zipper of her dress. In less than a heartbeat, the dress pooled around her feet, and she was naked—save for a pair of black silk panties. She kicked the dress aside, still dancing, still moving and spinning.

A thong. She was wearing thong panties, black silk against her skin so creamy and white.

And still she danced.

For him.

I've died, Joe thought, *and gone to heaven.*

She moved closer to him, smiling at the look he knew damn well was on his face. He was hypnotized. Stupefied. Totally overcome. And extremely aroused.

Still moving, she held out her hands to him. "Dance with me."

It was not an invitation he needed to hear twice. He set his beer on the nearest end table and rose to his feet. And then, God, she was in his arms, moving with him and against him to that bluesy melody.

Her skin was so smooth, so silky beneath his hands. He touched her everywhere. Her softly rounded bottom, her full breasts, her flat stomach, her long, willowy arms. He was still in his uniform and she was nearly naked, and he had never, *never* been so turned on in his entire life. They were dancing so close, their legs were intertwined. He could feel the heat between her legs against his thigh. She could surely feel his arousal—she pressed against him, her slow, sexy movement driving him crazy, and the sight of her, nearly naked in his arms, making him throb with need.

"Ronnie..."

Somehow she knew that he'd had nearly all he could take. She lifted her mouth to his and kissed him. Joe heard himself groan. He couldn't get enough of her.

He felt her fingers unbuckling his belt and swiftly unfastening his pants. And then he was in her hands. It was good, but it wasn't good enough.

"Ronnie, I need—"

"I know."

She covered him with a condom she'd procured from God-knew-where, and slipped out of her panties as she kissed him again.

"Lift me up," Veronica murmured.

"Yes," he breathed. She wrapped her arms around his neck and her legs around his waist as he ensheathed himself in her wonderful, smooth heat. "Oh, baby..."

She moved on top of him, against him, with him. She was in his arms, in his heart, in his very soul. This passionate, fiery woman, who could be blazing hot one moment and gently sweet the next, this woman with the sharp sense of humor and quiet touch that hid a will of steel—a will that was ruled by the kindest heart he'd ever known—this was the one woman he'd been waiting for all his life. All the love he'd made, all the women he'd known before, had meant nothing to him. No one had moved him. No one had even come close to holding him. He'd always been able to close the door and walk away from a woman without looking back.

But there was no way he'd ever be able to walk away from Veronica. Not without leaving his heart behind—ripped from his chest.

He clung to her, holding her as tightly as she held him, plunging himself deeply into her again and again.

He loved her. He wanted to tell her, but the words—those three simple little words—didn't come easily. The truth was, saying them scared him to death. Now, wasn't that funny? He was a SEAL. He'd faced platoons of enemy soldiers, he'd looked death in the teeth without batting an eye more times than he could count, yet the thought of uttering one very simple sentence made him sweat.

Ronnie's fingers were in his hair. Her mouth was covering his face and lips with kisses.

"Joe," she breathed, "Joe. I want more—" He moved, backing her up against the wall to anchor her in place, and she tipped back her head. "Yes . . ."

Her release was incredible. She cried out as he drove himself into her, giving her all she'd asked for. Her arms tightened around his neck, her fingers clutched him.

"I love you," Veronica cried. "Oh, Joe, I love you!"

Her words pushed him over the edge. She loved him. She really did. He exploded in a blinding white burst of pleasure so exquisite, so pure that the world seem to disintegrate around him.

Baby, I love you, too.

Chapter 19

Joe slowly became aware of his surroundings.

Ronnie's head was resting on his shoulder, her breath warm against his neck. His own forehead leaned against the wall. And his knees were damned shaky.

He could feel Veronica's heart beating, hear her soft sigh.

He didn't want to move. He'd never made love quite like this in his life, and he didn't want it to end. Of course, it had ended, but as long as they stayed right here, in this same position, these remarkable feelings could linger on.

It was, needless to say, incredibly exhilarating. His future looked so different, so much brighter, with Ronnie in the picture. For the first time in his life, Joe found himself actually considering the possibility of having children. Not for a good long time, of course. He wanted Ronnie all to himself for years and years and *years*. But down the road, making a baby, creating a new life would be exciting in a way he'd never imagined before. Fifty percent him and fifty percent her, with two hundred percent of their love...

The jeweler's box he carried in his pocket dug into his ribs and Joe had to laugh. He hadn't even asked Ronnie to marry him yet, and here he was, practically naming their kids.

"You didn't have to say that, you know," she whispered.

She lifted her head and lowered herself to the floor. The spell was broken. Or was it? Joe still felt an incredible warmth in his chest. He used to think it felt like a noose, he realized, but now it was a good feeling, a warmth surrounding his heart, giving him an amazing sense of peace and belonging.

"Didn't have to say what?" he asked.

Veronica moved away from him slightly, giving him room to adjust his clothes. She was still naked, but she seemed unaware of that as she gazed at him, concern darkening her blue eyes.

"You didn't have to say that you love me, too," she said.

Joe froze, hands stilled on the buckle of his belt. Had he actually spoken those words out loud?

"I'd rather that you be honest with me," she continued. "Don't say things you don't mean. Please?"

Veronica turned away, unable to continue looking into Joe's eyes, unable to keep up the brave front. But, bloody hell, here she'd just spoken of being honest.... "The truth is, Joe," she said, her voice shaking slightly, "I'm going to miss you terribly when you're gone, and—"

Joe drew her into his arms, moving with her so they sat on the sofa, Veronica on his lap. "Who says I'm going anywhere?" he asked softly, smoothing her hair back from her face and kissing her gently on the lips.

Veronica felt her eyes fill with tears. Damn! She blinked them back. "Tomorrow I'm flying to Seattle and you're—"

He interrupted her with another gentle kiss. "And who says when I said...what I said, that I wasn't being honest?" He ran his free hand down the curve of her hip and back up again, then cupped her breast. It was impossible not to touch her.

"You love me." Her disbelief was evident in her voice.

"Is that really so hard to believe?"

Veronica touched the side of his face. "You're so sweet," she said. At the mock flare of indignation in his eyes, she added quickly, "I know you don't think so, but you *are.* You're incredibly *kind,* Joe. And I know you have...feelings for me, but you don't have to pretend that they're more than—" She stared down in silence at the small black velvet box Joe pulled from his pocket and held out to her. "What's this?"

"Open it," he said. His face looked so serious, so hard. His eyes were so intense.

"I'm afraid to."

Joe smiled, and it softened his face. "It's not a grenade," he said. "Just open it, Ron, will ya?"

Slowly, she took it from him. It was small and square and black and furry. It looked an awful lot like a jeweler's box. What was he giving her? She couldn't even begin to imagine the possibilities. Her heart was pounding, she realized. She took a deep breath to steady herself. Then, gazing into Joe's beautiful eyes, looking for some sort of clue as to what was inside, she opened the box.

She glanced down and her heart stopped. It was a ring. It was an enormous, beautiful, glittering diamond ring.

"Marry me," Joe said huskily.

"Dear Lord!" Veronica breathed.

As she stared up into his eyes, her expression of shock made Joe smile. "I guess you weren't expecting this, huh?"

She shook her head.

"Neither was I," he told her honestly. "But that ring's not pretend, Ronnie. And neither is what I feel. I...you know...love you—" God, he'd said it and he wasn't struck by lightning. "And I want to make this thing we have permanent. You follow?"

She was silent. Her eyes were as large as dinner plates as she gazed at him. She was still naked, and he couldn't have kept from touching her, from stroking her soft skin, if his life depended on it. She was lovely, and he was already uncomfortably aroused again. God, he'd just had the best sex of his life, and already he wanted her again. He couldn't get enough of her. He never would.

But why wouldn't she answer? Why wouldn't she tell him that she wanted to marry him, too?

"Say something, baby." Joe tried to disguise his insecurity, but knew that he'd failed miserably. It showed in his eyes, in his voice. "The suspense is killing me. Tell me what you think. Good idea? Bad idea? Have I gone crazy, here?"

Veronica was dumbfounded. Joe Catalanotto—Lt. Joe Catalanotto of the U.S. Navy SEALs—wanted to *marry* her. He'd meant it when he'd said that he loved her. He loved her.

He *loved* her, and dear Lord, she should be ecstatic. She should be hearing wedding bells and picturing herself in a gorgeous white wedding dress, walking down the aisle of a church to meet this man at the altar. The one man that she truly loved.

But she couldn't picture herself at a wedding. She could only see herself at a funeral. *Joe's* funeral.

"When . . ." she started, then cleared her throat. She shivered slightly, suddenly aware of the chill of the air-conditioning against her bare skin. Joe ran his hand up and down her arm, trying to warm her. "When are you planning to retire?"

He stared at her blankly. "What?"

"From the SEALs," she explained. "When are you going to retire from active duty?"

Veronica could see that he didn't get how this pertained to his wedding proposal, but he shrugged and answered her anyway. "Not for a long time," he said. "I don't know. Not for another fifteen years. Twenty if I can manage it."

Her heart sank. Fifteen or twenty years. Two decades of watching the man she loved leave on countless high-risk missions. Two decades of not knowing whether or not he would return. Two decades of sheer *hell*. If he lived that long . . .

"I'm career navy, Ronnie," Joe said quietly. "I know I'm no prince, but I *am* an officer and—"

"You *are* a prince." Veronica kissed him swiftly on the lips. "I've never met anyone even half as princely as you are."

He was embarrassed. So of course, he tried to turn it into a joke. "Well, damn," he said. "All the naked women tell me that whenever I get them on my lap."

Veronica had to smile. "I *am* naked," she said. "Aren't I?"

"I noticed," he said, lightly touching her breast.

"Do you want me to put on some clothes?"

"I was thinking more along the lines that I should get rid of mine," Joe murmured, bringing his lips to where his hand had just been. But he only kissed her gently before lifting his head again. "Try it on."

The ring. He meant the ring.

She knew she shouldn't. She had no idea what her answer was going to be. She was so utterly, totally torn.

Still, Veronica took the ring from the box and slipped it onto her left hand. It was a little bit too large.

"Say the word, and we can get it sized," Joe said. "Or, if you want, you can pick out something different...."

Veronica looked at the ring's simple, elegant setting through a haze of tears. "This is so beautiful," she said. "I wouldn't want anything else."

"When I saw it," Joe said quietly, "I knew it belonged to you." He lifted her chin up toward him. "Hey. Hey, are you crying?"

Veronica nodded her head, yes, and he drew her even closer to him. He pulled her mouth to his and kissed her sweetly. She wanted so very much to tell him, "Yes, I'll marry you." But she wanted to go to bed every night with him beside her. And she wanted to wake up every morning knowing that he was going to be there again the next night. She didn't want a Navy SEAL, she wanted a regular, normal man.

But maybe if she asked, he'd leave the SEALs. Lord knows, he could do damn near anything, get any kind of job he wanted. He was an expert in so many different fields. He could work as a translator. Or he could work as a mechanic, she didn't care. Let him get covered with engine grease every day. She'd learn to do the bloody laundry if that's what it took. She just wanted to know that he would be safe. And alive.

But Veronica knew she couldn't ask him to leave the SEALs. And even if she *did* ask him, she knew that he wouldn't quit. Not for her. Not for anything. She'd seen him at work. He loved the risk, lived for the danger.

"Please, Joe," she whispered. "Make love to me again."

He stood, holding her in his arms, and carried her into the bedroom.

Veronica wanted desperately to marry Joe. But Joe was already married—to the Navy SEALs.

As Veronica slept, curled up next to him in the bed, Joe stared at the ceiling.

She hadn't said yes.

He'd asked her to marry him, and she'd asked him a bunch of questions in return, but she hadn't said yes.

She hadn't said no, either. But she'd taken off the ring and put it back in the box. She gave him some excuse about how she was afraid it was going to fall off. She was afraid she was going to lose it.

But if Ronnie had given *him* any kind of ring that meant that she wanted him forever, that she loved him "till death do us part," Joe would damn sure be wearing it, regardless of the size.

It was entirely possible that he was heading full steam ahead into an emotional train wreck. It was entirely possible that although Veronica had said that she loved him, she didn't love him enough to want "forever." Hell, it was entirely possible that although she had said she loved him, she didn't love him at all.

But no. He had to believe that she loved him. He'd seen it in her eyes, felt it in her touch. She *did* love him. The sixty-four-thousand-dollar question was, how much?

Across the room, from the chair where he'd thrown his clothes, his pocket pager shrilled.

Joe extracted himself from the bed, trying not to wake Veronica, but as he moved swiftly across the room, she stirred and sat up.

"What was *that?*" she asked.

"My pager," he said. "I'm sorry. I've got to make a phone call."

Veronica leaned forward and snapped on the light, squinting at him in the sudden brightness. As she watched, he sat back down on the edge of the bed, running his fingers through his short hair before he picked up the telephone. He quickly dialed—a number he had memorized.

"Yeah," he said into the phone. "Catalanotto." There was a pause. "I'm still in Phoenix." Another pause. "Yeah. Yeah, I understand." He glanced back at Veronica, his face serious. "Give me three minutes, and I'll call right back." Another pause. He smiled. "Right. Thanks."

He dropped the receiver into the cradle and faced Veronica.

"I can get a week's leave, if I want it," he said bluntly. "But I need to know right now if I should take it. And I don't want to take it if you can't spend the time with me. Do you know what I'm saying?"

Veronica glanced at the clock. "You get called at four-thirty in the morning about whether or not you want *leave?*" she asked in dismay.

Joe shook his head. "No," he replied. "I get called and ordered to report to the base at Little Creek. There's some kind of emergency. They're calling in all of SEAL Team Ten, including the Alpha Squad."

Veronica felt faint. "What kind of emergency?"

"I don't know," he said. "But even if I *did* know, I couldn't say."

"If we were married, could you tell me?"

Joe smiled ruefully. "No, baby. Not even then."

"So you just pack up and leave," Veronica said tightly, "and maybe you'll come back?"

He reached for her. "I'll always come back. You gotta believe that."

She sat up, moving out of reach, keeping her back to him so that he couldn't see the look on her face. This was her worst nightmare, coming true. This was what she didn't want to spend the next twenty years doing. This fear, this emptiness was exactly what she didn't want to spend the next two decades feeling.

"I either have to officially take leave, or go check in with the rest of the team. What do you think?" he asked again. "Can you get time off, too?"

Veronica shook her head. "No." Funny, her voice sounded so cool and in control. "No, I'm sorry, but I have to be on the cruise ship with Prince Tedric, starting tomorrow."

She could feel his eyes on the back of her head. She sensed his hesitation before he turned back to the telephone.

He picked it up and dialed. "Yeah, it's Joe Cat again. I'm in."

Veronica closed her eyes. He was in. But in for what? Something that was going to get him killed? She couldn't stand it. Not knowing where he was going, what he'd be doing, was awful. She wanted to *scream....*

"Right," he said into the phone. "I'll be ready."

He hung up the phone, and she felt the mattress shift as he stood.

"I have to take a quick shower," he said. "There's a car coming in ten minutes."

Veronica spun around to face him. "Ten *minutes!*"

"That's how it works, Ronnie. I get a call, I have to leave. Right away. Sometimes we get preparation time, but usually not. Let me take a shower—we can talk while I'm getting dressed."

Veronica felt numb. This wasn't her worst nightmare. This fear she felt deep in her stomach was beyond anything she'd ever imagined. She wanted to tell him, *beg* him to take the leave. She would quit her job if she had to. She would do anything, *any*thing to keep him from going on that unnamed, unidentified, probably deadly emergency mission.

And then what? she wondered as she heard the sound of the shower. She stood and slipped into her robe, suddenly feeling terribly chilled. She would lose her job, her reputation, her *pride*, for one measly week of Joe's company. But after that week of leave was up, he would be gone. He'd go where duty called, when duty called, no matter the danger or risk. Sooner or later it would happen. Sooner or later—and probably sooner—he was going to kiss her goodbye, leaving her with her heart in her throat. He would leave her alone, watching the clock, waiting, praying for him to return. Alive. And he wouldn't come back.

Veronica couldn't stand it. She wouldn't be able to stand it.

The water shut off, and several moments later Joe came out of the bathroom, toweling himself dry. She watched silently as he slipped on his briefs and then his pants.

"So," he said, rubbing his hair with the towel one last time, glancing over at her. "Tell me when you'll be done with the Ustanzian tour. I'll try to arrange leave."

"It won't be for another two or three weeks," Veronica said. "After the cruise, we'll be heading back to D.C., and then to Ustanzia from there. By then, Wila will have had the baby, and—" She broke off, turning away from him. Why were they having this seemingly normal-sounding conversation, when every cell in her body was screaming for her to hold him—hold him and never let go? But she couldn't hold him. A car was coming in five minutes to take him away, maybe forever.

"Okay," Joe was saying. She could hear him slipping his arms into his jacket and buttoning it closed. "What do you say I meet you in Ustanzia? Just let me know the exact dates and—"

Veronica shook her head. "I don't think that's a good idea."

"Okay," he said again, very quietly. "What *is* a good idea, Ronnie? You tell me."

He wasn't moving now. Veronica knew even without looking that he was standing there, his lean face unsmiling, his dark eyes intense as he watched her, waiting for her to move, to speak, to do something, *any*thing.

"I don't have any good ideas."

"You don't want to marry me." It wasn't a question, it was a statement.

Veronica didn't move, didn't say anything. What could she possibly say?

Joe laughed—a brief burst of air that had nothing to do with humor. "Hell, from the way it sounds, you don't even want to *see* me again."

She turned toward him, but she wasn't prepared for the chill that was in his eyes.

"Boy, did I have *you* pegged wrong," he said.

"You don't understand," Veronica tried to explain. "I can't live the way you want me to live. I can't take it, Joe."

He turned away, and she moved forward, stopping him with a hand on his arm. "We come from such different worlds," she said. His world was filled with danger and violence and the ever-present risk of death. Why couldn't he see the differences between them? "I can't just . . . pretend to fit into your world, because I know I won't. And I know you won't fit into mine. You can't change any more than *I* can, and—"

Joe pulled away. His head was spinning. Different worlds. Different classes was more like it. God, he should have known better. What was he thinking? How could he have thought a woman like Veronica St. John—a wealthy, high-class, gentrified lady—would want more from him than a short, steamy affair?

He'd been right—she'd been slumming.

That was all this was to her.

She had been slumming. She had been checking out how the lower class lived. She had been having sex with a blue-collar man. Officer or not, that was what Joe was, what he would always be. That was where he came from.

Veronica was getting her hands dirty, and Joe, he'd gone and fallen in love. God, he was a royal idiot, a horse's ass.

He took the ring box from where it still sat on the bedside table and dropped it into his pocket. Damned if he was going to let her walk away with a ring that had put a serious dent into his life savings.

"Try to understand," Veronica said, her eyes swimming with tears. She stood in front of the door, blocking his exit. "I love you, but...I can't marry you."

And all at once Joe *did* understand. She may have been slumming—at first. But she'd fallen in love with him, too. Still, that love wasn't enough to overcome the differences between their two "worlds" as she called it.

He should walk away. He *knew* he should walk away. But instead he touched her face and brushed his thumb across her beautiful lips. And then he did something he'd never done before. He begged.

"Please, Ronnie," Joe said softly. "This thing between us...it's pretty powerful. Please, baby, can't we try to work this out?"

Veronica stared up into Joe's eyes, and for a second, she almost believed that they could.

But then his pager beeped again, and the fear was back. Joe had to go. Now. Reality hit her hard and she felt sick to her stomach. She turned and moved away from the door.

"That's your answer, huh?" he said quietly.

Veronica kept her back to him. She couldn't speak. And she couldn't bear to watch him leave.

She heard him open the bedroom door. She heard him walk through the hotel suite. And she heard him stop, heard him hesitate before he opened the door to the corridor.

"I thought you were tougher than this, Ron," he said, a catch in his voice.

The door clicked quietly as it closed behind him.

Chapter 20

The guys in Alpha Squad were avoiding Joe. They were keeping their distance—and it was little wonder, considering the black mood he was in.

The "emergency" calling them all back to Little Creek had been no more than an exercise in preparedness—a time test by the powers that be. The top brass were checking to see exactly how long it would take SEAL Team Ten to get back to their home base in Virginia, from their scattered temporary locations around California and the Southwest.

Blue was the only man who ignored Joe's bad mood and stayed nearby as they completed the paperwork on the exercise and on the Ustanzian tour operation. Blue didn't say a word, but Joe knew his executive officer was ready to lend a sympathetic ear, or even a shoulder to cry on if he needed it.

Early that evening, before they left the administration office, there was a phone call for Joe. From Seattle.

Blue was there, and he met Joe's eyes as the call was announced. There was only one person in Seattle who could possibly be calling Joe.

Veronica St. John.

Why was she calling him?

Maybe she'd changed her mind.

Blue turned away, sympathy in his eyes. Damn it, Joe thought. Were his feelings, his hope for the impossible *that* transparent?

There was no real privacy in the office, and Joe had to take the call at an administrator's desk, with the man sitting not three feet away from him.

"Catalanotto," he said into the phone, staring out the window.

"Joe?" It *was* Veronica. And she sounded surprised to hear his voice. "Oh, Lord, I didn't think I'd actually get through to you. I thought... I thought I'd be able to leave a message with your voice mail or...something."

Terrific. She didn't actually want to speak to him. Then why the hell had she called? "You want me to hang up?" he asked. "You can call back and leave a message."

"Well, no," she said. "No, of course not. Don't be silly. I just...didn't think you'd be there. I thought you'd be...shooting bad guys...or something."

Joe smiled despite the ache in his chest. "No," he said. *"Yesterday* I shot the bad guy. Today I'm doing the paperwork about it."

"I thought..."

"Yes...?"

"Aren't you shipping out or...something?"

"No," Joe said. "It was an exercise. The brass wanted to see how fast SEAL Team Ten could get our butts back to Little Creek. They do that sometimes. Supposedly it keeps us on our toes."

"I'm glad," she said.

"I'm not," he stated flatly. "I was hoping they were sending us down to South America. We're *still* no closer to nailing Diosdado. I was looking forward to tracking him down and having it out with him once and for all."

"Oh," she said very softly. And then she was silent.

Joe counted to five very slowly, then he said, "Veronica? You still there?"

"Yes," she replied, and he could almost see her shake her head to get herself back on track. But when she spoke, her voice was no less tentative. "I'm sorry, I...um, I was calling to pass on some news I received this afternoon. Mrs. Kaye called from Washington, D.C. Cindy died this morning at Saint Mary's.''

Joe closed his eyes and swore.

"Mrs. Kaye wanted to thank you again,'' Veronica continued, her voice shaking. She was crying. Joe knew just from the way her voice sounded that she was crying. God, his arms ached to hold her. "She wanted to thank both of us, for your visit. It meant a lot to Cindy.''

Joe held tightly to the phone, fighting to ignore the six pairs of curious eyes and ears in the room.

Veronica took a deep breath, and he could picture her wiping her eyes and face, adjusting her hair. "I just thought you'd want to know,'' she said. She took another breath. "I have to run. The cruise ship sails in less than an hour.''

"Thanks for calling to tell me, Veronica,'' Joe said.

There was another silence. Then she said, "Joe?''

"Yeah.''

"I'm sorry,'' she said falteringly. "About . . . you and me. About it not working out. I didn't mean to hurt you.''

Joe couldn't talk about it. How could he stand here in the middle of all these people and talk about the fact that his heart had been stomped into a million tiny pieces? And even if he could, how could he admit it to her—the woman responsible for all the pain?

"Was there something else you wanted?'' he asked, his voice tight and overly polite.

"You sound so . . . Are you . . . are you all right?''

"Yeah,'' he lied. "I'm great. I'm getting on with my life, okay? Now, if you'll excuse me, I'll get back to it, all right?''

Joe hung up the phone without waiting to see if she said goodbye. He turned and walked away, past Blue, past the guard at the front desk. He walked out of the building and down the road, heading toward the empty parade grounds. He sat in the grass at the edge of the field and held his head in his hands.

And for the second time in his adult life, Joe Catalanotto cried.

Standing at the pay phone, Veronica dissolved into tears. She hadn't expected to speak to Joe. She hadn't expected to hear his familiar voice. It was such a relief to know that he wasn't risking his life—at least not today.

But he'd sounded so stilted, so cold, so unfriendly. He'd called her Veronica, not Ronnie, as if she were some stranger he didn't know. He was getting on with his life, he'd said. He clearly wasn't going to waste any time worrying about what might have been.

That was the way she wanted it, wasn't it? So why did she feel so awful?

Did she actually *want* Joe Catalanotto carrying a torch for her? Did she *want* him to be hurt? Did she *want* his heart to be broken?

Or maybe she was afraid that by turning him down, she'd done the wrong thing, made the wrong choice.

Veronica didn't know. She honestly didn't know.

The only thing she was absolutely certain of was how terribly much she missed him.

Joe sat in the bar nursing a beer, trying not to listen to the endless parade of country songs about heartbreak playing on the jukebox.

"At ease, at ease. Stay in your seats, boys."

Joe looked into the mirror behind the bar and saw Admiral Forrest making his way across the crowded room. The admiral sat down at the bar, next to Joe, who took another sip of his beer, not even looking up, certainly not even smiling.

"Rumor has it you survived your mission," Mac said to Joe, ordering a diet cola from the bartender. "But it looks to me like you extracted without a pulse or a sense of humor. Am I right or are you still alive over there, son?"

"Well, gee whiz, Admiral," Joe said, staring morosely into his beer. "We can't all be a barrel of laughs all the time."

Mac nodded seriously. "No, no, you're right. We can't." He nodded to the bartender as the man put a tall glass of soda on the bar. "Thanks." He glanced down the bar and nodded to Blue McCoy, who was sitting on Joe's right. "Lieutenant."

Blue nodded back. "Good to see you, Admiral."

Forrest turned back to Joe. "Hear you and some of your boys had a run-in with Salustiano Vargas two days ago."

Joe nodded, glancing up at the older man. "Yes, sir."

"Also hear from the Intel grapevine that the rumor is, Vargas was disassociated from Diosdado and the Cloud of Death some time ago."

Joe shrugged, drawing wet lines with the condensation from his mug on the surface of the bar. He exchanged a look with Blue. "Vargas wasn't able to verify FInCOM's information after we had it out with him. He was too dead to talk."

Admiral Forrest nodded. "I heard that, too," he said. He took a long sip of his soda, then set it carefully back down on the bar. "What *I* can't figure out is, if Salustiano Vargas was *not* working with Diosdado, why did earlier FInCOM reports state that members of the Cloud of Death were unusually interested in Prince Tedric's tour schedule?"

"FInCOM isn't known for their flawless operations," Joe said, one eyebrow raised. "Someone made a mistake."

"I don't know, Joe." Mac scratched his head through his thick white hair. "I've got this gut feeling that the mistake is in assuming the reports are true about this rift between Vargas and Diosdado. I think there's still some connection between them. Those two were too close for too long." He shook his head again. "What I can't figure out is *why* Salustiano Vargas— Diosdado's number-one sharpshooter—would set himself up as a suicide assassin. He didn't stand a chance at getting out of there. *And* he didn't even hit his target."

Joe took another slug of his beer. "He had the opportunity," he said. "I was on that stage, with my back to the bastard when he fired his first shot. It wasn't until the second shot went into the stage next to me that I realized he was shooting from behind me and—"

Joe froze, his glass a quarter of an inch from his lips. "Jesus, Mary and Joseph." He put his beer back on the counter and looked from Blue to the admiral. "Why would a sharpshooter of Vargas's caliber miss an easy target in broad daylight?"

"Luck," Blue suggested. "You moved out of the way of the bullet at the right split second."

"I didn't," Joe said. "I didn't move at all. He *deliberately* missed me." He stood, knocking his barstool over. "I need the telephone," he said to the bartender. "Now."

The bartender moved fast and placed the phone in front of Joe. Joe pushed it in front of the admiral.

"Who am I calling?" Forrest asked dryly. "*Why* am I calling?"

"Why would Salustiano Vargas deliberately miss his assassination target?" Joe asked. He answered his own question. "Because the assassination attempt was only a diversion, set up to make FInCOM's security force relax. Which they immediately did, right? I'm out of the picture. The rest of Alpha Squad is out of the picture. Mac, how many FInCOM agents are with Prince Tedric's tour now that the alleged danger has passed?"

Mac shrugged. "Two. I think." He leaned forward. "Joe, what are you saying?"

"That the *real* terrorist attack hasn't happened yet. Damn, at least I hope it hasn't happened yet."

Mac Forrest's mouth dropped open. "Jumping Jesse," he said. "The cruise ship?"

Joe nodded. "With only two FInCOM agents onboard, that cruise ship is a terrorist's dream come true." He picked up the telephone receiver and handed it to the admiral. "Contact them, sir. Warn them."

Forrest dialed a number and waited, his blue eyes steely in his weathered face.

Joe waited, too. Waited, and prayed. Veronica was on that ship.

Blue stood. "I'm gonna page the squad," he said quietly to Joe.

Joe nodded. "Better make it all of Team Ten," he told Blue in a low voice. "If this is going down, it's going to be big. We're going to need all the manpower we've got. While you're at it, get on the horn with the commander of Team Six. Let's put in a request to put them on standby, too."

Blue nodded and vanished in the direction of the door and the outside pay phone.

Please, God, keep Veronica safe, Joe prayed. *Please, God, let him be really, really wrong about the situation. Please God . . .*

Forrest put his hand over the receiver. "I got through to the naval base in Washington State," he said to Joe. "They're hailing the cruise ship now." He lifted his hand from the mouthpiece. "Yes?" he said into the telephone. "They're not?" He looked up at Joe, his eyes dark with concern. "The ship's not responding. Apparently, their radio's down. The base has them on radar, and they've gone seriously off course." He shook his head, his mouth tight with anger and frustration. "I believe we've got ourselves a crisis situation."

Veronica watched a second helicopter land on the sundeck.

This couldn't be happening. Five hours ago, she'd been having lunch with Ambassador Freder and his staff. Five hours ago, everything had been perfectly normal aboard the cruise ship *Majestic*. Tedric had been sleeping in, as was his habit. She'd been forcing down a salad even though she wasn't hungry, even though her stomach hurt from missing Joe. Lord, she didn't think it was possible to miss another person that badly. She felt hollow, empty, and hopelessly devoid of life.

And then a dozen men, dressed in black and carrying automatic rifles and submachine guns, jumped out of one helicopter and swarmed across the deck of the cruise ship, declaring that the *Majestic* was now in their control, and all her passengers were their hostages.

It seemed unreal, like some sort of strange movie that she was somehow involved in making.

There were fewer than sixty people aboard the small cruise ship, including the crew. They were all on deck, watching and waiting as the second helicopter's blades slowed and then stopped.

No one made a sound as the doors opened and several men stepped out.

One of them, a man with a pronounced limp who was wearing a baseball cap and sunglasses, smiled a greeting to the silent crowd. He had a wide, friendly, white-toothed smile set off by a thick salt-and-pepper beard. Without saying a word, he gestured to one of the other terrorists, who pulled the two FInCOM agents out in front of them all.

The terrorists had cuffed the two security agents' hands behind them, and now, as they were pushed to their knees in front of the bearded man, they fought to keep their balance.

"Who are you?" one of the agents, a woman named Maggie Forte demanded. "What is this—"

"Silence," the bearded man said. And then he pulled a revolver from his belt and shot both agents in the head.

Senator McKinley's wife screamed and started to cry.

"Just so you know our guns are quite real," the bearded man said to the rest of them in his softly accented voice, "and that we mean business. My name is Diosdado." He gestured to the other terrorists around him. "These men and women all work for me. Do as they say, and you will all be fine." He smiled again. "Of course, there are no guarantees."

Veronica stared at the bright red blood pooling beneath the FInCOM agents' bodies. They were dead. Just like that, a man and a woman were dead. The man—Charlie Griswold, he'd said his name was—had just had a new baby. He'd shown Veronica pictures. He'd been so proud, so in love with his pretty young wife. And now . . .

God forgive her, but all she could think was *Thank God it wasn't Joe.* Thank God Joe wasn't here. Thank God that wasn't Joe's blood spreading across the deck.

Diosdado limped toward Prince Tedric, who was standing slightly apart from the rest of them.

"So we finally meet again," the terrorist said. He used his submachine gun to knock the Stetson cowboy hat Tedric was wearing off his head.

Tedric looked as if he might be ill.

"Did you really think I'd forget about the agreement we made?" Diosdado asked.

Tedric glanced toward the two dead agents lying on the deck. "No," he whispered.

"Then where are my long-range missiles?" Diosdado demanded. "I've been waiting and waiting for you to come through on your part of the deal."

Veronica couldn't believe what she was hearing. Prince Tedric, involved in arms smuggling? She wouldn't have believed he had the nerve.

"I said I'd *try*," Tedric hissed. "I made no promises."

Diosdado made tsking sounds. "Then it was very bad form for you to keep the money," he said.

Tedric straightened in shock. "I sent the money back," he retorted. "I wouldn't have kept it. *Mon Dieu,* I wouldn't have . . . dared."

Diosdado stared at him. Then he laughed. "You know, I actually believe you. It seems my good friend Salustiano intervened more than once. No wonder he wanted you dead. He'd intercepted two million of my dollars that you were returning to me." He laughed again. "Isn't this an interesting twist?" He turned to his men. "Take the other hostages below, and His Highness to the bridge. Let's see what a crown prince is worth these days. I may get my long-range missiles yet."

Navy SEAL Team Ten was airborne less than thirty minutes after Admiral Forrest contacted the naval base in Washington State. Joe sat in the air-force jet with his men, receiving nearly continuous reports from a Blackbird SR-71 spy plane that was circling at eighty-five thousand feet above the hijacked cruise ship, over the northern Pacific Ocean. The Blackbird was flying so high the terrorists and hostages on board the *Majestic* couldn't have seen it even with high-powered binoculars.

But with the Blackbird's high-tech equipment, Joe could see the cruise ship. The pictures that were coming in were very sharp and clear.

There were two bodies on the deck near two high-speed attack helicopters.

Two bodies, two pools of blood.

More detailed reports showed that one of the bodies was wearing a skirt, her legs angled awkwardly on the deck.

One man, one woman. Both dead.

Joe studied the picture, unable to see the woman's features for all the blood. Please, God, don't let it be Veronica! He glanced up to find Blue looking over his shoulder.

Blue shook his head. "I don't think it's her," he said. "I don't think it's Veronica."

Joe didn't say anything at first. "It could be," he finally said, his voice low.

"Yeah." Blue nodded. "Could be. And if it's not, it's someone that somebody else loves. It's already a no-win situation, Cat. Don't let it interfere with what we've got to do."

"I won't," he said. He smiled, but it didn't reach his eyes. "That bastard Diosdado isn't gonna know what hit him."

Veronica sat in the dining room with the other hostages, wondering what was going to come next.

Tedric sat apart from the others, staring at the walls, his jaw clenched tightly, his arms crossed in front of him.

It was funny, so many people had seen Joe and thought that he was Tedric. But to Veronica, their physical differences were so clearly obvious. Joe's eyes were bigger and darker, his lashes longer. Joe's chin was stronger, more square. Tedric's nose was narrower, and slightly pinched looking at the end.

Sure, they both had dark hair and dark eyes, but Tedric's eyes shifted as he spoke, never settling on any one thing. Veronica had worked for hours and *hours*, trying to teach the prince to look steadily into the TV cameras. Joe, on the other hand, always looked everyone straight in the eye. Tedric was in constant motion—fingers tapping, a foot jiggling, crossing and uncrossing his legs. Joe's energy was carefully contained. He could sit absolutely still, but one could feel his leashed power. He nearly throbbed with it, but it didn't distract—at least, not all the time.

Veronica closed her eyes.

Was she ever going to see Joe again? What she would give to put her arms around him, to feel his arms holding her.

But he was in Virginia. It was very likely that he hadn't even heard about the hijacking yet. And what would he think when he found out? Would he even care? He'd been so cold, so formal, so distant during their last conversation.

Diosdado had opened communications with both the U.S. and the Ustanzian governments. Ustanzia was ready to ship out the missiles the terrorists wanted, but the U.S. was against that. Now the two governments were in disagreement, with the U.S. threatening to drop all future aid if Ustanzia gave in to the terrorists' demands. But Senator McKinley was on board the *Majestic,* too. So between the senator and Crown Prince Tedric, Diosdado had hit a jackpot.

But jackpot or not, Diosdado was losing patience.

He limped into the room now, and all of the hostages tensed.

"Men on one side, and women on the other," said the leader of the Cloud of Death, drawing an imaginary line down the center of the room with his arm.

Everybody stared. No one moved.

"Now!" he commanded quite softly, lifting his gun for emphasis.

They all moved. Veronica stood on the right side of the imaginary line with the rest of the women. There were only fourteen women on board, compared to the forty men on the other side of the dining room.

Mrs. McKinley was shivering, and Veronica reached down and took the older woman's icy fingers.

"Here's how it's going to work," Diosdado said pleasantly. "We're going to start with the women. You're going to go up to the bridge, to the radio room, and talk to your government. You're going to convince them to give us what we want, *and* to keep their distance. And you're going to tell them that starting in one hour, we're going to begin eliminating our hostages, one each hour, on the hour."

There was a murmur in the crowd, and Mrs. McKinley clung more tightly to Veronica's hand.

"And," Diosdado said, "you may tell them that once again we're going to start with the women."

"No!" one of the men cried.

Diosdado turned and fired his gun, shooting the man in the head. Several people screamed, many dove for cover.

Veronica turned away, sickened. Just like that, another man was dead.

"Anyone else have any objections?" Diosdado asked pleasantly.

Except for the sound of quiet sobbing, the hostages were silent.

"You and you," the terrorist said, and it was several moments before Veronica realized he was talking to her and Mrs. McKinley. "To the radio room."

Veronica looked up into the glittering chill of Diosdado's dark eyes, and she knew. She was going to be the first. She had only one more hour to live.

One very short hour.

Even if Joe knew, even if Joe cared, there was nothing he could do to save her. He was on the other side of the country. There was no way he could reach her within an hour.

She was going to die.

Chapter 21

Joe stood in the briefing room of the USS *Watkins,* and tried to work out a plan to get SEAL Team Ten onto the *Majestic,* and the hostages off.

"Infrared surveillance shows the majority of the hostages are in the ship's dining hall," Blue reported. He pointed to the location on a cutaway schematic of the cruise ship that was spread out on the table among all the other maps and charts and photographs. "We can approach at dusk, going under their radar with inflatable boats, climb up the sides of the *Majestic,* and bring the hostages out without the terrorists even knowing."

"Once everyone's clear of the cruise ship," Harvard said with a hard smile, "we kick their butts all the way to hell."

"We'll need air support," Joe said. "At the first sign of trouble, Diosdado is going to split in one of those choppers he's got on the deck. I want to make sure we've got some fighters standing by, ready to shoot him down if necessary."

"What you *need,*" Admiral Forrest said, coming into the room, "is a go-ahead from the president. And right now, he wants to sit tight, wait and see what the terrorists do next."

The intercom from the bridge crackled on. "We have a report from the *Majestic,*" a voice said over the loudspeaker.

"Another hostage is dead. The terrorists say they'll kill one hostage every hour until they get either twenty million dollars or a shipment of long-range missiles."

Another hostage was dead. Joe couldn't breathe. God help Diosdado if he so much as *touched* Veronica. He looked around the room at the grim faces of his men. God help that bastard, anyway. SEAL Team Ten was after him now.

The telephone rang, and Cowboy picked it up. "Jones," he said. He held the receiver out to the admiral. "Sir, it's for you." He swallowed. "It's the president."

Forrest took the phone. "Yes, sir?" He nodded, listening hard, then looked up at Joe. He spoke only one word, but it was the word Joe had been waiting for.

"Go."

As the sun began to set, Mrs. McKinley was taken back to the dining room, leaving Veronica alone with Diosdado and one of his followers.

"Right about now, you're wondering how you ever got into this mess," Diosdado said to Veronica, offering her one of the cigarettes from his pack.

She shook her head.

"It's okay," he said. "You can smoke if you want." He laughed. "After all, you don't have to worry about dying from lung cancer, right?"

"Right about now," Veronica said with forced calm, "I'm wondering what your head would look like—on a pike."

Diosdado laughed, and touched her on the cheek. "You Brits are so bloodthirsty."

She pulled her head away, repulsed. He just laughed again.

"They're all going to die," he said. "All of the hostages. You should be thankful *your* death is going to be painless."

Joe met Blue's eyes in the dimness of the corridor outside the dining hall. They both wore headsets and mikes, but at this proximity to the terrorists, they were silent. Joe nodded once and Blue nodded back.

They were going in.

The door was open a crack, and they knew from looking in that both guards had their backs to them. Both guards were holding Uzis, but their stances were relaxed, unsuspecting of trouble.

Joe smiled grimly. Well, here came trouble with a capital *T.* He pointed to Blue and then to the guard on the left. Blue nodded. Joe held up three fingers, two fingers, one . . .

He pushed the door open, and he and Blue erupted into the room as if they were one body with a single controlling brain. The guard on the left spun around, bringing his Uzi up. Joe fired once, the sound of the shot muffled by his hush-puppy. He caught the Uzi as the man fell, turning to see Blue lower the other guard, his head at an unnatural angle, to the ground.

The hostages didn't make a sound. They stared, though. The entire room reeked of fear.

"Dining room secure," Blue said into his microphone. "Let's get some backup down here, boys." He turned to the hostages. "We're U.S. Navy SEALs," he told them in his gentle Southern accent as Joe searched the crowd for Veronica. "With your continued cooperation, we're here to take y'all home."

There was a babble of voices, questions, demands. Blue held up both hands. "We're not out of danger yet, folks," he said. "I'd like to ask you all to remain silent and to move quickly and quietly when we tell you to."

Veronica wasn't here. If she wasn't here, that meant . . .

"Veronica St. John," Joe said, his voice cracking with his effort to stay calm. Just because she wasn't here didn't necessarily mean she was dead, right? "Does anyone know where Veronica St. John is?"

An older woman with graying hair raised her hand. "On the bridge," she said in a shaky voice. "That man, that murderer, is going to kill her at six o'clock. They took the prince somewhere else, too."

The clock on the wall said five fifty-five.

Joe's watch said the same.

He turned to look at Blue, who was already speaking into his headset. "Harvard and Cowboy, get your fannies down here on the double. We've got to get these people off this ship, pronto, and you're the ones who're gonna do it."

With Blue only a few steps behind, Joe slipped the strap of the Uzi over his shoulder along with his HK machine gun and headed back down the corridor at a run.

"I'm sorry," Diosdado said into the radio, sounding not one bit sorry. "Your promise to deliver twenty million to my Swiss bank account isn't enough. I gave you plenty of time to get the job done. Maybe you'll do it before the *next* hostage is killed, hmm? Think about it. This communication has ended."

With a flick of his wrist, he turned the radio off. He took a sip of coffee before he faced Veronica.

"I'm so sorry," he said. "Your government has let you down. They don't think you're worth twenty million dollars."

"I thought you wanted missiles," Veronica said. "Not money."

It was 6:01 p.m. Maybe if she could keep him talking, maybe if she could stall him, something, some miracle would happen. At the very least, she'd live a few minutes longer. She'd already lived one minute more than she'd thought she would.

"Either one would be fine," Diosdado said with a shrug. He turned to his guard. "Where is our little prince? I need him in here."

The man nodded and left the room.

Veronica felt incredibly calm, remarkably poised, considering that, miracles aside, she was going to get a bullet in her head in a matter of minutes.

She wasn't going to see another sunrise. She wasn't going to see Joe's beautiful smile, hear his contagious laughter again. She wasn't going to get a chance to tell him that she'd been wrong, that she wanted him for however long he was willing to give her.

Facing her own death made her see it all so clearly. She loved Joe Catalanotto. So what if he was a Navy SEAL. It was who he was, what he did. It was quite probably the reason she'd fallen in love with him. He was the best of the best in so many different ways. If by being a SEAL, he had to live on the edge and cheat death, so be it. She would learn to cope.

But she wasn't going to have a chance to do that. Because of her own fears and weaknesses, she'd pushed Joe away. She'd given up the few moments of happiness she could have had with him. She'd given up a lingering kiss goodbye. She'd given up a phone call that could have been filled with whispered "I love you's" instead of stilted apologies and chilly regrets.

How ironic that *she* was the one who was going to die a violent and horrible death.

Four minutes past six.

"What could be taking them so long?" Diosdado mused. He smiled at Veronica. "I'm so sorry, dear. I know you must be anxious to get this over with. I'd do it myself, but when Prince Tedric comes in, we're going to play a little game. Do you want to know the rules?"

Veronica looked into the eyes of the man who was going to kill her. "Why do you do this?" she asked.

"Because I can." The eyes narrowed slightly. "You're not afraid, are you?" he asked.

She was terrified. But she was damned if she was going to let *him* know that. She replied, "I'm saddened. There's a man that I love, and he's never going to know just how much I really do love him."

Diosdado laughed. "Isn't that tragic," he said. "You're just as pathetic as the rest of them. And to think, for a moment I was actually considering sparing you."

Five minutes past six.

He'd never had any intention of sparing her. It was just another of his head games. Veronica didn't allow any expression to cross her face.

"You didn't let me tell you about this game we're going to play," the terrorist continued. "It's called 'Who's the Killer?' When Prince Tedric comes in, I'll put a gun on the table over here." He patted the tabletop. "And then, with *my* gun on him, I'll order him to pick up that gun and fire a bullet into your head." He laughed. "Do you think he'll do it?"

"You aren't afraid he'll turn and use the gun on you?"

"Prince Tedric?" Diosdado blew out a burst of disparaging air. "No. The man has no . . . backbone." He shook his head. "No, it will be *your* brains on these nice windows, not mine."

The door was pushed tentatively open, and Prince Tedric came onto the bridge. He was still wearing his cowboy hat, pulled low over his face. But his jacket was unbuttoned. That was odd—surely a sign of his despondency. Veronica had never seen him look anything but fastidious.

"Your Royalness," Diosdado said. He swooped low in a mocking bow. "I believe you are familiar with Miss Veronica St. John, yes?"

Tedric nodded. "Yes," he said. "I know Ronnie."

Ronnie?

Veronica looked up at Tedric in surprise—and met Joe's warm brown gaze.

Joe! Here?

The rush of emotions was intense. Veronica had never been so glad to see anyone in her entire life. Or so frightened. *Lord, please, don't let Joe be killed, too. . . .*

"Get down," Joe mouthed silently.

"We're going to play a little game," Diosdado was saying.

"I've got a game for you," Joe said in Tedric's Ustanzian accent. "It's called 'Show-and-Tell.'"

He pulled the biggest machine gun Veronica had ever seen in her life out from under his open jacket and aimed it at Diosdado.

"I show you my gun," Joe finished in his regular voice, "and you freeze. Then tell your army to surrender."

Diosdado didn't freeze. He lifted his gun.

Veronica dove for the floor as Joe opened fire. The noise was incredible, and the smell of gunpowder filled the air. But just as quickly as it started, it stopped. And then Joe was next to her on the floor, pulling her into his arms.

"Ronnie! God, tell me you're all right!"

She clung to his neck. "Oh, Joe!" She pulled back. "Are *you* all right?" He seemed to be in one piece, despite all of the bullets that had been flying just moments earlier.

"He didn't hurt you, did he?"

Veronica shook her head.

He kissed her, hard, on the mouth and she closed her eyes, pulling him closer, kissing him back with as much strength and passion. She welcomed his familiar taste, giddy with relief and a sense of homecoming she'd never experienced before. He'd come to save her. Somehow he'd known, and he'd come.

"Well," Joe said, his voice husky as he drew back. "I guess this is probably the one situation where you'd be indisputably glad to see me, huh?" He smiled, but there was a flash of remorse in his eyes as he took off Tedric's jacket, revealing some kind of dark uniform and vest underneath.

He was serious. He honestly thought the only reason she was so happy to see him was because he had come to save her life. "No, Joe—" she said, but he stopped her, standing and pulling her to her feet.

"Come on, baby, we've got to get moving," Joe said. "In about thirty seconds, this place is going to be crawling with tangos who heard that gunfire. We've got to get out of here."

"Joe—"

"Tell me while we're moving," he said, not unkindly, as he pulled her toward the door. She hesitated only a second, glancing back over her shoulder at where Diosdado had stood only moments before.

"Is he . . . ?"

Joe nodded. "Yeah." Holding her hand, he led her gently down the corridor. She was shaking slightly, but otherwise seemed okay. Of course, it was entirely possible that the shock of what she'd just been through hadn't set in. Still, they had to move while they could. "Can you run?" he asked.

"Yes," she said.

They set off down the corridor at an easy trot.

She was still holding his hand, and she squeezed it slightly. "I love you," she said.

Joe glanced at her. Her eyes were bright with unshed tears, but she managed to smile as she met his gaze. "I didn't think I'd get the chance to tell you that ever again," she explained. "And I know we're not out of danger, so I wanted to make sure you knew, in case—"

Veronica was right—they *weren't* out of danger. They were at the opposite end of the ship from the extraction point, and the tangos had surely been alerted to the fact that there were intruders on board. They had surely noticed that their hostages were missing and their leader was dead. SEAL Team Ten had stirred up one hell of a hornet's nest—and Joe and Veronica were still in the middle of it.

But Joe wasn't about to tell Veronica that. They *could* pull this off. Damn it, they *would* pull this off. He was a SEAL and he was armed to the teeth. Several dozen terrorists didn't stand a chance against him. Hell, with stakes this high, with the life of the woman he loved at risk, he could take on several hundred and win.

Joe slowed, peering around a corner, making sure they weren't about to run head-on into a pack of terrorists. Veronica loved him, and even though she didn't love him enough to want to marry him, he didn't care anymore. He honestly didn't care. If he'd been five minutes later, if that evil bastard Diosdado hadn't wanted to play games with his victims, if any number of things had been different, he would have lost Veronica permanently. The thought made him crazy. She could have been killed, and he would be alone, without her forever and ever.

But she hadn't been killed. They'd both been given a second chance, and Joe wasn't going to waste it. And he wanted to make his feelings clear to her—now—before she walked away from him again.

"When this is all over," he said almost conversationally, "after you're off this ship and safely back onshore, you're going to have to get used to me coming around to visit you. You don't have to marry me, Ronnie. It doesn't have to be anything permanent. But I've got to tell you right now—I have no intention of letting this thing between us drop, do you follow?"

Silently, she nodded.

"Good," Joe said. "You don't have to go out with me in public. You don't have to acknowledge our relationship at all—not to your friends, not to your family. I'll keep sneaking in your back door, baby, if that's the way you want it. You can just go on slumming, indefinitely. I don't give a damn, because I love you." To hell with his pride. To hell with it all. He'd take her any way he could get her.

"Slumming?" Veronica echoed, surprise in her voice. "What—"

"Beg your pardon, Romeo," came Blue's voice over Joe's headset, and Joe held up his hand, cutting Veronica off, "but I thought you might want to know that I've extracted with my royal luggage. Ronnie's the last civilian on board. The tangos know something's up, so move it, Cat—fast. The USS *Watkins* is moving into position, picking up the IBS's with the hostages. I'm coming back to the *Majestic* to assist you—"

"No," Joe interrupted. Veronica was watching him, with that look on her face that meant she was dying to speak. He shook his head, touching his headset as he spoke to his XO. "No, Blue, I need you to stay with the prince," he ordered. "But make sure there's a boat waiting for me and Ronnie at the bottom of that rope at the bow of this ship."

"You got it," Blue said. "See you on the *Watkins*."

"Check," Joe replied.

Veronica watched Joe. *Slumming?* What had he meant? Then her words came back to her. *Different worlds.* She'd talked about their different worlds when she'd turned down his marriage proposal. She'd been referring to the differences between his matter-of-fact response to danger, his thrill for adventure, and her fears of letting him go. Had he somehow misunderstood her? Had he actually thought she'd been talking about their supposed class differences—assuming something as absurd as class differences even existed? Could he actually have thought she was put off by something as ridiculous as where he came from or where he grew up?

Veronica opened her mouth, about to speak, when suddenly, from somewhere on the ship, there was an enormous, swooshing noise, like a rocket being launched.

"What was *that?*" Veronica breathed.

But Joe was listening again, listening to the voices over his headset.

"Check," he said into his microphone. He turned toward Veronica. "The T's are firing artillery at the hostages. Return fire," he ordered. He listened again. "You're gonna have to," he said tersely. "We're down below, outside the game room, but that's gonna change real soon. I'll keep you informed of my position. You just use that high-tech equipment and make sure you aim when you shoot. Fire now. Do you copy? Fire *now.*"

"My Lord!" Veronica said. Joe had just given an order for the men on the USS *Watkins* to return fire at the cruise ship—while she and Joe were still on board!

A deafening explosion the likes of which Veronica had never heard before thundered around them. The missile from the USS *Watkins* rocked the entire ship, seeming to lift it out of the water and throw it back down.

Joe grabbed Veronica's hand and pulled her with him down the hallway.

"Okay, *Watkins,*" he said over his headset. "We're heading away from the game room, toward the bow of the ship." There was a flight of stairs leading up toward the deck. Joe motioned for Veronica to hang back as he crawled up and peeked over the edge. He motioned with his hand for her to follow him. "Heading toward the recreation deck," he said into his microphone as he climbed up the steps and got his bearings, hanging back in the shadows and looking around. Veronica wasn't sure what he saw, but it didn't make him happy. "We're not going to make it to the extraction point," he said. "We've got to find another way off—"

Then Joe saw it—the perfect escape vehicle—and smiled. Diosdado's helicopters were sitting there, waiting to be hijacked. But this time by the good guys.

They were twenty yards from the helicopter. Twenty yards from freedom.

"Heading for the choppers up on the deck," he said into his mike. "Keep those missiles coming in, but keep 'em clear of us."

Fifteen yards. Ten. God, they were going to make it. They were—

All hell broke loose.

It was a small squad of T's—only about five of them—but they came out of nowhere.

Joe had his gun up and firing as he stepped in front of Veronica. He felt the slap of a bullet hit him low in his gut, beneath the edge of his flak jacket, but he felt no pain, only anger.

Damn it, he wasn't going to let Ronnie die. No way in *hell* was he going to let her die. Not now. Not when he was so close to getting her to safety...

His bullets plowed through the terrorists, taking them down, or driving them away from him to cover. But the sound of gunfire drew more of them toward him.

His mind registered the first sensations of pain. *Pain?* The word didn't come close to describing the white-hot, searing agony he felt with every step, every movement. He was gutshot, and every pounding beat of his heart was pumping his blood out of his body. It wouldn't be long before he bled to death. Still firing his gun, he tried to stanch the flow. He'd been trained as a field medic—all SEALs were. He'd been trained to provide first aid to his men, and even to himself. He needed to apply pressure, but it was tough with a wound this size. The bullet had penetrated him, leaving an exit wound in his back, through which he also bled.

God, the pain.

Through it all, he kept going. If they could reach the chopper, he could still fly Ronnie out of here. If they could reach the chopper, bleeding or not, dying or not, he could get her to the *Watkins*.

The door to the bird was open—God was on his side—but Joe didn't seem to have the strength to push Veronica in. "Dear Lord, you're bleeding," he heard her say. He felt her push him up and into the cockpit. And then, damned if she didn't grab his extra gun, and turn and fire out the open door, keeping the T's at bay while, through a fog, Joe started the engine. He could fly anything, he told himself over and over, hoping that the litany would somehow make his brain respond. They didn't make a chopper he couldn't handle. But his arms felt like lead and his legs weren't working right. Still, he had to do it. He had to, or Veronica was going to die alongside him.

And then, miracle of miracles, they were up. They were in the air and moving away from the ship.

"We're clear of the *Majestic*," Joe rasped into his microphone. "Launch a full-scale attack."

The world blurred for a second, and then snapped sharply into focus.

That was smoke he saw coming from the engine. Sweet Jesus, the chopper must have sustained a direct hit. Somehow, Joe had gotten the damned thing up, but it wasn't going to stay in the air too much longer.

"Tell them you need a medic standing by," Veronica said.

"We've got bigger problems," Joe told her.

She saw the smoke, and her eyes widened, but her voice didn't falter as she told him again, "You've been shot. Make sure someone on the *Watkins* knows that, Joe."

"We're not going to make it to the *Watkins*," Joe said. He spoke into his microphone. "Blue, I need you, man."

"I'm here, and I see you," Blue's familiar Southern drawl sounded in his ears. "You're leaving a trail of smoke like a cheap cigar, Cat. I'm coming out to meet you."

"Good," Joe said. "Because I'm going to bring this bird low, and Ronnie's gonna jump out into the water, you copy?"

"I'm not going anywhere without you," Veronica said, adding loudly, loud enough for Blue to hear, "Joe's been hit, and he's bleeding badly."

"I have a medic standing by," Blue said to Joe. "Is it bad, Cat?"

Joe ignored Blue's question. "I'm right behind you, Ronnie," he said to Veronica, knowing damn well that he was telling her a lie. "But I'm not going to ditch this bird until you're clear."

He could see her indecision in her eyes. She didn't want to leave him.

God, he was getting light-headed, and this chopper was getting harder and harder to handle as he hovered ten feet above the water's surface. The combination was *not* good.

"Go," he said.

"Joe—"

"Baby, *please* . . ." He couldn't hold on much longer.

"Promise you'll be right behind me?"

He nodded, praying to God for forgiveness for his lie. "I promise."

She slid open the door. "I want us to get married right away," she said, and then she was gone.

The water was cold as ice.

It surrounded Veronica, squeezing her chest as she surfaced and tried to take in a breath of air.

But then a boat was there, and hands reached for her, pulling her up.

Veronica ignored the cold as she turned to watch the chopper, hovering above the waves, its whirling blades turning the ocean into choppy whitecaps. Someone wrapped a blanket around her— Blue, it was Blue McCoy, Joe's executive officer.

The plume of smoke from the helicopter was darker, thicker. And the chopper seemed to lurch instead of holding still.

"Why won't he jump?" she wondered aloud.

Before she finished speaking, the helicopter jerked forward and down—into the water.

She could hear shouting—it was Blue's voice—and she couldn't believe that the noise—some noise, *any* noise, wasn't coming from her own throat.

The helicopter was sinking beneath the waves, taking Joe with it, taking all her hopes and dreams for the future away from her.

"No!" she cried, the word torn from her raggedly.

"I'm going in after him." It was Blue. "Pull this boat closer."

"Sir, I can't let you do that," said a young man in a naval uniform. His face was pale. "If the chopper doesn't pull you under, the water's so cold, it'll kill you. You won't last more than five minutes before hypothermia sets in."

"Pull the damned boat closer, Ensign," Blue said, his voice as cold as the Alaskan water. "I'm a SEAL, and that's my commander down there. I'm going after him."

The water was cold as ice.

It roused Joe from his fog as it splashed him in the face.

Damn, he'd gone down. He didn't remember going down. All he remembered was Ronnie—

Ronnie telling him that she wanted to . . . marry him?

The last pocket of air bubbled out of the helicopter cockpit.

No way was he going to die. Ronnie wanted to *marry* him. No way was he going to *drown. Or bleed to death,* damn it.

The water was cold as hell, but it would slow his bleeding.

All he had to do was get his arms and legs to work.

But he hurt.

Every single cell in his body hurt, and it took so much goddammed effort to lift even a finger.

This was worse than anything he'd ever experienced, worse even than Hell Week, that torturous final week of SEAL training that he'd lived through so many years ago.

He'd never wanted anything as badly as he'd wanted to be a SEAL. It had kept him going through the nonstop exertion, through the pain, through the torturous physical demands. *"You got to want it badly enough,"* one of his instructors had shouted at them, day after day, hour after hour. And Joe had. He'd wanted to be a SEAL. He'd wanted it badly enough.

He'd wanted to be a SEAL almost as much as he wanted Veronica St. John.

And she was there, up there, above the surface of that freezing water, waiting for him. All he had to do was kick his legs, push himself free and he would have her. Forever. All he had to do was want it badly enough....

Veronica stared at the water, at the place where first the helicopter and then Blue had disappeared.

Please, God, if you give me this, I'll never ask for anything ever again....

Seconds ticked into one minute. Two. Three . . .

Was it possible for a man to hold his breath for this long, let alone search for a wounded, drowning man . . . ?

Please, God.

And then, all at once, a body erupted from beneath the surface of the water. Veronica peered into the area lit by the searchlights. Was that one head or . . .

Two! Two heads! Blue had found Joe!

A cheer went up from the sailors on board the boat, and they quickly maneuvered closer to the two men, and pulled them out.

Dear God, it *was* Joe, and he was breathing. Veronica stood aside as the medics sliced his wet clothes from his body. Oh, Lord, he'd been shot in the abdomen, just above his hip. She watched, clutching her own blanket more tightly around her as he was wrapped in a blanket and an IV was attached to his arm.

"Cat was coming up as I was going down after him," Blue said, respect heavy in his voice. "I think he would have made it, even without me. He didn't want to die. Not today."

Joe was floating in and out of consciousness, yet he turned his head, searching for something, searching for...

"Ronnie." His voice was just a whisper, but he reached for her, and she took his hand.

"I'm here," she said, pressing his fingers to her lips.

"Did you mean it?" He was fighting hard to remain conscious. He was fighting, and winning. "When you said you'd marry me?"

"Yes," she said, fighting her own battle against the tears that threatened to escape.

Joe nodded. "You know, I'm not going to change," he said. "I can't pretend to be something I'm not. I'm not a prince or a duke or—"

Veronica cut him off with a kiss. "You're my prince," she said.

"Your parents are going to hate me."

"My parents are going to *love* you," she countered. "Nearly as much as I do."

He smiled then, ignoring his pain, reaching up to touch the side of her face. "You really think this could work?"

"Do you love me?" Veronica asked.

"Absolutely."

"Then it will work." The boat was pulling up alongside of the USS *Watkins,* where a doctor was waiting. From what Veronica had gathered from the medics, they believed the bullet had passed through Joe's body, narrowly missing his vital organs. He'd lost a lot of blood, and had to be stitched up and treated for infection, but it could have been worse. It could have been *far* worse.

Joe felt himself placed onto a stretcher. He had to release Ronnie's hand as he was lifted up and onto the deck of the *Watkins.*

"I love you," she called.

He was smiling as the doctor approached him, smiling as the nurse added painkiller to his intravenous tube, smiling as he gave in to the drug and let the darkness finally close in around him.

Joe stared up at the white ceiling in sick bay for a good long time before he figured out where he was and why he couldn't move. He was still strapped down to a bed. He hurt like hell. He'd been shot. He'd been stitched up.

He'd been promised a lifetime filled with happiness and Veronica St. John's beautiful smile.

Veronica Catalanotto. He smiled at the idea of her taking his name.

And then Blue was leaning over him, releasing the restraints. "Damn, Cat," he said in his familiar drawl. "The doc said you were grinning like a fool when he brought you in here, and here you are again, smiling like a fox in a henhouse.''

"Where's Ronnie?" Joe whispered. His throat was so dry, and his mouth felt gummy. He tried to moisten his dry lips with his tongue.

Blue turned away, murmuring something to the nurse before he turned back to Joe, lifting a cup of water to his friend's lips. "She's getting checked by the doctor," he told Joe.

Joe's smile disappeared, the soothing drink of water forgotten. "She okay?"

Blue nodded. "She's just getting a blood test," he said. "Apparently she needs one."

"Why?"

"Because I'm hoping to get married," Ronnie said, leaning forward to kiss him gently on the mouth. "That is, if you still have that ring. If you still want me."

Joe gazed up at her. Her hair was down, loose and curling around her shoulders. She was wearing a sailor suit that was several sizes too large, white flared pants and a white shirt, sleeves rolled up several times. She was wearing no makeup, and her freshly scrubbed face looked impossibly young—and anxious—as she waited for his answer. "Hell, yes," he somehow managed to say.

She smiled, and Joe felt his mouth curve up into an answering smile as he lost himself in the ocean color of her eyes. "Do you still want *me?*"

Blue moved quietly toward the door. "I guess I'll leave you two a—"

Ronnie turned then, looking up at Joe's XO and best friend. "Wait," she said. "Please?" She looked back at Joe. "I'll marry you, but there's one condition."

Blue shifted his weight uncomfortably.

"Anything," Joe said to Veronica. "I'd promise you anything. Just name it."

"It's not something *you* can promise me," she said. She looked up at Blue again, directly into his turquoise eyes. "I need Blue's promise—to keep Joe safe and alive."

Blue nodded slowly, taking her words seriously. "I'd die for him," he said, matter-of-factly.

Veronica had seen them in action. She'd seen Blue dive into the icy Alaskan waters after Joe, and she knew he spoke the truth. It wasn't going to make her fear for Joe's safety disappear, but it *was* going to make it easier.

"I didn't want to marry you because I was—I am—afraid that you're going to get yourself killed," she said, turning back to Joe. "I knew I couldn't ask you to leave the SEALs and..."

She saw his eyes narrow slightly as he understood her words. "Then..."

Veronica felt more than saw Blue slip from the room as she leaned forward to kiss Joe's lips. "I wasn't 'slumming.'" She mock shuddered. "Nasty expression, that."

He laced his fingers through her hair, wariness and concern in his eyes. "I can't leave the SEALs, baby—"

She silenced him with another kiss. "I know. I'm not asking you to. I'm not going to quit my job and become a career navy wife, either," Veronica told Joe. "I'll travel and work—the same as you. But whenever you can get leave time, I'll be there."

As she gazed into Joe's midnight-dark eyes, the last of his reservations drained away, leaving only love—pure and powerful. But then he frowned slightly. "Your ring's back in Little Creek," he said.

"I don't need a ring to know how much you love me," Veronica whispered.

Joe touched his chest, realized he was wearing a hospital gown, then pressed the call button for the nurse.

A young man appeared almost instantly. "Problem, sir?"

"What happened to my uniform?" Joe demanded.

"There wasn't much left of it after the medics cut it off you, sir." The nurse gestured toward a small table just out of reach of the bed. "Your personal gear is in that drawer."

"Thanks, pal," Joe said.

"Can I get you anything, sir?"

"Just some privacy," Joe told him, and the nurse left as quickly as he had come.

Joe turned to Veronica. "Check in that drawer for me, will you, baby?"

Veronica stood up and crossed to the table. She pulled open the drawer. There were three guns inside, several rounds of ammunition, something that looked decidedly like a hand grenade, a deadly-looking knife, several bills of large denominations, a handful of change . . .

"There should be a gold pin," Joe said. "It's called a 'Budweiser.'"

A gold pin in the shape of an eagle with both an ocean trident and a gun, it was Joe's SEAL pin, one of his most precious possessions. He'd gotten it on the day he graduated, the day he became a Navy SEAL. Veronica took it from the drawer. It felt solid and heavy in her hand as she carried it to Joe.

But he didn't take it from her. He wrapped her fingers around it. "I want you to have it."

Veronica stared at him.

"There are two things I've never given anyone," he said quietly. "One is this pin. The other is my heart." He smiled at her. "Now you got 'em both. Forever."

He pulled her head down to him and kissed her so gently, so sweetly, so perfectly.

And Veronica realized again what she'd known for quite some time.

She had found her prince.

*   *   *   *   *

COMING NEXT MONTH

#721 WILD BLOOD—Naomi Horton
Wild Hearts

Jett Kendrick was untamable, and Kathleen Patterson had the broken heart to prove it. She hadn't even been able to hold on to their baby before tragedy struck. So why, fifteen years later, was Jett looking at her with guilt—and longing—especially when his teenage boy was near?

#722 BORROWED BRIDE—Patricia Coughlin

One minute Gabrielle Flanders was wedding-bound, the next she'd been abducted from the church! Connor DeWolfe claimed she was in grave danger—that he was the only man she could trust. But Gaby didn't think her "honeymoon" was the time to find out...or was it?

#723 THE ONE WHO ALMOST GOT AWAY—Alicia Scott
The Guiness Gang

She always got her man—and Jake Guiness was no exception. The infuriating playboy was Regina O'Doul's only lead in the case of her life, so she got *close*. But somehow pretending to be lovers had led to the real thing—and to very real danger for them both....

#724 UNBROKEN VOWS—Frances Williams

Ex-SEAL David Chandler had nothing left to give—but for Cara Merrill, he would certainly try. The gutsy beauty needed his soldiering skills to locate her ex-fiancé. But amid their dangerous jungle mission, David found himself wanting Cara all for himself....

#725 HERO IN HIDING—Kay David

Mercy Hamilton had one rule about Mr. Right: she had to trust him. Then dark, handsome Rio Barrigan challenged her beliefs. He was all mystery—at times warm and loving, at others almost deadly. And though he broke her cardinal rule, Mercy couldn't help but believe in him—and their love.

#726 THE BABY ASSIGNMENT—Cathryn Clare
Assignment: Romance

Agent Jack Cotter knew about guns, bad guys...but babies? On that subject he knew absolutely nothing. But single-mom-on-the-run Shelby Henderson and her bouncing baby girl taught him all he needed to know about family and fatherhood. Jack only hoped they would all survive to put what he'd learned into practice.

Take 4 bestselling love stories FREE

Plus get a FREE surprise gift!

This July, watch for the delivery of...

An exciting new miniseries that appears in a different
Silhouette series each month. It's about love,
marriage—and Daddy's unexpected need for
a baby carriage!

Daddy Knows Last unites five of your favorite authors
as they weave five connected stories about baby
fever in New Hope, Texas.

- **THE BABY NOTION** by Dixie Browning
  (SD#1011, 7/96)

- **BABY IN A BASKET** by Helen R. Myers
  (SR#1169, 8/96)

- **MARRIED...WITH TWINS!**
  by Jennifer Mikels
  (SSE#1054, 9/96)

- **HOW TO HOOK A HUSBAND (AND A BABY)**
  by Carolyn Zane
  (YT#29, 10/96)

- **DISCOVERED: DADDY** by Marilyn Pappano
  (IM#746, 11/96)

Daddy Knows Last arrives in July...only from

DKLT

SILHOUETTE... Where Passion Lives

Add these Silhouette favorites to your collection today!
Now you can receive a discount by ordering two or more titles!

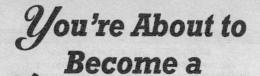

You're About to Become a

Privileged Woman

Reap the rewards of fabulous free gifts and benefits with proofs-of-purchase from Silhouette and Harlequin books

Pages & Privileges™

It's our way of thanking you for buying our books at your favorite retail stores.

PROOF OF PURCHASE
SIM-PP148
Offer expires October 31, 1996

Pages & Privileges ™

Harlequin and Silhouette—
the most privileged readers in the world!

For more information about Harlequin and Silhouette's PAGES & PRIVILEGES program call the Pages & Privileges Benefits Desk: 1-503-794-2499

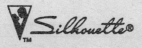

Silhouette®

SIM-PP148